STORM'S JUSTICE

AMELIA STORM SERIES: BOOK SEVEN

MARY STONE
AMY WILSON

❀ Created with Vellum

Mary Stone

To my readers, who are the best ever. You mean the world to me. Thank you from the bottom of my grateful heart.

Amy Wilson

To my one and only, my husband and best friend, and the best boys a mother could dream of, who all worked with me to make this all possible.

DESCRIPTION

Taking justice into your own hands can be deadly...

After receiving a mysterious note from the man claiming to be her brother's confidential informant, Special Agent Amelia Storm decides to trust fellow agent Zane Palmer with the truth. But as Amelia tells Zane about her murdered brother's activities and her own ties to the mafia world, they're called into work. A federal judge, along with her husband and daughter, have been murdered execution-style. The case reeks of mafia involvement, but several aspects of the case hint at something more personal.

There's no doubt the hit was premeditated and carefully planned...except for one crucial fact. The killer left a witness behind, and though traumatized by the events she witnessed, the girl shares a few important details. The killer was a man...and he wasn't alone.

Driven to settle a score and dictate their own brand of justice, the killers aren't finished yet. As Amelia soon learns, they have a score to settle...and one of the Bureau's own is next.

From the wickedly dark minds of Mary Stone and Amy Wilson comes Storm's Justice, book seven of the Amelia Storm Series. Be careful who you aggravate. They may take justice into their own hands.

1

Kate Denson hurried down the sidewalk, only slowing her pace when she reached the wooden stairs of the front porch. Her breath came in white puffs, and thanks to her desire to be fashionable, the light peacoat she'd chosen for her night out did little to ward off the late December chill.

Glancing over her shoulder, she offered a wave goodbye to the black Honda idling beside the curb. Her best friend since elementary school had convinced her boyfriend to be their designated driver for an evening of barhopping, but Kate wasn't even sure she'd attained a buzz.

She certainly hadn't attained any fun.

Two days after Christmas, the nearest bar scene had been far more packed than she'd anticipated, and she and Marlee had been forced to wait a good half hour for their second drink. They'd quickly lost interest in getting drunk and used the time to nurse drinks while catching up on their respective college semesters.

Kate's throat was still hoarse from shouting to be heard over the music, but the time with her friend had been worth the trouble. She and Marlee both attended schools in Chicago, but their busy schedules hadn't allowed much hang-out time lately.

As Kate fished her house keys from her handbag, she noted that the Civic hadn't left. Her heart lightened at the sight. Ever the protective friend, Marlee wouldn't let Jared leave until she made sure Kate had gotten inside safely. Kate was grateful for the watchfulness, especially since the temperature had dipped below twenty. Their night together had ended earlier than either had planned, but the stillness of the evening made the time feel far later than ten forty-five. Heck, her parents might even still be awake.

Though a golden glow seeped through a couple windows of the house next door, all the lights of her parents' place were dark. She remembered her mom mentioning the blackout curtains they'd installed in their first-floor bedroom. Her mom had claimed it was both for privacy and to help them sleep when they turned in early. Kate couldn't imagine going to bed when it was still light out.

"Hope I never get old like that."

Easing open the screen door, she slid her key into the lock like she was a thief in the middle of a diamond heist. The hinges creaked, and Kate flashed a thumbs-up to Marlee and Jared before she ducked into the shadowy foyer. If she'd forgotten her keys, she'd have been in for a long, cold stay on the porch while she waited for someone to wake up to get the damn door. Neither Anna Denson nor Stephen Denson had ever been what Kate would call night owls, and Kate's younger sister, Kelly, had followed their lead.

Not Kate, though. She was the opposite of her parents and sister in just about every way possible.

The quiet din of the city was replaced by silence as Kate gingerly closed the door. She rushed to the keypad to silence the anticipated beeping, but there were no beeps to be heard.

That's weird. Why wasn't the alarm system armed?

Fear made the tiny hairs all over her body prickle, but she shook off the moment of worry. She'd told her mom that she would probably have a few drinks with Kristen and that Jared would be their designated driver. Her parents probably assumed she'd be too inebriated to properly punch in the code.

Kate snorted. She hoped her parents never learned of all the things she could do while wasted. They'd probably both have a heart attack.

She paused to let her eyes adjust to the lack of light. As she'd suspected, the only sources of illumination were a few strategically placed nightlights throughout the house. Her parents and her sister were all fast asleep.

After making sure her cell was on silent, Kate tucked it into her pocket and set her purse on a bench that ran the short length of the wall. She shrugged off her coat and hung the garment on the one free hook.

With her few drinks spread out over the evening and her night out cut short, she wasn't the least bit tired. A junior at Chicago's Northwestern Illinois University, Kate had become accustomed to late nights of cramming for exams and scrambling to make last-minute adjustments to papers and projects. It was still early as far as she was concerned.

Maybe she and Marlee should have tried a different location for their post-Christmas festivities, or maybe they should have gone with Marlee's initial idea of attending a dance club.

Kate shivered. Her last time at a club hadn't gone well. She'd damn near gotten into a fistfight with some pervert who'd groped her on the dance floor.

His reasoning for being such a creep? Kate had smiled at him.

"Sorry I've got manners, dipshit." Her response had earned a

scowl, followed by a rant about how women were all teases or some such nonsense. Kate had been ready to clock the fool, but her friend had jumped between her and the grope-happy perv.

She heaved a mental sigh and pushed aside the memory. No more dance clubs. Not until she had a black belt, or until she got off her ass and went to one of those Krav Maga sessions Marlee had told her about.

For tonight, she'd just have to find a way to entertain herself until she fell asleep. At least she'd be in her own bed and not on Marlee's uncomfortable couch.

Stretching both arms above her head, Kate padded past the open living room toward the kitchen. Even in the darkness, she knew how to navigate around the furniture without stubbing a toe or bruising a shin. Fortunately, her parents hadn't rearranged the room in some time. Kate lived in her dorm for most of the year, but when she stayed at home, she always found herself sneaking around the place in the dark.

Not that her parents had an issue with her going to a bar with some friends. She *was* twenty-one, after all. But like she'd pointedly advised the moron from the club, she'd been raised with manners. Just because her stomach growled like clockwork for a late-night snack didn't mean she would parade through the kitchen like a human-sized tornado and wake everyone.

A cartoon image of her as the Tasmanian Devil from *Looney Toons* popped into her mind, and she stifled a laugh. Marlee was going to school for art. Maybe Kate could convince her to draw the silly picture.

As Kate reached for the handle of the stainless-steel refrigerator, she froze.

What the hell was that?

From the direction of the dark hall that led to her parents' room, she could have sworn she'd heard a noise. Was it her dad snoring? Farting in his sleep?

Despite the humorous thought, cold needles of dread prickled the back of her neck. Kate couldn't attribute the sensation to the usual concern over whether or not she'd woken her mom or dad on her way to the kitchen, either.

It's nothing. Probably the furnace or something.

She was about to concede to the rationalization when another bizarre groan drifted from the hall. A groan or a grunt?

Either way, the noise had definitely *not* come from one of the household appliances. Was it a movie?

One hand resting on the fridge handle, Kate peered into the dark hallway past the kitchen. A slat of faint light fell from the half-closed door, not quite bright enough to be the overhead light but not dim enough to be the television. She waited for a flicker that might indicate a scene change, but the golden glow remained steady.

Not a movie or a television show. Did her parents even keep a TV in their room? Kate wasn't sure. As an adult, the instances when she visited her parents' bedroom were few and far between.

The next noise was a cross between a grunt and a moan, and a sudden realization dawned on Kate.

Were her parents having sex?

Oh god, please no.

Her gut twisted, her appetite vanished. Why in the hell had they left the damn door open? Kate didn't live at home full-time, but her sister was still a senior in high school. Just because Kelly was likely asleep upstairs didn't mean their mom and dad would leave their room open when they were getting it on. They'd known Kate was out and that she'd be home eventually.

Did they want to gross her out? Was this some weird

display of dominance, an effort to remind Kate whose house this was?

No, that was ridiculous.

Heart in her throat, Kate remained rooted to the spot as the needles of dread morphed into full-on daggers.

College campuses could be a hostile environment for a young woman, and Kate had learned to trust her instincts when it came to her fellow students and faculty members. If her gut told her a house party was bad news, she'd collect her friends and leave. Any time a frat boy regarded her with that predatory glint in his eyes, she was always tempted to remind the creep that her mother was a federal judge for the Northern District of Illinois.

One in five girls were raped during their college careers, and Kate was determined to leave NIU with her degree, a few new friends, and nothing else. She was already a statistic thanks to a former friend's father, and she'd be damned if some dipshit frat boy made her check another box on her list of lifelong traumas.

She'd learned to trust her instincts, and right now, her instincts were screaming something was very wrong with this situation. With those...*sounds*.

Swallowing the sandpaper that had become her throat, Kate finally let go of the refrigerator. Even if this turned out to be nothing, she'd lost her appetite.

Though every neuron in her brain was trying to convince her nothing was amiss, Kate took a tentative step toward the hall. She didn't want to walk in on her parents screwing, but at the same time...she wasn't so sure that was what was happening.

She needed to know her parents were okay. That a burglar hadn't broken in to tie them up while they rifled through the family's valuables, or worse.

Almost as an afterthought, Kate paused and pulled a

butcher knife from the magnetic rack hanging beside the stove. Feeling slightly more confident now that she was armed with the same weapon Michael Myers used to torment Haddonfield, Illinois in the *Halloween* films, she slowly made her way to the hall.

Another grunt and moan were followed by a muffled whimper, sending a jolt of fear through Kate's already tense body.

She wanted to turn around, go up to her room, and crawl under her blankets like a small child hiding from the monsters under their bed.

Should she call 911?

And tell them what? That you heard some weird noises from your parents' bedroom?

She needed to witness for herself what was happening.

Clamping her hand as tightly around the knife handle as she could manage, Kate forced herself to take the next few steps. The soft glow spilling through the door was no longer warm. Instead, the illumination had morphed into the twisted light signaling the transition to a villain's lair in a horror film.

Ever so slightly, she tested each part of the hardwood before settling her weight more fully. Burglar or not, she didn't want to alert anyone to her presence.

The trip to the partially open doorway seemed to take far too long. Her heart clamored against her chest like it was trying to escape from her body, and any semblance of moisture had left her mouth. Even if she managed to avoid all the creaky parts of the floor, she was convinced the *thud-thud-thud* of her heart would alert anyone nearby of her presence.

Finally, after the agonizingly slow trek down the hall, she stopped short of the doorway. The noises were more distinct now, and Kate knew they were definitely not normal sex sounds.

For starters, the moans and groans of pleasure, or whatever in the hell they were, belonged to a male. And the, ugh...*pained* whimpers, well, those were male too.

Moving the knife behind her back and out of sight, Kate held her breath and hesitated. She wanted her brain to talk her out of this...whatever in the hell *this* was. She wished she could convince herself her parents were swingers, that they were into some kinky shit, or that their preference in porn had taken a turn for the nontraditional.

But all the rationalizations fell short of the sickening ball of dread sinking in her stomach.

One quick look. That's all she needed.

Poke your head around the corner, see what kind of weird stuff Mom and Dad are into, and then get the hell out of here and pretend like none of this ever happened.

Before she convinced her muscles to follow through with the plan, Kate knew she was standing at the precipice of an event that would permanently alter the rest of her life.

Just like she had when she'd spent the night with her friend Ginny for the first time. When she'd joined Gin and her father for dinner, the man had shot her a sneaky wink from across the table.

The alarm bells in the back of Kate's head had told her to text her mom and ask for a ride home. To lie and say she didn't feel well. To get the hell out of that house.

But she hadn't. She'd ignored her instincts, and she'd paid the price. Much like tonight, she'd seen the yawning chasm ahead of her for what it was...something that would change her forever.

When Ginny's father had woken her in the middle of the night and taken her to his room, that was the same sense of impending dread that now flowed through every vein, every capillary in her entire circulatory system. She hadn't known he'd put a mild sedative in his own daughter's food to make her sleep through his intrusion.

Now, an inexorable force propelled Kate forward. The inexplicable knowledge that no matter how she reacted, nothing would ever be the same.

Clenching her teeth together so tightly her jaw ached, Kate put her back to the drywall and moved forward until her shoulder was flush with the doorframe. She flexed her fingers on the grip of the knife, took in a silent breath, and inched her head forward.

The sole source of illumination was the light from the walk-in closet. Otherwise, the heavy, forest green curtains had been drawn to block out the picture window overlooking the backyard.

Kate didn't need an overhead light to realize something terrible had happened.

No, something terrible *was happening*.

In the little alcove that housed the window, Kate's mother was slumped in front of the settee where she liked to curl up to read on a rainy day.

Instead of a book in her hands, her wrists were bound together. The silver duct tape was smeared with blood, likely from the fresh gash on her forehead. Tears ran down her cheeks, streaking through the crimson staining the tape over her mouth. Though Kate's mother could have spotted her if she'd turned her head, she wasn't able to do so. Duct tape ran across her forehead, binding her to a table leg. And her eyes...they'd been taped wide open.

Kate was sure the scene couldn't get much worse, and she held onto that certainty until her eyes moved to the king-sized bed.

The green and white patterned blankets Kate's dad always took such care to straighten each morning were a disheveled bundle at the edge of the mattress, and at least half the collection of pillows was strewn across the floor. A darker bundle rested next to the comforter, the details shrouded in the shadow cast by a person standing over the bed.

It took Kate a moment to notice the supposed bundle wasn't bedding at all. It was her father.

And the man standing over the bed…

She clamped a hand over her mouth to suppress a gasp. Or a sob, she wasn't really sure.

The metal of a belt clinked as the broad-shouldered man pulled his pants up over what Kate suddenly realized was his bare ass.

That couldn't be right, could it? Those couldn't have been the sounds she'd heard as she was creeping down the hall. The moaning and the whimpering. Had that man brutalized her *father*?

Kate's head spun like a dreidel. Her stomach lurched, bile racing its way up the back of her throat. Before she risked making a sound that would give her away, she slowly backed out of the doorway.

Squeezing her eyes shut, she tightened her hand over her mouth, the other still desperately clutching the butcher knife.

What did she do now?

What *could* she do?

The figure hulking over her parents' bed was easily over six-foot, and he was built like a linebacker. On a good day, Kate reached five-nine—one inch shy of her mother's five-ten, and five inches shorter than her father.

She'd put on her freshman fifteen a few years ago and then a little more to boot. Though she diligently attended the gym four days a week, she'd barely managed to lose ten pounds, much less hammer out a physique that could compete with a six-foot-plus, muscle-bound man.

Even if she'd gone to those damn Krav Maga lessons, was

she really any match for the rapist now towering over her poor father?

Her parents had a few guns, but there was one problem. And it was a major one.

The guns were in their bedroom.

All Kate had was the butcher knife, but she wasn't indestructible. She wasn't Michael Myers, and this wasn't the town from *Halloween*. It was Chicago.

Do something. You have to do something to help them. Is he going to kill them? Is he going to rape Mom next? What about Kelly?

Each thought whipped through her brain like rounds from a plasma rifle in one of those shooter games Marlee and Jared liked to play.

Focus!

She snapped her eyes open, half-expecting to be face-to-face with the man from the bedroom.

Instead, she saw only the gray-blue drywall of the hallway wall across from her parents' bedroom and the trio of evenly spaced family photos that adorned it. Pictures of her, Kelly, Mom, and Dad. All staged, of course, but their smiles were genuine.

Kate's vision blurred as tears stung the corner of her eyes. Christ, how long had she been standing here, clutching so desperately at the threads of a reality that was threatening to unwind?

Too long. She needed to do something.

But what? Call the cops? The man in the room would hear her. She needed to get out of this part of the house if she wanted to call 911.

Just as Kate was preparing to take her first step away from the doorway, an unfamiliar voice stopped her dead in her tracks.

"How does it feel to watch someone you love suffer like that, Anna?"

Terror pulsed through Kate's body like lightning. The man wasn't addressing her, though.

He was talking to her mom.

"Now you know what we had to endure. Or, at least, you will know. Soon."

We?

There were two of them?

Kate's knees had turned to rubber, and her stomach threatened to expel her earlier drinks and snacks from her night out. Was a second man in the closet? Was that why the light had been turned on?

Desperate to make sense out of what was happening, Kate dipped her head through the doorframe before she could think better of the action. Her eyes darted from her mother to the bed and then to the man whose back still faced the doorway.

One, two, three...where was the accomplice?

Hidden. Out of sight. What did it matter?

What if he was somewhere else in the house? Had he gotten to Kelly?

Before Kate retracted to hide behind the wall, the intruder produced an item from his coat. A handgun, one that had been fitted with a sound suppressor.

By now, Kate was numb to the sheer horror that had threatened to consume her only moments ago. She was pointedly aware this wasn't a nightmare, but she also knew she was missing something. Chances were, she'd die before she ever found out what that something was.

"It's a shame, Anna." The man leveled the weapon to where Kate's father was still facedown on the bed. "You had such a beautiful family. You know what that's worth these days, don't you? But you squandered it. You squandered it by ruining another family. And now, you'll pay for it."

A soft *pop* came after the cryptic remark, followed almost immediately by a muffled wail of agony from her mother.

Mom. Dad. Why was this happening?

Her feet acted of their own volition, carrying her down the hall and avoiding all the creaky boards she'd crept past on her way to the kitchen. Adrenaline and abject terror fueled Kate's movements, and she was propelled forward by her primal instinct to survive.

She was across the open-air living area in seconds and had her hand on the front door before reality returned.

Kelly. She needed to go get Kelly. After that, she'd call the cops and get them both the hell out of there.

Turning from the door, she realized the stairs posed a brand-new challenge. Though the house had been renovated with modern appliances and a more functional floor plan, the place was still more than eighty years old, and the hardwood was original.

During her high school years, Kate had committed the squeaky parts of the steps to memory. As the sole night owl of the family, she'd utilized all her stealth to make her way to and from the kitchen while everyone else was asleep.

The intruder in her parents' room might not have been able to hear the creak of the steps if she landed in the wrong spot, but she still had no idea where the other man was. If he was creeping through her dad's study or through the upstairs bedrooms, then she didn't want to alert him of her presence. Right now, stealth was her only defense.

As she reached the top landing, a sliver of relief pierced through the fog of dread. Kelly's room was the second door on the right—directly across from Kate's. Once she got Kelly, they could hide in the attic, a closet, their shared bathroom, *somewhere*, and Kate could call the cops.

She wasn't so sure they could risk a trip downstairs, but if she minimized the volume on her phone and hid behind a closed door, she could get through to 911 without alerting the intruders. If a phone call wasn't an option, then she could always send a text message to Marlee and Jared to ask them to call the cops on her behalf. As long as the two weren't getting it on or sleeping...

Kate shut down the slew of what-ifs. She had to focus. She needed to get her sister the hell out of here.

Kelly's door was closed, a habit she'd picked up around thirteen. Before then, they'd all slept with their doors open so the family's two cats could migrate from place to place overnight. Once the beloved pets had passed, Kate was off to college, and Kelly had begun to value her privacy like a normal teenager.

Keeping her breathing as quiet as humanly possible, Kate glanced back and forth to ensure no one was about to creep up on her. As she twisted the doorknob, she clenched her jaw like it would prevent extraneous noise.

She threw another paranoid look over her shoulder, pushed the door open just wide enough to slide through, and closed it behind herself. Though Kelly's room was as dark as a cave, Kate didn't have time to pause to let her vision adjust. They needed to get the hell out of this house, and they needed to do it *now*.

As Kate crept along the carpeted floor, she strained her hearing for any signs that the madman from downstairs might have decided to change targets.

The room was quiet. *Too* quiet.

Without the quiet hum of the furnace in the background, Kelly's room was as silent as a tomb.

Cold fingers of dread began to close in around Kate's heart. Shouldn't she hear Kelly breathing? Snoring? *Something*?

Maybe she went over to a friend's house. She might not even be here.

Kate clung to the dim beacon of hope as she advanced another few steps. As much as she wanted to quietly call out to her sister, she resisted the urge. With her luck, the moment she spoke would be the same instant one of the psychopaths downstairs decided to patrol the hall.

The approximate shape of her sister's bed was about all she could make out in the darkness. If she wasn't careful, she'd trip or run into a piece of furniture and alert the intruders.

With a trembling hand, Kate reached to her back pocket to retrieve her cell. Entering in the PIN to unlock the screen was an arduous task, and she almost dropped the damn phone twice. Crime shows on television never showed people in a panic struggling to perform basic functions, like entering a six-digit code on a touch screen.

Tears of frustration and panic stung the corners of her eyes, but Kate refused to let them fall. Grating her teeth together, she held her breath and willed her thumb to cooperate.

Come on. 8-8-6-4-7-2.

A wave of relief washed over her as the numpad finally disappeared. The starry sky background was one of the most welcoming sights Kate had ever laid eyes on.

She didn't hesitate to turn the device over to shine the screen on the floor in front of her feet. She had a flashlight app, but she never used the damn thing, and she didn't want to waste precious time trying to find the right buttons. Besides, it was so dark in Kelly's room that she only needed the glow from the home screen.

Sure enough, she was only a few steps away from the foot of Kelly's bed. Tendrils of hope snuck in beside the panic and terror. If she could get herself and her sister the hell out of here, then...

As she shifted the phone to illuminate Kelly's bed, her breath caught in her throat.

No.

The white and green striped comforter was pulled up over the pillows, but a darker shade of crimson had soaked through the fabric.

Kate began to reach for the blanket, but she had no idea what she hoped to find. Best case scenario was...what, exactly? A bloody nose? A spilled drink? A head injury?

An iron tang filled her nostrils. She knew what she'd find, but she had to be sure.

At the same time she lifted the blanket, the creak of the stairs ripped her attention away from the sight of her sister's still form.

Someone was coming.

Tears blurred her vision again, her pulse pounding in her ears as she glanced to the bed. Kelly was facedown, but there was no mistaking the head of dark brown hair. The meager light of Kate's phone glinted off coagulating blood that coated not only the back of her sister's head but part of the comforter that Kate had lifted.

She threw the blanket back over her sister like it was a venomous animal that had bitten her. Her heart felt like it was coated in ice. Guts churning, Kate clamped a hand over her mouth to silence a sob.

Kelly was dead. Shot, undoubtedly by the same people who'd assaulted and killed her father downstairs. And her mom, what about her mom?

Someone's coming. Focus. Hide.

Using the faint light of her phone, Kate picked her way over to the door of Kelly's closet. Her motions were robotic as she twisted the knob, her entire body numb, mind reeling.

Before she could pry open the door, the floorboards outside Kelly's room alerted her to someone's presence.

Metal creaked as the person in the hall turned the knob.

This was it. Because Kate had been frozen by the sight of her dead sister for so long, she was about to be caught in front of a closet door by a lunatic. She was a sitting duck.

No. Not like this. I won't let him catch me standing here like a dumbass.

Survival instincts she didn't even know she possessed took over. A computer desk Kelly used more for gaming than homework rested against the wall perpendicular to the closet. When their parents had given Kelly the desk, Kate remembered thinking Kelly's choice of placement was at least partially strategic.

From where it sat beside the doorway, her parents wouldn't have time to glimpse what was on the monitor before Kelly had a chance to minimize anything she didn't want them to see. Smart, but no surprise considering the source. Kelly had always been the better student between the two Denson girls, but she'd preferred video games to homework just about any day of the week. All the coursework had come easily to Kelly, leaving her plenty of time to game.

Kate shoved her grief back into the darker recesses of her mind. Holding her breath, she ducked away from the closet and crouched in the kneehole of the desk. She'd be dead if the man on the other side of the door decided to take a thorough gander around the room, but she had no other options.

Tucking both knees up to her chest, she took in a breath as quietly as she could manage and turned off her phone to darken the screen.

The door creaked open, and a handful of muffled footsteps followed. When they stopped, Kate hugged herself a little tighter, praying to any deity that would listen that her phone was still on silent.

"Kelly Denson." The man's voice seemed to echo through the room like sound bouncing off slab walls in a mausoleum. "I'm sorry this had to happen, but we don't get to pick our family, do we?"

Kate pressed her face into her knees and swallowed against the fading sting of bile in her throat.

Just leave. Just leave, please. Please. Please. Please.

The man took another step, but Kate couldn't be sure if he was moving closer or farther away. Seconds dragged by with each passing moment like a tally mark on a prison cell wall.

Kate wasn't sure how much more she could take. For a beat, she wondered if she'd be better off if the man in her sister's room just killed her.

She shut the sentiment down as soon as it had formed. No, someone had to tell the authorities what had happened here. Kate's sister, dad, and probably her mother were all dead, and she was the only one who would ever be able to speak on their behalf.

She had to survive.

Tightening her grip on the butcher knife, Kate closed her eyes and thought back to the affirmations she and Marlee had come up with during their second semester in college.

I am resilient. I am strong. I will get through this.

She repeated them before adding a new affirmation. *I'll survive, and I'll tell my family's story.*

Her hand ached from her death grip on the knife.

She wasn't as formidable a force as Michael Myers, but she *was* strong. Like Laurie Strode, the protagonist of the original *Halloween*, Kate would persevere against unthinkable odds.

I'm going to survive this. Just breathe in and out. Slow and quiet. He doesn't know I'm here.

When the man cleared his throat, Kate nearly leapt in surprise. "Yeah, I'm coming. Just a second."

How long had she been curled up beneath her sister's desk, waiting for this evil prick to leave? Long enough to lose herself in the abyss of her thoughts, apparently.

Though Kate hadn't heard the person who'd beckoned him, she was grateful that *someone* had convinced him to leave.

The man let out a long breath and lowered his voice. "Sorry again, Kelly Denson. Sometimes this is just the way it goes. We don't get to pick our family, do we?"

Hinges creaked as he closed the door, leaving Kate alone in the dark with her sister's body.

2

Special Agent Amelia Storm paced back and forth in front of her apartment's granite breakfast bar, tugging at locks of her dark, blonde-tipped hair as she went. Twirling or pulling on her hair was a long-standing nervous tic, and right now, nervous was the name of her game. In fact, she couldn't remember the last time she'd been this anxious to talk to another human being.

At quarter 'til midnight, she was waiting for her friend and fellow FBI special agent, Zane Palmer. She could now add "lover" to that list, though they hadn't officially established their relationship. Not that the lack of labels was a bad thing. In fact, it was far from the source of her anxiety.

Taking in a deep breath, she rested a hand over her rapidly beating heart and turned to the open living room. She smiled at the long-haired calico perched on one arm of the sectional couch.

"How're ya doing, sweet girl?" Amelia's tension eased as she approached the cat and stroked Hup's soft fur.

A half meow, half purr was the cat's only response,

though she did lift her chin so Amelia could better reach her favorite scratching spot.

"That good, huh? I wish a good scratch could solve some of my problems."

The cat yawned and rolled over to expose her chest to the ministrations.

Amelia huffed. "You might want to work on your listening skills."

Amelia had taken Hup in after solving a big case earlier that year, and she hadn't regretted bringing her furry roommate home since that fateful day.

Home.

Being back in Chicago was a blessing and a curse. It's where she'd lived for her entire childhood. It was where her father, her sister-in-law, niece, and nephew were. During the decade she'd spent in the military, she'd been in Chicago less and less, though her absence was largely by design.

After all, she hadn't left Chicago at eighteen because she *wanted* to leave. She'd left because the father of her then-boyfriend had threatened to do unspeakable things to her if she remained in the city.

Parents threatening the significant others of their children wasn't particularly uncommon. Amelia had witnessed plenty of pudgy, middle-aged men wearing t-shirts that read "rules for dating my daughter" or some other equivalent nonsense.

But most of the men and women wearing those stupid shirts weren't highly renowned mafia commanders, and most of their sons weren't their prodigy in the same illicit line of work. Luca Passarelli, the father of Amelia's high school sweetheart, Alex Passarelli, had been, still *was,* mafia royalty. A filthy commoner like Amelia Storm had threatened Luca's ideal for his son's future—a future that would carry on the lineage of the D'Amato and Passarelli families.

Twisting a piece of hair around her index finger, Amelia paced to the kitchen before turning her attention back to the cat. Though Hup sat perfectly upright, her eyes were closed, and she looked more serene than Amelia had ever felt.

Amelia envied the feline's ability to shut out the world and sleep for sixteen hours per day. "Must be rough, being a cat."

One orange and black ear twitched, but otherwise, Hup didn't acknowledge the human's presence.

"The only time you're ever anxious is when you can see the bottom of your food bowl. I bet you'd be freaking out a little too if you were about to tell your…boyfriend? Is that what he is?" Amelia waved a dismissive hand like she was talking to another human being who was paying attention to her, and not a cat that was half-asleep. "Whatever he is, I'm going to tell him about the note I got a week ago."

She paused in her rant. Was it a week ago? No, almost two weeks ago.

It had been nearly fourteen days since Amelia had arrested the serial killer James Amsdell, whom the media had dubbed The New Moon Killer due to his deranged religious motivation, which included carving Bible verses into the flesh of each victim. He'd even dumped two people into Lake Michigan. After his arrest, Amelia had emerged from a coffee shop to find a handwritten note beneath one of her car's windshield wipers.

Agent Storm,

I need to talk to you. I've been putting this off for far too long, and it's time you know the truth about what happened to Trevor. I was his confidential informant in the Gianna Passarelli case. Don't waste your time looking for my name. You won't find it.

Please understand this is very risky for me. There are fates much worse than death that await me if I'm caught. I want to meet with you. Be at this address in two weeks.

And the writer of the note? Someone who alleged to be her brother's confidential informant during a mafia-related kidnapping case.

A case that had led up to Trevor Storm being shot and killed by a still-unknown assailant. A case that Trevor had worked off the books for the D'Amato family—one of Chicago's two major Italian crime families.

The time to meet up with the supposed informant was nearing, and Amelia hadn't heard another peep from the CI. Not a text, an email, a phone call, or even another damned note.

They'd given her an address to meet, but aside from stipulating "two weeks," they hadn't provided a specific timeframe. When it came to a person who might have information pertaining to her brother's murder, she wasn't willing to deal in approximations. She wanted a specific date and time, but she didn't have the first clue how to get either.

"Don't waste your time looking for my name. You won't find it."

She'd ignored the pointed suggestion altogether, and her first order of business had been to search for the damn name by scouring every case Trevor had ever worked on, hoping something might pop out at her. What kind of investigator would she be if she'd just taken the note at its word?

Then, there were the photos she'd been given of fellow special agent Joseph Larson on a yacht with a former trafficking suspect, Brian Kolthoff—also known as The Shark. Kolthoff was a former venture capitalist turned D.C. lobbyist, a billionaire, and Amelia strongly suspected, a sex trafficker. If the man was in cahoots with one of the FBI's own, then the relationship could have dire implications.

Blowing out a frustrated sigh, she leaned against the granite bar and scrutinized the open floorplan of her apartment. Hup's tail swished.

"Don't you swish your tail at me. This is my apartment. I can sigh as much as I want. You don't pay rent here."

The calico's ears flattened slightly, and Amelia wondered if she'd understood the sarcasm.

Amelia threw her arms up in the air. "Then get a job and pay rent."

Another tail flick was followed by a squinty stare.

"You didn't like that idea very much, did you?" An outside observer might have thought Amelia was insane for holding a conversation with her cat, but there were times Amelia thought Hup must have been a person in a previous life.

Hup tucked her front paws beneath herself until she resembled a loaf. As the cat closed her eyes, Amelia resumed pacing.

The day before, Amelia had chickened out when she'd decided to tell Zane, the man who may or may not be her significant other, about the note.

Or maybe she hadn't chickened out as much as she'd been swept up in the heat of a moment that had come with their reunion after his three-day trip to visit family on the East Coast. Amelia had spent the Christmas holiday with her dad and her sister-in-law, but she and Zane had both agreed it was premature to drag the other out to meet parents and siblings.

Either way, she'd planned to tell him yesterday, but she hadn't succeeded.

On the surface, discussing the mysterious note with someone she trusted as much as Zane shouldn't have bothered her. And it wouldn't have, except revealing the person who claimed to be Trevor's confidential informant meant unearthing all the skeletons that went along with her brother's final years.

Namely, the fact that he was a corrupt cop working for the D'Amato family. And if she revealed Trevor's relationship with the D'Amatos to Zane, then she'd have to explain *her* affiliation.

If anyone other than Zane found out she'd used information obtained from a D'Amato family capo to arrest the creeps responsible for an underage sex trafficking ring, it might mean the case could be reopened and the conviction potentially overturned.

It didn't stop there, either. Alex Passarelli had provided valuable information that helped her locate sixteen-year-old Leila Jackson from within Emilio Leóne's sex trafficking ring. While CIs were used all the time and only rarely had their identities revealed, the optics of being seen with a mafia capo could derail Amelia's credibility and her career.

They don't have to find out. Zane won't tell anyone. I know he won't. I trust him.

Amelia gnawed at her bottom lip. Fortunately, her brain didn't have much more time to spiral into the land of what-ifs before she caught a pair of headlights glinting through the half-closed blinds. Heart *thud-thudding* against her chest, Amelia quickly strode over to check the parking lot from her second-story vantage point.

Relief, mixed with a touch of trepidation, flooded her as she spotted the familiar silver Acura.

Twenty minutes ago, Zane had sent her a text to tell her he was on his way to her place. Zane had been invited to the engagement party of one of the younger men who were part of the cleaning crew that maintained the FBI building.

In Zane's nine months in Chicago, he'd befriended most of the field office's janitorial staff. Even now, Amelia was fairly sure Zane had more friends on the cleaning crew than he did in the actual Bureau.

He'd asked Amelia to accompany him to the evening's festivities, but she'd declined in the interest of spending her evening napping and watching television. Now that the

Amsdell case had wrapped up, she'd been grateful for the moments of respite.

To her chagrin, all she'd done instead was mentally go over the upcoming conversation. Over. And over. And over. She'd imagined all the ways the dialogue could go horribly wrong, but few instances where the discussion went well.

Seeming to sense another person would soon encroach on her territory, Hup opened her eyes and twitched her ears.

As Amelia made her way to the foyer, she pointed an accusatory finger at the cat. "You don't pay rent, remember? You don't get to decide when we have company. Go nap somewhere else if you don't like it."

In response, Hup yawned.

Flicking the deadbolt, Amelia glanced back toward the breakfast bar. She'd stuffed the note, as well as the two printed images of Larson and Kolthoff, into a manila envelope. Partially because she didn't want to languish in front of them any more than she already had, and partially because she couldn't help but wonder if they were connected.

Had Trevor been on Kolthoff's radar? On *Joseph's* radar?

Anger bubbled in Amelia's veins at the thought. She'd never been one to put much stock into coincidence. Even in a city the size of Chicago, there were only a few degrees of separation for the average Joe.

When it came to criminal activity, just about everyone had something to say about everyone else. No one operated on any noteworthy scale without piquing the attention of one of the major players in the city's seedy underbelly. The San Luis Cartel, the Veracruz Cartel, the D'Amato family, the Leóne family, or the Russians.

Amelia rubbed her temples and forced the doubts from her head. Squinting through the peephole, she caught sight of Zane as he ascended the last few steps at the end of the hall.

The sight of him lifted her spirits and drove away a portion of her worries.

Now that she could *see* him, somehow, she felt more confident about presenting the note and the pictures to him.

He'd understand why she hadn't said anything until now. Both of them harbored secrets, and they'd learned to trust that the other would reveal them if or when it became relevant.

Well, it's relevant now, isn't it?

Pulling open the door, she permitted a wide smile to make its way to her face.

At six-three, a height attained thanks in part to his Nordic ancestry, Zane stood more than half a foot taller than Amelia's five-eight. With his professed hatred of shaving, a couple days' worth of stubble almost always darkened his cheeks. Aside from his scruffy face, however, every aspect of his appearance was always meticulous. Tonight was no exception.

Parted to the side, his dark blond hair was brushed forward and styled as fashionably as ever, and his usual black frock coat made him look every bit the part of an FBI agent. Even if he was just coming from an engagement party.

His gray eyes met hers, and his lips parted in a wide smile that revealed perfectly straight white teeth.

That showstopping smile still made her feel as giddy as a lovestruck teenager. "Hey, you. How was the party?"

He stepped past her as she closed and locked the door. "Good. They did a potluck thing, which I guess is a tradition in their family." He patted his belly. "Lots of homemade food. I stuffed my face."

Amelia laughed, permitting herself to soak up the moment of good humor. No matter the hardships she'd faced since returning to Chicago, she was truly glad to be in the presence of a wonderful person like Zane Palmer.

She waited until he'd shucked off his coat and shoes before she wrapped him in a tight embrace. "I'm glad you had a good time."

Tucking two fingers beneath her chin, he lifted her face for a light, loving kiss. This was the point yesterday where Amelia had lost her will to broach the subject of the note and the D'Amato family, electing instead to press herself against his lean, muscular frame and usher him in the direction of the bedroom.

Tonight was different, however. Time was growing short, and her meeting with Trevor's supposed CI was right around the corner. In order to lock in her commitment to discuss the subject with Zane, Amelia had even sent him a text advising that she had a dilemma she wanted to run by him. That way, even if she tried to procrastinate or dodge the subject, he'd have enough curiosity to prod an answer out of her.

Provided he remembered, that was. But when a girlfriend or partner or whatever she was sent a message asking to talk something through, what man or woman *could* forget?

Not Zane. He might act like a goofball, but he had a mind like a steel trap.

Just rip off the band-aid. Show him the pictures and the note and get this shit out in the open already.

As they separated, Amelia took a step toward the dining table and cleared her throat. "So, um, there's something I wanted to ask you about."

He cocked an eyebrow, his gaze following her every movement. "Oh? Is it about...us?" He gestured to her and then himself. "Whether or not we're a thing?"

A pang of guilt stabbed at Amelia's heart. She hadn't wanted her message to cause him any worry, but she didn't miss the trepidation in his voice. "That wasn't it, no. But we are, aren't we? Or do we want to be?"

His expression brightened a notch. "Of course *I* want to be. What say you, Ms. Storm?"

Even the way he still spoke with a slight Jersey accent was endearing. Despite the heavy subject matter ahead of them, she grinned at his response. "I say yes, we're a thing."

He held up an invisible glass and returned her smile. "Here's to being a thing, then."

Amelia couldn't remember the last time she was this happy. It would be so easy to forget about the damn D'Amatos and the cryptic note and just enjoy her night with this man. But she knew herself, and she knew the CI's message would eat away at her until it drove her insane.

Happiness later. For now, she needed to get this over with.

Motioning to the manila envelope, she took a couple more steps toward the matte black table. "I...have something to show you. Something I might need your help with."

His face went from jovial to focused in a fraction of a second. With a silent nod, he followed her to the dining area next to the breakfast bar.

Amelia's pulse picked up speed, and her palms were suddenly clammy.

It's been three years since Trevor was killed, and you haven't talked about it with anyone other than the detectives who worked his case. It's time to put this shit out in the open. Time to get some answers, and by now, it ought to be obvious you might need a little help with that.

Following the mental pep talk, a surge of determination chased away the nervousness. Revealing vulnerabilities and asking for help had never come naturally to Amelia. Ever since she was a kid and her mother died, she'd shouldered every one of her life's emotional burdens by herself.

With an alcoholic father—who was currently four years sober—she hadn't been granted many resources to navigate her emotional hardships. Trevor had helped, but there was only so much she'd been comfortable sharing with her older brother. And then, of course, he'd been killed.

The inner contemplation lasted for only a moment, and when she returned her focus to the room, she was confident she was doing the right thing. Not only was Zane an important person in her life, but he was also a former CIA operative. He'd never said the words specifically, but Amelia had deduced enough in their conversations to conclude his ten-plus years with the Bureau hadn't actually been spent with the FBI.

Amelia cleared her throat a second time and scooped up the manila envelope. "It's…sort of work-related, I guess? Part of it is. Part of it isn't."

Though an irrational part of her worried he'd grow impatient with all her postponement, Zane's expression changed little as she fumbled with the metal clasp.

Pulling in a deep breath, she pulled out the note and plunked it down on the table. "Remember when I grabbed sandwiches from Herman's after the Amsdell takedown?"

Zane's gaze flicked from the paper to Amelia and back. "Yeah. Herman's was Steelman's recommendation, and we've been back there, like, five times since then."

Her spirits lifted a little at the comment, and she reminded herself this wasn't an excuse to get side-tracked. She tapped the note for emphasis. "Cassandra and I were at the café near the office, and when I went out to my car, this was under the windshield."

Assistant U.S. Attorney Cassandra Halcott had taken point on prosecuting the New Moon Killer. The discovery of a new serial killer who'd been active for more than four years had been a national media sensation, and to Amelia's relief, Halcott had taken on the entirety of the spotlight.

Unless public relations were part of their job description,

FBI agents in Organized Crime weren't often exposed to the media, save for official press conferences. Such a public profile would render undercover work nearly impossible, though Amelia had already crossed that bridge when she'd been framed by a fellow agent.

Former Special Agent Glenn Kantowski, a member of the Bureau's Public Corruption Unit, had disseminated doctored photos of Amelia screwing a city councilman. Thanks to the quick work of Cassandra Halcott and the U.S. Attorney's office, the Bureau had nipped the scandal in the bud before it could become a nationwide headline. However, the story had been picked up by every local news outlet, which meant Amelia's days of in-depth undercover work had ended before they'd begun.

A crease gradually deepened between his eyebrows as Zane scanned the sheet of notebook paper. "Someone left this on your car in broad daylight, at a coffee shop?"

His tone was non-accusatory, but Amelia was still struck with a reflexive pang of defensiveness. "I know, it sounds ridiculous, doesn't it?"

He shook his head. "No, not really. It's the same concept as hiding in plain sight. It's just..." he paused and ran a hand through his sandy brown hair, "for the person to do something that ballsy, it shows some level of confidence. It makes me wonder who in the hell this is."

Amelia had to admit his point was valid. She'd mulled over the mystery person's identity more times than she could count. "I was thinking the same thing. It makes me wonder if..." She worried at her bottom lip. The theory was a little out-there, but considering the crux of what she was dealing with, nothing was too farfetched. "If they're an FBI agent."

Scratching his unshaven cheek, Zane pulled out a chair and dropped down to sit. "I wouldn't rule it out. But it says they're your brother's old CI, so that wouldn't make any sense. Why would an agent be a CI to a city detective?"

"I don't know. I thought the same thing. It just seemed like a convenient theory, I guess. But…" Now came the hard part. The context behind the note. Secrets Amelia had kept buried since she was a teenager…since she fled Chicago and joined the military.

Through the doubt that clawed at the back of her mind, she took a seat, angling the chair to face Zane. His face was a mask of concern, and it struck her that this was perhaps the most vulnerable he'd ever been in her presence.

Typically, Zane Palmer was unbothered by just about anything. He wore his insecurities on his sleeve, or at least, that's what he wanted people to believe. Despite his never-ending supply of embarrassing middle school stories, there were deeper struggles he faced that Amelia doubted he'd shared with another living soul.

For him to be so worried was bizarre. Like Amelia had awoken to find the earth spinning in the wrong direction.

She took in a deep breath and straightened her back. "There's more to it. To Trevor, and to me too, I guess."

He lifted an eyebrow, some of the anxiety giving way to curiosity. "I know, and it's okay. Does it have something to do with this note? And with how your brother was killed?"

Amelia should have known someone as sharp as Zane would have put two and two together by now. "Yes. Well, at least, I think it does. There's not really any other explanation. Look, this is going to sound bad no matter how I go about it, so I'll cut right to it. My brother was…he wasn't exactly on the straight and narrow."

Zane pulled the note closer and scrutinized it before he turned back to Amelia. "He was dirty?"

The base of Amelia's skull prickled, and she fought the rush of defensiveness and anger the simple statement brought to light. Blowing out a long sigh, she massaged her temples.

Before she could speak, Zane lifted a hand. "Sorry. I didn't mean it like...*that*. I'll shut up now."

"No, it's okay." The irritability subsided as she returned her attention to him. "It's true. He wasn't a bad guy, but he was dirty. He worked with the D'Amato family."

Saying the words out loud was surreal. For a beat, Amelia wasn't sure if she was in the real world or some form of *The Twilight Zone*. Until now, she was the only person—aside from the D'Amatos, of course—who'd known about Trevor's extracurricular activities during his tenure with the Chicago Police Department.

The pain beginning to pulse in her temples was a reminder that this was, in fact, reality. "I don't know what exactly he did for them. Probably the usual, at least for the most part. But I do know of one thing he was doing for them when he was killed. The detectives who worked his case didn't find anything that pointed to either the D'Amatos or the Leónes, but we both know how well those families can hide something they don't want people to find."

Zane snorted quietly. "That's no shit."

Half smiling, Amelia threaded her fingers together to keep herself from wringing her hands. "Well, that's why no one ever found what I'm about to tell you. Because the D'Amatos didn't want them to. And because I didn't want them to."

He kept his gaze fixed on hers, his gentle expression a silent bid to continue. A reminder he wouldn't judge her.

"When I was in high school, five years after my mom died, I got a job at a movie theater. My dad blew all his money on booze, and the only way I was going to get anything I wanted was to buy it myself. I was only fifteen, so

I got shit for hours and was always assigned to the concession stand."

Zane chuckled, but Amelia could tell the laugh was mostly for her sake.

She pushed her hair back from her face and locked her fingers behind her neck. "Sorry. I digress. That's where I met the guy I dated throughout high school." She licked her lips and mentally braced for the words she was about to say aloud. "That guy was Alex Passarelli."

For only a split second, Zane's eyes shot open wide. In the silence that followed, however, the surprise dissipated from his face, replaced by understanding. "I can see why you wouldn't want the Bureau to know about that. Good thing that was before social media got as big as it is now, huh?"

His lighthearted tone was like music to Amelia's ears. Finally, after the nine and a half months they'd known one another, Amelia's darkest secrets were out in the open.

More importantly, she'd been right. Judgment or anger was nowhere to be found in Zane's expression. As he tilted his head to the side, he tapped his index finger on the note. "That's how your brother got his start with the D'Amatos, right?"

"Yeah." She held out her hands. "I don't know when, and I don't know how. Trevor took all that information with him when he died, and god knows Alex won't ever tell me the truth."

Zane rubbed his chin. "You've been in contact with him?"

"Professionally." Amelia's tone was crisper than she'd intended, and warmth crept up her cheeks. "Sorry, I couldn't tell if you were asking as a...boyfriend, or you know."

To her relief, he flashed her one of his patented grins. "Asking *professionally*."

Huffing with feigned indignation, Amelia crossed her legs and arms. "I mean, I couldn't just show back up in Chicago to work in Organized Crime *without* consulting my mob boss ex-boyfriend."

Zane laughed. "True. Seems like he'd be a valuable source of information on the Leónes too."

"The world's weirdest CI." If Amelia didn't make light of the situation, she was sure the borderline dissociation would swallow her whole. "He gave me information in the Leila Jackson case. He provided Giorgio Delusso's identity and the location of Emilio Leóne's hideout."

Zane offered an approving nod. "We take those. That's what the kids are saying, isn't it? Ex-boyfriend, mob boss, who gives a shit when it helps you lock up a sex trafficker at the end of the day. Trust me, I've gotten information from shadier sources."

She didn't doubt him. The entire purpose of the CIA was to gather intelligence on issues related to national security. They took their leads where they got them.

Now that revealing the tangled mess that was her relationship with Alex Passarelli was out of the way, renewed determination rushed through Amelia's veins. She grabbed the manila envelope, pulled out the two photos of Joseph Larson and Brian Kolthoff, and set them just above the note.

Zane sucked in a sharp breath. "What the hell? Is that... Larson? And Brian Kolthoff? The fucking Shark?" His gaze snapped back up to hers. "Where did you get these?"

"Alex Passarelli." Amelia took stock of the pictures.

Both depicted Larson and Kolthoff on the upper deck of a luxurious yacht, though the vessel was different in each photo. In the older of the pair, the men each held drinks, their colorful button-down shirts and shades giving off a vacation vibe.

As for the second, newer image, Kolthoff was in the middle of laughing, presumably at something Joseph had said. Their attire was more formal this time—more "cocktail party" and less "spring break."

"Shit." Zane drew the word out from one syllable to more than five. "These are two different locations, yeah?"

"Right." She gestured to the image of the two creeps in their Hawaiian getup. "That one is from four years ago, or at least that's what Alex said. The other is more recent. It's from a few *months* ago."

"Shit." Zane nearly spit the word that time. "That means when we worked the Leila Jackson case, Larson was already pals with The Shark?"

"Exactly. This proves it." She wrapped a piece of hair around her index finger, finally giving in to the tic. "The only problem is I can't exactly take these in and sit them down in front of SAC Keaton, you know? I need to corroborate them, which is what I've been working on. I just haven't had any luck."

"I can help with that."

Gratitude seized Amelia's throat. Moments when Amelia was rendered speechless weren't common, but she struggled to find a suitable response to Zane's assurance.

Sure, she'd *wanted* to ask him for his expertise on the situation. She'd *hoped* he might have an old contact in the CIA who could give them some more background, but she hadn't been prepared for him to come out and offer his assistance right off the bat.

He leaned closer to the table, his eyes flitting from one picture to the next. "We know these aren't Larson's boats, so they're probably Kolthoff's. Kolthoff's a billionaire, and if I remember right, he's got one of the top fifty largest yachts in the world. Boats have to dock somewhere, right? Usually, those places are..." he made a show of weighing his hands, "heavily monitored, to say the least. I think I might have someone that could help us out."

Amelia opened and closed her mouth a couple times before shaking off the moment of surprise. Of course he'd help her. What else should she have expected? "Thank you. I really appreciate that."

He smiled and rested a hand on her forearm. "You know I've got your back. This might be what we need to finally get Larson the hell out of the FBI. If we can do it before he applies for Spencer's spot, I think we'd be doing the Bureau a favor."

After Joseph had tried and failed to blackmail Amelia into sleeping with him, she'd just as soon send him to a prison cell. What for, she still wasn't sure. However, his relationship with Brian Kolthoff and his subsequent involvement in the Leila Jackson investigation—and his failure to disclose his friendship with Kolthoff after the man had become their prime suspect—was most definitely an offense worthy of firing.

She'd take what she could get.

Scooting to the edge of her chair, Amelia pointed to the note. The most difficult part of the conversation was over, but there was still a significant problem to solve.

Zane's gaze followed hers to the paper. "Right. What's the background for this?"

"When my brother died, he was investigating a kidnapping. Gianna Passarelli's case. The cops who worked it initially had shelved it by that point. It was a cold case, and the D'Amatos paid my brother a pretty penny to reopen it off the books. Apparently, they thought he'd have access to a lot of resources they didn't, and he could make some headway in the case where the previous detectives had failed."

Zane nodded his understanding. "What did he find?"

Amelia lifted a shoulder and let it fall. "I don't know. Nothing, as far as I can tell."

"They, whoever 'they' is, wouldn't have killed him if he'd

found nothing." The surety with which Zane spoke the words insisted he was speaking from experience.

"That's what I think too. I tried to find any record of who this CI might be, but like they said in the note, there's nothing. Whoever they are, they're a ghost. I got this thing almost two weeks ago, and I still have no idea what time or what specific day they expect me to meet with them."

"How about the address? Did you find anything from it?"

She slumped down in her seat. "Nothing. It's just a park east of the city. There's a pond, and Google reviews of the place say some mean geese like to hang out there during the spring and summer."

"This person has to give you something more than 'meet me in two weeks.' That leaves way too much to interpretation. Is it exactly two weeks, or do they mean two business weeks? And what time? Are you just supposed to spend your entire day out in bum fuck nowhere waiting for this person who may or may not show while fending off geese from hell?"

"Your guess is as good as mine." She propped an elbow on the table and dropped her cheek into her hand. "I really want to know who in the hell wrote this, but like you said, I can't spend an entire day out of the city just sitting on my hands."

"Yeah, I know." Zane reached for the pocket of his black slacks. As he produced his cell, he shot Amelia a sheepish look. "Sorry. I didn't think I'd be getting any calls at midnight."

With a reassuring smile, she gestured to the living room. "Mine is sitting in there with the volume turned on. We're in the same boat so don't feel bad."

Zane turned his phone so she could view the screen. "Speaking of work, that's who's calling."

"Well, you'd better answer it." Amelia's mood sank a notch at the idea of Zane being summoned to work. Their job wasn't just a typical nine-to-five grind. If the FBI was calling late at night on a Sunday, then the reason was important.

Mouthing an apology, Zane swiped the screen and raised the phone to his ear. "This is Agent Palmer."

A tinny voice responded immediately, but Amelia could only make out enough to discern that the caller was their boss, Spencer Corsaw.

"Uh-huh." Zane's face grew somber. "A judge?"

Goose bumps rose on Amelia's forearms.

"Okay. Yeah, I'll grab Agent Storm, and we'll head to the scene. All right. Thanks, you too. Bye."

No, Zane wasn't being called into work. They *both* were. "That didn't sound good."

Zane shoved to his feet and pocketed his cell. "It's not. A federal judge and her family were just found murdered in their home."

Amelia followed his lead and stood, her emotions and hopes for the evening taking a back seat as she donned her Agent Storm persona. "Let's go."

3

As Zane Palmer ducked beneath the yellow crime scene tape, Amelia only a couple steps behind him, he was struck by the sheer amount of personnel milling about the Denson residence. He'd counted five patrol cars, an ambulance, the medical examiner's van, a couple unmarked vehicles, and then three crime scene vans. The city and the Bureau's response had been swift and comprehensive.

Such an undertaking came with the territory when they were dealing with the murder of high importance.

According to Spencer Corsaw, the 911 call had only come in twenty minutes before the FBI was alerted. Since one of the three victims was a federal judge for the Northern District of Illinois, the case automatically fell into federal jurisdiction. Though city police officers had been the first to respond and secure the scene, they'd wasted no time in calling in the cavalry.

Not that Zane could blame them. A triple homicide wasn't an investigation many cops wanted on their desk. City cops already had a hell of a workload as it was.

Aside from a small cluster of about ten people milling on

the street in front of the two-story gray stone house, the media presence so far was minimal, though he knew that wouldn't last long. Even though it was nearly one in the morning, Zane noted a couple civilians holding up their phones to capture video or photos of the Denson house.

He barely kept himself from shouting at them as he and Amelia flashed their badges to the pair of uniformed officers at the front door.

What great neighbors. They come out in the middle of the night after you and your entire family are murdered because they want to get a scoop for their social media accounts. These people would sell their kids for a "like."

Studying the crowd, Zane was also aware that many killers had a voyeuristic tendency. The old adage of returning to the scene of a crime was cliché for a reason.

Pausing at the threshold of the front door, Zane turned back to the taller of the two officers. "You've got someone keeping an eye on that crowd, right?"

The officer, a clean-shaven fellow with striking green eyes, nodded. "Sure do. We made sure to get that set up right away after securing the property."

Zane returned the man's nod. "Appreciate it."

As the pair went back to their vigil, Zane eased the door closed to keep the cold December wind from entering the house. From his limited vantage point at the edge of the foyer, he spotted a couple members of the CSU making their way through the living room, their camera shutters clicking as they documented each and every item, never knowing an item's significance.

After taking off their coats, he and Amelia both accepted a pair of booties and gloves from a petite blonde tech who'd been stationed in the foyer. Once they'd signed in and donned the protective apparel, she pointed down a hallway. "The downstairs bedroom is just down the hall past the kitchen. It's where Judge Denson and her husband's bodies were found. There's another bedroom upstairs where the youngest daughter's body was located."

Amelia peered around the corner before shifting her attention to the tech. "Who else is on the scene so far? Any detectives, other agents?"

"The officers who responded to the 911 call are still here. The two of them were in the kitchen, last I knew. The medical examiner got here a few minutes before you two did. I believe she's in the downstairs bedroom right now."

"Okay. Thank you." With a slight smile, Amelia turned to Zane. "Let's talk to the officers first, and then the M.E.?"

"Sounds good."

Picking their way through the spacious living area, Amelia and Zane set off in the direction indicated by the tech at the front door. The information Zane had received from Spencer was minimal—only that the judge, her husband, and their youngest daughter had been killed. No mention of the cause of death, or any other details. Spencer had also advised he was personally en route to the Denson house, but his commute was a bit longer.

Hopefully, the responding officers could shed some more light on the situation.

As Zane rounded an angled breakfast bar, he locked gazes with an officer who could have been SAC Keaton's younger sister. Her black hair was pulled into a neat, low bun, and her brown eyes were as astute as any agent at the FBI.

To her side, standing a full head taller than the woman, who was five-four on a good day, was the man who must have been her partner. His face was youthful, but his dark blue eyes belied a person who'd been through his fair share of battles.

Zane went to reach for his badge but stopped himself, remembering partway through the motion that he was wearing vinyl gloves for a reason. "Evening, Officers. I'm Special Agent Palmer, and this is my partner, Special Agent Storm."

The man started to reach for a handshake, but like Zane, caught himself and dropped his arm back to his side. "Evening, Agents. I'm Officer Redfield."

"And I'm Officer Hernandez." The woman inclined her chin, her expression as unflinching as a statue. "We were the first on the scene. We've already gone over our movements with the crime scene techs. Nothing much to note about our arrival, though. We didn't disturb anything, just went directly to the witness and then cleared the house."

Anticipation flared in Zane's chest. "A witness? Where'd they go?"

Redfield glanced to his partner, to the hall at their backs, and then to Amelia and Zane. "Hospital to get checked out. Densons' eldest daughter home from college. She said she wasn't injured, but it's standard procedure."

"She was in shock." Hernandez tapped her temple. "Psychological shock, I mean. We see it pretty often in folks who just witnessed something traumatic. She was coherent and all, but she had that look in her eyes."

Zane's heart squeezed. "The thousand-yard stare. Poor kid."

Redfield raised a shoulder. "We asked her some questions, but she sounded like a robot."

Amelia dug in her coat for a miniature notepad and a pen. She'd have to replace her gloves before she handled any object in the house, but Zane was grateful for her foresight. At least they could read her handwriting. Any time he took notes, Amelia always had to ask for clarification on what each chicken scratch meant.

Redfield crossed his arms, glancing up at the ceiling as he appeared thoughtful. "We asked her if there was anyone else in the house other than her, and she said she didn't think so. She thought she'd heard them leave but said she couldn't be completely sure. That's why we did a full clear of the place."

Amelia scribbled a few words on her notepad. "Them? Did she say there was more than one person involved?"

"We asked, and she said she wasn't sure." Redfield touched his silver name plate—either a normal mannerism or a nervous tic. Despite his mask of indifference, Zane suspected the night's events had gotten under his skin.

Though Zane had been hopeful learning of a witness, his spirits were sinking like a ship that collided with an iceberg. "She wasn't sure? Did she actually see anything?"

Redfield shook his head. "You're going to have to talk to her about that, Agent. We didn't get into an in-depth conversation with her. We just asked if she was hurt and if there was anyone else in the house. She said no to the former and wasn't sure about the latter. Otherwise, we just asked her name and if she knew what day it was. Standard stuff to make sure she wasn't suffering from a brain injury."

Before Zane could pose another query, Amelia jumped in. "All right. We'll save those questions for her. What did you two see when you were sweeping the house?"

Redfield's finger went back to the name plate, and Hernandez looked down at her feet. When her gaze returned to Zane and Amelia, her face was calm. Not an honest, serene expression, but the forced sort of calm a person used to keep their cards close to the vest. "One vic upstairs, and two downstairs. The male, Stephen Denson, appeared to have been shot in the back of the head, but he was disrobed from the waist down."

Now, Zane understood why she was wearing a mask of dispassion. "Sexual assault?"

Hernandez blew out a breath. "We can't say for sure. I'm just telling you what we saw."

Zane offered her a sympathetic glance. "Sorry. Go ahead."

"The female in the downstairs bedroom, Anna Denson, was also dead from what appears to have been a single shot to the head." The officer's jaw tightened before she continued. "The third vic was upstairs. Kelly Denson, seventeen, a high school senior. A shot to the back of her head, possibly while she was sleeping."

An entire family, minus one daughter, murdered, execution-style. No, not just any family, but the family of a damn *federal judge*. Zane now understood why Organized Crime had been called to the scene. So far, the description provided by Hernandez and Redfield reeked of mafia involvement.

However, the possible sexual assault of Stephen Denson muddied the waters. Was he the target, or was his wife?

Zane filed the questions away to be reexamined later. "All right. Let's see if we can get some officers to canvass the neighborhood. Ask anyone nearby if they heard or saw anything."

A portion of the tension left Redfield's stance. "We can do that. We think some of the people out front are from this block."

Hernandez snorted. "What lovely neighbors."

Amelia put away her pen and paper. "Just stay close by. We might have more questions for you after we talk to the medical examiner."

"Can do." Redfield touched his hat, and he and his partner left the open-concept kitchen.

Neither Zane nor Amelia spoke as they made their way to the master bedroom, passing yet another crime scene tech. Though Zane hadn't expected the FBI to be called on an open and shut case, the systematic murder of a judge and her family was a quagmire. Less than ten minutes in and he already felt the ground beginning to swallow him.

As he and Amelia entered the master suite, two familiar

faces turned toward them. Sabrina Ackerly, one of Cook County's youngest appointed medical examiners in recent history, might have rolled out of bed fifteen minutes ago. The woman with her, Shanti Patel, was the assistant who'd helped with the autopsy of the first victim in Zane and Amelia's previous case.

He lifted a hand to greet the pair. "Dr. Ackerly, Ms. Patel. I wish I could say it's nice to see you."

Sabrina managed a strained smile as she stepped away from the corpse strewn across the bed. Zane and Amelia had dealt with another pathologist from Cook County, Dr. Adam Francis, on their last case. Apparently, with a judge as the victim, they'd decided to bring out the head honcho.

Her long, platinum blonde hair was fastened atop her head in a messy bun, and the dark circles beneath her pale blue eyes hinted at a lack of sleep. "Hello, Agent Palmer. Agent Storm."

Double-checking the floor to ensure he didn't disturb an evidence marker, Zane took a few cautious steps toward the M.E. and the body. "What have you got so far?"

Dr. Ackerly snapped off her gloves and rested both hands on her hips. "Stephen Denson was sexually assaulted. There are some small tears and congealed blood around his anus. There are no visible signs of semen, but I'll check that once I get him back to my lab. It's possible a foreign object was used. I should be able to determine that later." The M.E. sighed and glanced between the bodies. "I just finished taking his liver temperature, and it confirms the daughter's account of the time of death. His body temp indicates he's been dead for approximately two hours."

Amelia circled around the other side of the bed. "Right. We've got officers canvassing the neighborhood to see if there are any witnesses who might've seen something. The houses around here are pretty close together, though, and there weren't any reports of a gunshot. None that we've heard of yet, anyway."

Shit. A triple homicide committed with a silenced weapon. Zane gritted his teeth. Spencer was right. So far, this case reeked of mafia involvement. "Based on the lack of a mess, I'm guessing it was small caliber?"

Ackerly's gaze drifted back to Stephen Denson's corpse. "Right. Either a .22 or a nine-mil. We'll know once we dig out the slugs and get them over to ballistics."

One of Amelia's eyebrows shot up. "No shell casings?"

"Not that I saw."

In tandem, Zane and Amelia jerked their heads to where the voice had come from the adjoining bathroom. Yet another familiar face, a seasoned FBI crime scene tech named Norman Odgers, emerged from the doorway, an SLR camera in his gloved hands.

The implication of the tech's words marinated in Zane's brain. "No shell casings. None, anywhere?"

Odgers pressed his lips together and slowly shook his head. "Not that we've seen so far. We'll tear this place apart after we've got it all bagged and tagged, but something tells me we aren't going to find those casings."

Amelia swore. "Triple homicide, all shot in the back of the head with a low-caliber weapon using a suppressor. And the unsub policed his brass."

"Tell me we're dealing with a mafia hit without telling me we're dealing with a mafia hit." Zane immediately regretted the words. The sarcastic remark had been made to himself, and he hoped the comment didn't make him come across as aloof or uncaring.

When it came to professional hits, however, solving a case was a tremendous undertaking. Contract killers rarely, if ever, had a relationship with the people they killed. Considering most homicide cases were cracked wide open upon discovering a personal feud, the impersonal nature of a hitman left them with little more than the physical evidence.

And if the hitman knew what they were doing, then that evidence was minimal.

Zane rolled his shoulders, hoping to ease some of the tension that had begun to cramp his muscles. "From what Officer Redfield said, the vic wasn't disrobed by you, was he, Dr. Ackerly?"

"No. I haven't moved him or disturbed the body at all. He was lying on his stomach already, and all I've done is visually assess the body and make the incision to take his liver temperature." Dr. Ackerly snapped on a new pair of gloves and waved at the crumpled form beneath a window.

Zane turned to the woman's body at the foot of a beige settee.

At least, it had once been beige. Now, the front portion was stained with dark crimson spatter. Like Stephen, a good portion of Anna Denson's face was missing. Unlike Stephen, Anna was fully clothed.

Beside him, Amelia gasped. "Her eyes were taped open."

Zane felt ill. "And her head taped in place so that she was forced to watch."

"Mr. Odgers." Sabrina Ackerly gestured to the crime scene tech. "Could we get some more photos of the second victim before I move her body for my exam?"

As Odgers made his way to Anna Denson, Zane and Amelia exchanged grim looks before following.

The *click-click-click* of the shutter was the only sound in the room for several long moments. Zane waited for the tech to finish, knowing the M.E. could offer important details that might help them find the savage who had brutalized this family.

When Odgers had taken a sufficient number of photos, he stepped back to clear the space for Dr. Ackerly.

Kneeling beside Anna Denson's body, the medical examiner gingerly moved aside a clump of sandy brown hair that was stained with blood and liquified brain matter. Ackerly glanced to Amelia and Zane, then to Norman, who continued to snap photos of the newly exposed wound.

"Now, this is just a cursory examination, but this entry wound is about the same size as the one on our first vic." She gestured to the splatter that stained the settee. "And based on the amount of blood and tissue from the exit wound, I think it's safe to say we're dealing with the same small-caliber firearm."

Zane wasn't all that surprised. "A single shooter?"

Amelia lifted a finger. "A single weapon. Redfield said when he and Hernandez talked to Kate Denson, she thought there were two assailants in the house."

"Hitmen working together?" He mulled over the idea. This *was* a larger job. Killing a federal judge, including apparently bypassing the home's security measures, couldn't have been easy.

"We also haven't seen the victim upstairs. She could've been killed with a different weapon," Amelia said.

The reasoning made sense. Zane wasn't excited about working the scene of a seventeen-year-old girl's murder, but he also knew their theories couldn't be too specific just yet. They weren't operating with all the facts, and at this point, their hypotheses were just speculation.

Regardless, it was better to get the thoughts out in the open as they went through the house.

Dr. Ackerly adjusted her gloves. "I haven't found any evidence of defensive wounds. Of course, we'll bag the hands of all the victims and investigate whether there is any DNA material present under the fingernails or in their teeth. The usual. That will have to wait until the victims are back at the morgue." She glanced to Norman Odgers. "I'm going to turn her over now."

Readjusting the camera around his neck, Odgers crouched down closer to Ackerly's level and eased the duct tape away from the table leg holding the vic upright.

As the medical examiner slowly tugged on Anna Denson's shoulder, the cold grasp of unease closed around Zane's throat.

Most of the woman's forehead was gone, and in its place was a grisly, oozing crater of shattered bone and ruined brain tissue.

The gore wasn't what unnerved Zane. What unnerved him was her sightless stare. An expression of dread was permanently etched on her face. Duct tape covered her mouth, but the abject horror in her eyes was still present, even in death. Maybe the unsettling expression would wane once her honey-brown irises became white, Zane wasn't sure. He'd been face-to-face with dead bodies before, plenty of which had passed with their eyes open. Very few, however, had passed with the same visage of absolute terror as Anna Denson.

If Sabrina Ackerly was remotely fazed, she gave no indication. Cool as ever, she glanced up at Amelia and Zane and pointed to a dark circle beneath Anna's right eye. "Bruising here, as well as on her left cheek. That contusion appears more significant than the black eye, and I wouldn't be surprised if her cheekbone was broken."

Odgers snapped more photos as Zane and Amelia leaned closer.

Zane bit his tongue to keep a flurry of four-letter words at bay. "She was beaten?"

"She suffered several injuries to the head and neck, yes. I'll know more once she's on my table, but right now, 'beaten' seems to be an apt descriptor. Her wrists are also bound with zip-ties. Double bound, so whoever did it knew how to keep her from breaking free."

Zane's gut twisted. "Why tie her up? Why not just kill her?"

The question was rhetorical, but Amelia vocalized what they all must have been thinking. "Torture. Sending a message."

She was right.

Hitmen delivered messages all the time, but this felt personal.

4

Rubbing her tired eyes, Cassandra Halcott pried her attention away from the information on her laptop screen to check the small clock on her computer's task bar. Almost one in the morning. Great.

She set the computer on the coffee table and stretched both arms above her head, not stopping until she felt the satisfying *crack* between her shoulder blades. Ever since James Amsdell had turned down a plea agreement that would have given him life in prison without the possibility of parole —but would have taken the death penalty off the table— Cassandra had been swamped with pre-trial work. Amsdell might have been a psychopathic religious zealot, but the guy had enough money left over from his parents' estate to hire a competent defense attorney.

As soon as Cassandra had first read the man's name, she'd braced herself for a flurry of nonsensical motions, all attempting to institute bail for his client.

"Bail for The New Moon Killer." Saying the words aloud made the prospect even more ridiculous. Still, stranger things had happened within the American justice system.

Take Brian Kolthoff, for instance. What Cassandra felt should have been a slam-dunk case for child sex trafficking had been watered down to solicitation and then to nothing at all.

She'd know. She'd been sitting beside fellow Assistant U.S. Attorney Cyrus Osborne when he'd received the news. Most of the words he'd uttered couldn't be repeated in polite company, but Cassandra understood his frustration.

More than understood. She'd endured the same bullshitery plenty during her one-year tenure with the U.S. Attorney's office. Though she'd sought to become a prosecutor to ensure pricks like Kolthoff didn't walk away scot-free, she'd quickly learned one important lesson.

Money talks and bullshit walks.

Growing up, she'd heard the phrase plenty. Until she was a practicing lawyer, however, she'd never *truly* understood what the words meant.

Now, she got it.

Flopping onto her side, she let herself meld into the cushions of the overstuffed couch. Work was enough to deal with on most days, but tonight, she had the added stressor of dealing with her jackass boyfriend.

Soon to be ex-*boyfriend.*

Joseph Larson was an attractive, ex-military FBI agent who maintained the physique of a Greek god, but the man was a total and absolute prick.

A couple weeks ago, Joseph's former case partner, Agent Amelia Storm, had given Cassandra a cryptic warning about Joseph. According to Storm, Joseph had friends in low places. She had advised that Joseph was dangerous and had stressed that Cassandra needed to extricate herself from the relationship.

Cassandra didn't appreciate being left in the dark about what exactly made Joseph so damn dangerous, but conveniently enough, she'd already planned on dumping his sorry ass. Not long before the conversation with Agent Storm, Cassandra had found a condom and a receipt for a fancy Italian restaurant in Joseph's wallet.

Since Cassandra and Joseph no longer used condoms when they slept together, she'd known right away the rubber was meant for another woman. Coupled with his tendency to show up at her apartment hours later than scheduled, only to immediately take a shower...

Yeah. She was finished with his lying, cheating ass. No matter how nice that ass might be.

She just had to see the son of a bitch in person to make the breakup official.

Considering his most recent text message, received three hours ago, had advised he would be at her place no later than midnight, *seeing* him had become more of a challenge than it should have been.

Maybe he'd just *disappeared*. Perhaps the Langoliers—the beings that had devoured time itself in Stephen King's famous short story of the same name—had swallowed Joseph while he was en route to bang his side chick.

Cassandra snorted to herself. The sound was muffled from where she'd shoved her face in a throw pillow.

If only.

If Amelia Storm was to be believed, then the situation with Cassandra and her soon-to-be-ex was more dire than a run-of-the-mill relationship gone south. Joseph was dangerous, and Cassandra knew she shouldn't be lying on the couch mentally disparaging the man when he could likely kill her with little effort.

Was that what he did to Michelle Timmer? Did he kill her and bury her body somewhere in southern Illinois? Did he cut her up into little pieces like Dan Gifford did to Heather Breysacher?

If that was the case, then Cassandra was as good as dead.

Ugh. She needed to stop letting her mind race to such dark places. Joseph was a misogynist and asshole, but she had no reason to believe he was capable of murder.

Her gut didn't seem to agree.

She'd considered ending the relationship in a public place to ensure her safety, but there was one major problem with the strategy. Sure, she'd be safe in the immediate aftermath of the breakup, but what about afterward?

With Joseph's skillset, if he truly wanted her dead because she'd dumped him, she would be screwed no matter where or when the conversation occurred. Best to do it on her home turf.

And better to keep the focus on his suspected cheating instead of her growing unease whenever he was around.

Shoving herself to sit upright, Cassandra sighed, long and heavy. Her brain was taking her to strange places as the familiar sensation of anxiety built at the base of her skull. Long ago, she'd learned to make light of heavy situations by using humor. More than one of her colleagues had given her a strange, sideways glance after she'd let a morbid comment slip. She'd merely pretend the expressions didn't exist and move on about her business.

Most of the men and women in fancy suits hadn't spent their adolescence in foster care. In fact, the majority of Cassandra's colleagues were carrying on their parents' legacy. Law school attracted the sons and daughters of congresspeople, senators, governors, CEOs, and the like.

Plenty of them wouldn't know hardship if it smacked them in the face.

A heavy knock at the front door pulled Cassandra away from the musings, and she was on her feet almost immediately.

Speaking of smacking people in the face.

Once upon a time, she'd have double-checked her appearance before answering the door for Joseph Larson. Now, her track pants, black band t-shirt, and the messy bun that held her bright auburn hair would have to suffice. As she marched toward the door, she couldn't help but wonder if she ought to feel a sense of sadness or loss for what was about to happen.

Checking the peephole to confirm her visitor was indeed Joseph, she let her gaze linger on him as she dug deep for some semblance of affection.

His black suit jacket and matching slacks were neatly pressed, but he'd loosened the striped tie around his neck, and his hair appeared windblown. Never mind that it was approximately twenty degrees outside, and Joseph's wool coat was draped over one arm.

Even at this time of the morning, his pale blue eyes were shrewd. They were eyes that never missed their surroundings. The eyes of a competent investigator, or something more sinister?

Unease shifted in Cassandra's gut. She needed to rip off this band-aid and be done with the agent. She wouldn't stop trying to find out what had happened to Michelle Timmer, but she wanted this man as far away from her as humanly possible.

Straightening her back, Cassandra squared her shoulders and pulled open the heavy door.

A smile took over Joseph's face, but the expression didn't last long. The instant his eyes met Cassandra's, concern clouded his features. Feigned concern, she was sure, but concern nonetheless.

Unbidden, he stepped over the threshold and went to hang his coat on one of the wall-mounted hooks. As he started down the short hall, he tilted his chin in the direction of her room. "You mind if I shower quick?"

Cassandra paused at the opening of the living area and

rolled her eyes. "I do, actually."

He turned around and fixed her with a steely gaze. "What? Why?"

Genuine confusion. The man legitimately didn't understand what was about to happen. He thought he'd wrapped Cassandra around his little finger, and if he told her to jump, she'd ask how high.

Who had been manipulating whom, anyway?

She bit her tongue to keep a bark of mirthless laughter at bay. "We need to talk."

His posture stiffened, but he didn't move where he stood only a few feet away from her. "About what, exactly?"

Playing dumb. Of course he was.

Cassandra crossed her arms to give herself a firmer stance. "About this. About you showing up here late and running straight to the shower. Do you think I haven't noticed this pattern? Or do you think your dick is so magical I *wouldn't* notice? If it's the latter, then I'm sorry, but I've got some disappointing news for you, sweetheart."

Anger flashed across his face. "What?"

There it was. She'd gone and insulted his cock—the one sure-fire way to get under any man's skin.

Cassandra pretended to be interested in her cherry-red nails. She'd rather come across as aloof and uncaring than angry or heated. She didn't want to give him the impression she cared about what he had to say. "Don't insult my intelligence. There's only one reason you'd still carry a condom in your wallet, and there's only one reason you'd be so eager to take a shower the second you got here. I know you're screwing someone else. Montanelli's Steakhouse ring a bell?"

Jaw tightening, he clenched and unclenched one hand, a brief reminder to Cassandra about who exactly she was dealing with.

A federal agent. A combat veteran in prime physical

shape. Cassandra knew a few self-defense moves, but she wasn't some secret black belt. If Joseph wanted to pick a physical fight with her, he *would* win.

All she had on her side was a lack of fear. She'd been through it all—an abusive ex had done everything but kill her. If she'd been able to deal with him, then she could deal with anything.

After a tense silence, Joseph raked a hand through his hair. "What about Montanelli's? And a condom? We've only been together for, what? A couple months?" He shrugged noncommittally. "It was there before we got together. I never took it out. And just because we're dating, does that mean I'm not allowed to go to a nice restaurant by myself?"

Cassandra's eye twitched. The rebuttal was reasonable, and each question was one she'd already posed to herself. "What exactly do you buy for yourself that costs almost a hundred dollars *before* the gratuity? And does eating steak make you sweat so much you immediately need to shower when you get here?"

He threw his hands up in the air and laughed, though the sound was bitter. "I did that for you! I know how you are about hygiene. I thought maybe you'd appreciate I was making an effort, but here we are." He gestured back and forth between them. "What are you trying to tell me here, anyway? Care to stop the lawyer bullshit and just come out and say it?"

Her composure came close to cracking at his retort. She wanted to get in his face, to snap at him, to reiterate what a waste of time the last few weeks had been.

Joseph's got friends in low places. Be careful. She heard Amelia Storm's ominous warning as clearly as if the woman was standing right next to her.

She needed to remain aloof by staying as cool and composed as she could. Stick to the facts. "You've been sleeping with someone else, Joseph. This isn't my first rodeo. Besides, this, you and me, this was never meant to be serious. You know that, right? You don't exactly strike me as the type to settle down in a nice monogamous relationship."

He held his arms out at his sides. "Maybe for you it was. Maybe I was starting to fall in love with you."

On a younger, more impressionable woman, the line might have tugged at heart strings. Maybe for the woman he was banging on the side, such nonsense worked.

Cassandra was a lot of things, but she sure as hell wasn't naïve. That starry-eyed girl had died before she'd even finished law school.

She leveled a flat stare in Joseph's direction. "No, you're not. Cut the crap. You can't bullshit a bullshitter." She poked herself in the chest. "I'm a lawyer. I'm a master bullshitter, okay? We had our fun, and it's run its course. Clearly, since you've already found somewhere else to sleep at night."

Her superfluous remark stoked renewed ire in Joseph's pale eyes. For a beat, she was reminded of some words of wisdom she'd been given by a so-called foster "father."

Someday, that mouth of yours is gonna get you killed, girl.

As the jabs fell from her lips virtually unbidden, she couldn't help but wonder if the scumbag's prophecy would soon come true.

"I was ready to go the extra mile for you, you know that, right?" Joseph dropped his hands to his hips and tilted his head back, his gaze shifting to the ceiling. "I could've been in Florida, sailing around the Keys, enjoying the beaches and the beautiful women. I didn't tell you about that, but I could've transferred down there for six months. Instead, here I am. I stayed here for you!"

Where guilt would have sawed at a normal person's heart, Cassandra felt only…annoyance. Even if he was telling the truth, which she knew he wasn't, she wouldn't have felt any differently. Maybe she wasn't as far removed from the psychopaths she put away as she liked to think.

Or maybe it was just Joseph.

She shook off the concern. "That sounds like a *you* problem. Besides, you were stationed in Florida when you were in the Army. Don't act like it's some brand-new experience for you. If you wanted to be in Florida, you'd be there."

He started to respond, but Cassandra stopped him with an upraised hand.

"This is over, all right? Even if you take away all your condoms and weird showers and hundred-dollar dinners, it's still over. We're just not...compatible. You want someone who's going to *obey* you, and you ought to know by now I'm not her."

He jabbed an index finger at her, his expression contentious. "No, you aren't going to brush what you accused me of under the damn rug. You accused me of *cheating*!"

Cassandra suddenly wished she was a trained Ninja warrior so she could break his damn hand. Flares of anger were a regular occurrence for her—an aspect of herself she'd had to learn to rein in as she'd grown older. If she was confident in her physical prowess, she'd have snapped off Joseph's finger and punched him straight in his lying mouth.

That's not who you are. Find your center, Cassandra. Stay calm. Watch your mouth. This guy is dangerous.

Before she had a chance to respond one way or another, her phone buzzed against her leg. Taking a step away from Joseph, she pulled the device from her pocket and checked the screen.

Work was calling. Thank God.

Joseph guffawed. "You're getting a phone call? At one in the morning? And *I'm* the suspicious one here, yeah?"

She shot him a withering glare. "It's the U.S. Attorney."

Holding up the phone, she turned the screen toward him. "You want to talk to her? Or should I?"

His jaw tightened, but he didn't reply.

Swiping her thumb across the screen, Cassandra raised the cell to her ear. "This is Halcott."

"Cassandra, my apologies for the late-night call." Simone Julliard was a no-nonsense woman with an eye for serving justice, and unlike most seasoned lawyers, she didn't beat around the bush. Cassandra respected the hell out of her, and someday, she aspired to be half as imposing as Julliard.

Cassandra cleared her throat, pretending Joseph was elsewhere. Preferably on the moon or on the International Space Station. "No worries at all. I was just looking through the Amsdell case, actually."

"Well, I've got another one for you. Time sensitive. A judge for the Northern District, Anna Denson, was found murdered, along with her husband and seventeen-year-old daughter."

Cassandra was struck with a pang of grief for the family. Maybe she wasn't an unfeeling robot after all. "What do you need from me?"

"There's a witness. Anna Denson's older daughter, Kate Denson. She'll go to the FBI field office once the hospital clears her. The agents working the case will fill you in on the rest of the details when you get there." Simone Julliard didn't *ask* the attorneys in her office to attend to a case. She only hired those who knew their role, and Cassandra damn sure knew hers.

"Okay. I'll be there as soon as I can."

"I appreciate it. Drive safely."

"I will. Thanks."

As she ended the call, Cassandra was pointedly aware of Joseph's scrutiny. She wanted to scream at him, call him any name she could think of, and chase him out the door. The notification that a judge and her entire damn family had been murdered was a stark reminder that Cassandra had priorities that ranked much, much higher than a chiseled body and a nice smile.

"I have to go. I've got a case." She pointed to the door. "It's urgent, which means I need you to leave."

Joseph's eyes latched onto Cassandra, and for a beat, the chill of dread pulsed through her veins.

Was he going to leave? Or was he truly dead set on having the last word?

What the hell is he going to do? I just got off the phone with the U.S. Attorney. If I don't show up at the FBI office, more than a few people are going to notice.

Just before Cassandra was prepared to reiterate her order, Joseph shook his head. "This conversation isn't over."

Yes, it is. For once, she managed to keep the thought to herself. "I need to go to work. Goodbye, Joseph."

Jaw clenched, he turned toward the door. The seconds dragged as he took the first couple steps, and Cassandra held her stance until he was gone.

She didn't waste a second before she locked the deadbolt behind him.

The entire scenario was just...*off.* Between Amelia Storm's warning and Joseph's blatant attempt to gaslight her, Cassandra had a sinking suspicion her Joseph-related woes had only just started.

Where they'd end, she wasn't sure she wanted to know.

JOSEPH LARSON SANK LOWER in the driver's seat, keeping his eyes glued to the rearview mirror as a familiar silver sedan pulled out of the parking garage across the street. Since he'd only just left Cassandra's apartment ten minutes ago, he wasn't necessarily worried about her spotting his parked car. Even if she asked him what in the hell he was doing, his response would have been simple. He was collecting himself before the drive home.

Yeah, right.

That bitch liked to think she was something special. They *all* liked to think they were something special. That they were better than him, or they didn't need him.

The joke was on her. He'd already found a sweet little piece of ass to keep him warm at night. In fact, he was about to head over to her place to work out some of this frustration.

Despite the reprieve, anger simmered low in his chest. Gritting his teeth, Joseph smacked the steering wheel with the heel of his hand.

Where in the hell did that lawyer bitch get off thinking she was the one in charge here? He was done with her when *he* decided he was done with her, and not a damn second earlier.

And how had she known about Montanelli's? Had she been snooping through his things?

"Nosy bitch." The words came out as a low growl.

She'd told him this wasn't her first rodeo, but as luck would have it, this wasn't *his* first, either. Cassandra thought she held the reins here, but she was wrong. Just like Michelle had been wrong.

He couldn't wait to show her how wrong she was.

5

With one last glance at the haunted face of the girl who sat on the other side of the one-way glass, Amelia blew on her steaming mug of coffee. She'd been the only one desperate or brave enough to consume the break-room sludge. On her way back to her colleagues, she'd decided to quickly drop in on the sole witness to the triple homicide who had just landed in the FBI's lap.

As best as Amelia could tell, Kate Denson was in shock. Kate's clothes had been bagged as evidence, and she'd been given a gray hoodie and matching sweats. With her copper-colored hair pulled into a ponytail, the dark shadows beneath her haunted brown eyes were even more visible. Aside from answering the standard questions at the crime scene, Kate had been silent since arriving from the hospital.

As she spared one last glance at the girl, Amelia's heart clenched.

In the blink of those same eyes, her entire family had been taken from her. Though Amelia could relate to losing loved ones, she honestly couldn't imagine how alone Kate must feel as she sat in the undecorated interview room. Next to Kate sat an older woman from victim services. The woman was Martha Beech, but Amelia had never worked with her. She only hoped the woman's kind smile and motherly appearance offered some level of comfort to the stricken girl on the other side of the glass.

The sooner we get through the procedural stuff, the sooner she can get somewhere a little less...sterile.

Straightening her back, Amelia strode to the door across the hall. With the death of a federal judge and her entire family on their plate, the FBI had been quick to throw resources at the Denson case. In addition to Zane and Amelia's organized crime experience, SAC Keaton had assigned Violent Crimes agents Sherry Cowen and Dean Steelman to the investigation.

Though plenty of signs pointed in a mob-related direction, no possibility was being ruled out just yet. Like they'd done with the Dan Gifford case, the Bureau wanted to ensure every angle was covered—mafia and cartel, as well as everything non-mob related.

As Amelia let herself into the adjacent interview room, three familiar faces turned toward her. Dean Steelman's unshaven face was tired, but his sapphire blue eyes were alert. His whiskey brown hair was brushed straight back from his forehead, though the style wasn't quite as neat as Amelia was used to. Then again, it *was* almost two in the morning.

Sherry Cowen, on the other hand, appeared wide awake. Wavy ash blonde hair framed her fair face, though Amelia thought her skin was a shade tanner after she'd taken a vacation to Florida for her wedding.

Zane's gaze shifted to the mug in Amelia's grasp, a slight smile forming on his face. "Well, you're not dead, so that must mean the coffee on this floor is okay to drink."

"Not dead yet." Amelia took a sip of the bitter brew.

Steelman rubbed his eyes and stifled a yawn. "That's good news. I might need some of that shit with the way this night is going." The legs of a metal chair scraped the tile as he took a seat.

The brief moment of amusement over the breakroom coffee vanished like the steam coming off Amelia's mug. "Did I miss anything while I was gone? Any new theories?"

Zane leaned against a windowless, beige wall. "Nothing, really. How does Kate look?"

Amelia let out a sigh and took a seat beside Sherry. "No change. Victim Services is sitting with her for now, but she's still staring off into space with that haunted look in her eyes."

Sherry reached for a tablet and powered on the device. "The CPD finished canvassing the neighborhood." She tapped the screen a couple times. "Houses in that area are fairly close together, and no one reported hearing a gunshot. None of the neighbors noticed strange vehicles coming or going. Not tonight, and not any time recently. SSA Corsaw is compiling everything and working on tomorrow morning's press briefing."

Amelia was grateful for the thorough questions posed by the officers, and she was a little disappointed the door-to-door interviews hadn't yielded any useful information. "The CSU already swabbed Kate's hands for gunshot residue, and there was nothing. They've also sent all the family's firearms over to ballistics to rule them out. They were all locked up, but we're being thorough. Before she went quiet, Kate told the CPD she'd been out with a couple friends before returning home around ten-thirty."

"Right." Zane fished in his pocket and produced a pack of gum. "Marlee Hendricks and her boyfriend, Jared Olsen. Kate gave the CPD their names before she, well...you know."

Sherry swiped the screen of the tablet. "We got their statements on our way here, and it confirms Kate's alibi. We can pull security camera footage from the bars they visited too. Not that I think we need it, but we'll be thorough."

The more evidence they could get, the better. Regardless, Amelia tended to agree with Sherry. In addition to her hands, Kate's clothes had been tested for gunshot residue as well. Most people thought that GSR was confined to a person's hand and forearm, but in truth, the substance could show up on their shirt, pants, and even shoes.

Considering Kate's entire outfit had tested negative, the potential that she was the shooter was slim to none. In a less fact-based analysis, Amelia was confident Kate's traumatized reaction was one-hundred-percent genuine. There were no lies in her weary brown eyes, only fear and profound grief and shock.

Zane cleared his throat. "We'll need to pull the logs for the Densons' home security system. We can perhaps find out from that what time the system was disarmed and if it was by a passcode or another means."

Steelman nodded. "Good point. I'll get the paperwork started on that."

Amelia lifted a hand, refocusing on the room. "Kate's scared shitless, and she's the sole witness to a triple homicide. Her only remaining relative in the city is an aunt, but has the aunt been notified?"

Zane tapped a finger against the pack of gum, appearing thoughtful. "No, not yet. What're you thinking?"

"I don't think we should let anyone know where Kate is or that she's a witness." Amelia expected a rebuttal, figuring one of her three colleagues would mention freedom of the press or the public's access to information.

Instead, she received three approving nods.

Steelman stretched both arms above his head. "If we're dealing with any level of mob involvement, we're going to want to keep her in a safe house, yeah?"

Amelia was grateful they were all on the same page. "Yeah. And we're going to want to keep her out of the media. The press doesn't need to know there was a witness. All they need to know is what we give them at a press conference."

Scooting closer to the table, Sherry peered down at her tablet. "Question is, did anyone see her leaving the house?"

Amelia dared another drink of her too-hot coffee. "I don't think any of the looky-loos were there yet. Kate was gone before Palmer and I got there. The CPD had taken her to the hospital to get checked out."

"Perfect." Sherry gestured to the tablet. "We'll keep an eye on the news to make sure. She signed a HIPAA nondisclosure form at the hospital, so we shouldn't have to worry about any medical personnel talking to reporters."

A light knock at the door jerked their collective attention away from the discussion. Dean Steelman's eyebrows furrowed. "Who the hell is that?"

As Amelia opened her mouth to tell him she wasn't sure, the hinges creaked, revealing none other than Assistant U.S. Attorney Cassandra Halcott.

Like Sherry, Cassandra appeared to be wide awake. Amelia suspected this confirmed who the two night owls of the group were.

The lawyer's gaze flicked from one agent to another as she eased the door closed behind her. "Sorry to interrupt, Agents. SSA Corsaw told me I'd find you all in here. I just wanted to stop in and see what you've got so far."

With a welcoming smile, Sherry Cowen went through the evidence and statements collected so far.

Amelia braced herself. Though her fellow agents might have been fine with the idea of keeping Kate's identity secret, she wondered if some heretofore unknown legal precedent would stand in their way.

To her continued, pleasant surprise, Cassandra agreed. "She'll be going to a safe house, I assume?"

"Right." To Amelia's side, Sherry Cowen twisted her white gold wedding band. "Usually, witness protection goes to the U.S. Marshals, but since this is an active investigation, the Bureau will keep control of her safety."

Sherry's husband, Teddy Kielman, was a member of the aforementioned Marshal service, but if Amelia remembered correctly, the man specialized in fugitive recovery, not witness security.

"Okay, we'll keep her out of the press conference, then." Cassandra readjusted the messenger bag over her shoulder. "I appreciate the update. Keep me in the loop, if you don't mind. And let me know if I can help with anything."

As Sherry shot the lawyer another smile and a wave goodbye, Amelia wondered how often the two women had worked together in the past. Aside from the fact that Cassandra was dating a...a what? Wannabe rapist? Worse? Aside from her relationship with Joseph, Amelia didn't know much about the woman outside of her professional qualifications.

No, she's not dating him anymore, remember? She said she was going to dump his sorry ass.

Good. Amelia hoped she'd kicked him in the balls too. She couldn't imagine that a blow from one of Cassandra's Louboutin heels would feel great on a man's nether regions.

Once Cassandra had taken her leave, Zane pushed himself away from the wall. "Should we give it another shot? Talking to Kate before we get her to a safe house, I mean."

Glancing from Zane to Dean and back, Amelia pushed her coffee cup around in a circle. Agents Steelman and Palmer were most definitely two of the good guys, but Steelman only stood a hair shorter than Zane's six-three, and both men were imposing figures if a person didn't know them.

If Kate had just witnessed a man—which was the only real detail they knew about their suspect—murder members of her family, Amelia doubted the young woman would want to sit down in a tiny, sterile room with any man, no matter how decent he was.

"Maybe," Amelia looked between the three of them, "Agent Cowen and I should talk to her. I think two women might be better for talking to a traumatized girl."

If Amelia wasn't mistaken, Dean appeared to be more than a little relieved. She didn't blame him. "Good call, Storm. Palmer and I can watch from behind the two-way mirror."

Amelia flattened her palms on the table. "I figure it's at least worth a shot while she's still here. Plus, we're going to need to tell her about the safe house."

"Agreed," Sherry said. "We'll be waiting until tomorrow for most of the analyses and for the details of the crime scene and the autopsies. Might as well do what we can while we can."

The four of them made their way to the viewing room. To Amelia's disappointment, Kate's expression and stance had changed little. Her stare was still distant and haunted, almost like the young woman had been replaced with a wax figure of herself. She didn't even seem to realize the rep from victim services was in the room.

Zane and Dean took their spots, this time with Dean standing and Zane sitting. Amelia led the way to the interview room, Sherry on her heels.

Hand resting on the metal lever, Amelia turned back to Sherry. "I think we should tell her about the safe house first. That way, she'll hopefully feel a little more at ease."

The other agent brushed off the front of her sweater.

"Good idea. Then, after that, we can build on the questions the CPD already asked her. It might be easier on her if we approach it that way."

Amelia gently rapped her knuckles against the door before slowly pushing it open. FBI agents didn't always knock when they were about to interview a witness, but Kate Denson had been frightened enough for one night.

Kate's vacant stare snapped over to the doorway as Amelia and Sherry entered, but the same distant look remained in her eyes. Aside from shifting slightly in her chair, she did little to acknowledge Amelia and Sherry's presence.

Keeping her movements slow and purposeful, Amelia took a seat across from the traumatized girl. Once Sherry was situated, Amelia nodded to the victim services rep, who quietly excused herself from the room. Amelia produced the same notepad she'd used at the crime scene. "Hello, Kate. I'm Special Agent Storm. You can call me Amelia. This is my case partner, Special Agent Cowen."

Sherry folded her hands on the table and offered Kate a smile so reassuring that even Amelia felt more at ease. "Please call me Sherry. We're sorry you had to wait so long. Would you like anything to drink? We have plenty of water, some soda, or even coffee if you want."

Amelia knew the inviting tone was an effort to set aside the usual, cold professionalism in hopes of presenting Kate with an environment in which she felt safe to talk. "I'm not sure if you'd want any of that coffee, though. Most days, I'm pretty sure it's not even real coffee."

"True." Sherry chuckled.

Though the change could have been Amelia's imagination, she swore Kate's posture relaxed slightly. She'd love to continue the silly coffee banter until the young woman came out of her shell, but unfortunately, they had far grimmer business to address.

Clicking her pen, Amelia returned her attention to Kate. "We have some news that I'd like to get your opinion about. It's still early in the investigation, and since we don't know yet who did this to your family, we want to take certain precautions to be proactive."

A faint line appeared between Kate's eyebrows, and Amelia was pleased the young woman appeared to focus on her words. Though she said nothing, Amelia thought Kate understood the silent question.

Amelia's smile was gentle but confident. "Once we're done here, we want to take you to an FBI safe house."

Kate blinked a couple times, swallowed, but said nothing.

Sherry reached out a hand, but it sank to the table before touching Kate's arm. "You'll be safe there. We'll maintain a security detail twenty-four-seven, and before we go, we'll have the security team give you more information on what living in the safe house will be like. Can we do that?"

Licking her lips, Kate managed a slight nod.

The girl was here with them. Amelia mentally breathed a sigh of relief. Emotional trauma could do irreparable damage to a person, and in extreme cases, could even cause dangerous physiological complications. They were far from out of the woods with Kate, but at least she was aware of her surroundings and was able to process the information being given to her.

"Kate." Amelia was careful to keep her tone kind and gentle but not patronizing. She was speaking to a twenty-one-year-old woman, not a small child. "I know you've already answered some questions for the detectives with the Chicago police. Would it be okay if Sherry and I asked you a couple more?"

Kate's eyes shifted from Amelia to Sherry and back before dipping her chin.

Amelia was no psychologist, but she knew she'd be best served by sticking to close-ended questions. "Okay. Did you recognize the person in your house?"

The muscles in Kate's neck tightened and she blinked repeatedly, her eyes glassy as she shook her head.

Scribbling a few words on the notepad, Amelia deferred to Sherry for the next question. The majority of the CPD's inquiry had been to rule Kate out as a suspect, and the task of obtaining information from her now fell to the FBI.

"Did you see the person's face?" Like Amelia, Sherry's voice was soothing without the patronizing tinge that so often came with efforts to be accommodating.

Another head shake. As Kate swiped at her eyes, Amelia noticed the young woman's hand had begun to tremble. No, not just a tremor. More like a full-on earthquake.

Sherry seemed to notice the shake too but forged ahead with her next question. "Do you know of anyone who might have wanted to hurt you or your family?"

Another head shake.

Amelia pondered the phrasing of her next close-ended query as she eased back into the conversation. "Kate, was there more than one person in your home?"

Kate both nodded and offered an almost imperceptible shrug of her shoulders. The girl wasn't sure. Interesting.

Deciding that particular line of questioning might be futile in Kate's current nonverbal state, Amelia shifted gears. "Did you hear the stranger's voice?"

Kate didn't respond to the question at first. Amelia reached across the table with her palm up and offered her hand to the traumatized girl, although she didn't acknowledge its presence. Her faraway stare didn't waver as her head slowly nodded.

Now we're getting somewhere. What an amazing girl. She lost her whole family and is a wreck, but she is still offering information we might be able to use.

"Kate, you're doing great. I have one last question for you. The man you heard talk, did you recognize his voice?"

Kate wrapped both arms around herself, tears now flowing freely down her pale cheeks. Her body shook like she'd been caught in a snowstorm without a coat. As the tears dropped into her lap, one last time, Kate shook her head.

Amelia pulled a packet of tissues from the pocket of her hoodie. She hated the way her nose would start to run when she stepped out into the cold, so she always carried them during the winter months. After sliding the tissues to Kate, she shot Sherry a knowing glance.

They both knew this wasn't the time to press Kate for a full statement. If Amelia or Sherry directed the conversation in the wrong direction, Kate was liable to recede into her shell. And after what she'd been through, Amelia wasn't sure when she'd come out again.

"I'm so sorry you're going through this, Kate." Amelia scooted a couple inches closer to the victim. "I know that going to a safe house sounds intimidating, but I can promise you that you *will* be safe. We'll make sure of it, and we'll keep you safe until we find the person who did this."

Knuckles white from her grip on the tissue, Kate managed a nod as she dabbed at her cheeks. The poor girl was standing at the edge of a panic attack, or maybe worse.

Promising to find a perpetrator wasn't usually a good idea in Amelia's line of work, but she was compelled to say *something* to help ease the pain and terror eating away at Kate's psyche.

Then again, Amelia's words were accurate. They would keep Kate safe until they found who had killed her family, even if that meant sending her into Witness Security. After losing her family, maybe a fresh start wouldn't seem so bad to Kate, if worse came to worst. Amelia knew she'd prefer the chance at a new life if she were in Kate's shoes.

Of course, that was all provided the killer didn't have friends in high places. Amelia had learned early on in her time at the Chicago Field Office that not every FBI agent and CPD detective was here to serve the greater good.

Even her brother.

Amelia and Sherry each gave Kate their cards and assured her the security detail at the safe house would contact them on her behalf at any time. The best Amelia could do right now was ensure Kate knew there were people on her side, and she wasn't all alone in the world.

Whoever had killed Kate's family was a damn ghost.

But Amelia had dealt with plenty of specters, and she'd contend with this one too.

6

As I pulled into the grocery store parking lot, I kept an eye on the black sedan I'd followed for the past several miles. The driver and his family didn't have the first clue I was watching them, which was just the way I preferred the situation.

With only a few days to go before New Year's Eve, I'd expected the store to be busier at ten o'clock on a Monday morning. Kids were out of school for winter break, and plenty of their parents had also taken time off work.

Parents like Anna and Stephen Denson.

I scoffed aloud.

"What?" My brother's gravelly voice kept me from wandering down memory lane.

Shaking my head, I pulled into a parking spot approximately catty-corner to the black sedan. "Nothing. Just thinking."

"You need to think about this asshole we're following."

I mentally cringed at the casual reprimand. That's what older brothers were for, wasn't it? To keep you in line, keep you focused on the goal at hand. Keep you from daydreaming about the way that man had screamed through the duct tape that covered his mouth.

The way his wife had cried and pleaded before I'd taped her damn mouth shut too. At first, I'd wanted to hear her beg for mercy, but her repeated offering for me to take her instead, to spare her daughter, to just kill her and leave, had grown tiresome. Even my brother had gotten sick of her attempts at bargaining.

My mind had been made up, my goal set. No amount of Anna Denson's begging and rationalizing would change a damn thing.

I'd let her think her kid was still alive until right before I shot her in the head. It was an effective tactic to get her and her husband to keep their voices down before I was able to tape their mouths shut.

As long as Kelly Denson didn't hear anything, she wouldn't be considered a witness. And if she wasn't a witness, then I wouldn't have to *deal with* her.

Anna and her college professor husband had bought the story hook, line, and sinker.

Once I was done with Stephen, I'd knelt beside Anna, pressing close until I was an inch away from her ear. *"Your daughter's already dead. I shot her first. Such a shame too. What a beautiful girl."*

Before Anna could scream or cry or lash out, I'd stood and pulled the trigger, careful to get as little of the blood spatter on myself as possible. Not that it mattered. I'd thrown all the clothes in the fireplace when I'd gotten home, and then I'd taken a little trip north of the city to toss the murder weapon into Lake Michigan.

I'd covered my bases. And if I'd forgotten anything, my brother sure as hell would have reminded me.

"C'mon, kid." My brother's voice cut through the musing. "Get your head out of the clouds. I know you had fun last night. We both did. But we need to focus. What do we know about this guy?" He jerked a thumb over his shoulder to gesture to where a man, woman, and an adolescent girl had just emerged from the sedan.

Drumming my fingers against the steering wheel, I looked up to the rearview mirror to watch the family start toward the store. My brother was right. He usually was. We had a finite period of time to make good on our quest for vengeance, and we needed to use every minute efficiently.

I glanced to the passenger seat, where my brother watched me, patiently waiting for a response. "Cyrus Osborne, age forty-one, married to Mabel Osborne for twenty years in March. Their daughter, Julie, turned fourteen in October. Cyrus has been an assistant U.S. attorney for the past seven years, but as far as I can tell, he doesn't have ambitions to advance any further in that office. Probably not until the current U.S. Attorney retires."

"Good for nothing lawyers." My brother crossed his arms. "Are you sure you've nailed down his day-to-day routine as well as you did for Anna and Stephen? And that alarm system..."

I waved a dismissive hand. "Those things are kid's toys. I'll take one of those fancy-ass security systems over a trained German shepherd or pitbull any damn day. You can't sneak up on a dog and turn it off, but there're plenty of ways to turn off an alarm system."

Appearing thoughtful, my brother cocked his head. "Do we know if our lawyer pal has any guns?"

"Not sure, but he's got a membership for a firing range outside the city, so more than likely."

"A firing range? Then he probably knows how to use it. How'd you find that out?"

I chuckled. People were so lackadaisical about their digital lives when they thought they were safe behind a password. Take away the security measure, and you could lay their lives bare. "Social media. I hacked into his home Wi-Fi and got ahold of his personal calendar and emails. I also hacked their phones, so I know their every text and call. He doesn't go back to work for another week, not until after the New Year. He and his wife are hosting a small New Year's Eve party. They've only got a few guests and their kids planned as visitors."

My brother grunted his approval. "People store so much about themselves electronically. It's ridiculous what you can learn about a person when you know a little bit about computers."

I grinned. My brother and I hadn't been raised in a household big on reassurance, and his remark was as close to a compliment as I'd ever get. Even as a grown man, receiving praise from my older brother was still a source of pride.

The air of positivity didn't last long. Snapping his fingers, he pointed to the entrance of the store. "They're about to head inside. You got a plan?"

"Always." I twisted the white gold band around my left ring finger. I wasn't married. Never had been, but the ring put strangers at ease when they were talking to a guy like me.

One of my brother's eyebrows lifted, a faint trace of annoyance in his expression. "And? What's the plan?"

I sighed, ignoring the frown I received as I did. "I go in, buy some groceries, and run into the lawyer and his family. Stay close, and if the opportunity presents itself, I'll interact with them. If not, then I ought to at least pick up a little info while I'm nearby."

People were never on guard in public like they ought to be. They'd discuss their plans for the night, the week, even the month, never aware of who might be listening.

Rubbing his jaw, my brother slowly nodded. "All right. Don't get too close to them, got it? You were already pushing it last night by standing in the crowd in front of the Densons' house. You should have come to the van with me and left." His glare shot daggers. "You know, I had half a mind to take off and leave your ass there."

A combination of shame and longing overtook me at my brother's words. I'd never been one for the drug scene, but I could only imagine that addicts must have been chasing the same high I'd attained standing in front of that judge's house.

I'd changed my clothes in the van, ensuring there would be no suspicious blood spatter or any other substance of interest. As confident as I was that the cops didn't have the first clue who I was or why I was there, I couldn't let my guard down.

My brother was right. The decision to stay was stupid, but I'd missed out on the thrill the first time around. When we'd crossed the first name off our list—the names of those who had tried to ruin my brother's life—I'd left the neighborhood as soon as the deed was done. Killing Carla and Scott Graham had been satisfying, there was no doubt about that. But, to me, the experience had been missing...*some*thing.

I wanted to watch the aftermath of my handiwork. To watch the cops scramble to assemble a response, to watch the shock and awe on the faces of Carla's neighbors as the realization of her murder dawned on them. Or, better still, to spot the onlookers in the crowd who were like me. Who were there to revel in another person's pain and suffering, and who hid their sick pleasure with a thinly veiled mask of concern.

Those were my favorites. With a little push, I bet they'd be happy to live out their own dark impulses.

For me, the push had come in the form of revenge. These

people had tried their damnedest to ruin my brother's life, and I wasn't about to let them get away with it.

We wouldn't let them get away with it. They had to die. Every last one of them.

My brother was the only family I had left, and anyone who had tried to take him would suffer.

Cyrus Osborne in particular. I had a long list of punishments I'd like to exact on the hotshot lawyer. Though I doubted I'd be able to get through all of them, I'd make my time with Cyrus count.

Maybe, instead of shooting his kids in their sleep like I'd done with Kelly Denson, I'd wake them up. Who knew what type of suffering I could inflict on Cyrus if his kids were present?

The idea was a new one. So far, I'd eliminated my targets' children to avoid witnesses. Perhaps I needed to be more creative in my approach.

I pushed aside the thoughts. There I'd gone again, getting lost in my own damn head. This time, however, my brother didn't offer an admonishment. He had his own musings to attend.

Clearing my throat, I unfastened my seat belt. "You can stay here. This shouldn't take long."

"Yeah, all right. Remember to be careful in there." As my brother reached for the radio dial, I pulled up the collar of my coat and stepped into the chilly, late December air.

I knew my brother had a valid point about the risks involved with personally interacting with the Osborne family, but there was a part of our mission he didn't understand.

I *needed* this.

Being close to someone without them realizing you held their life in your hands was a thrill I'd never find anywhere else. It was complete and total control. Proof to myself that I alone held all the cards. Not Cyrus, even if he was a damn sharpshooter. Not even my brother.

For once, we were in my territory. This was my area of expertise.

I'd help my brother attain his vengeance, and I'd finally show him what I could do.

7

Cassandra Halcott tightened her grasp on the strap of her messenger bag and braced herself as the doors to the elevator slid open. Fortunately, she was on the fifth floor of the FBI Field Office—where the Violent Crimes Division was housed—and not the sixth floor, which was home to Organized Crime. And Joseph Larson.

The paranoid part of her brain expected to come face-to-face with her new ex-boyfriend the instant she stepped off the elevator. When she was instead greeted with the utilitarian beige walls, an empty leather bench, and silence, she breathed a sigh of relief.

That's what you get for shitting where you eat. Should've thought that through before *you went home with him. Just because you hadn't gotten any for a while didn't mean you needed to put yourself in this position.*

As obnoxious as Joseph's recent text messages had been and as irritating as he'd no doubt be for the next couple weeks, Cassandra was most disappointed in herself…for letting a good-looking guy and a mediocre lay mess with her equilibrium at work. She was a thirty-one-year-old woman with a promising career, not some high school girl trying to get a boy's attention.

The truth was more complicated than that, she knew. Cassandra hadn't just been yearning to scratch a physical itch. She'd been lonely. After more than a year in Chicago, she should have had friends, or at least acquaintances. She should have had more than her job.

For a naïve second, she'd honestly believed Joseph was the person he presented himself as. A blue-collar guy who'd risen above his family's lower-class station by joining the military and excelling. An honest face in the big, bad city.

That was the picture she'd *wanted* to believe, so she'd ignored her gut and gone along with the imagery she'd created in her mind. All because she was lonely and sad.

She should have listened to her instincts. Should have known Joseph's honest, hardworking appearance was all a façade.

Massaging her temples, she forced aside her personal issues and started down the hall. The morning's press conference was finished, but there was still plenty of work to be done. Though Cassandra might be friendless and loveless, at least her job allowed her to do some good for other people.

She'd been advised that the agents working the Denson case had established an incident room on the fifth floor of the building. After the post-press conference meeting with the U.S. Attorney, Cassandra had left for the FBI field office. The drive had taken a good half hour, and as she approached the incident room, she felt like a kid who was late for their first day of college classes.

She clenched her hands into fists as the bout of anxiety settled like a stone in her stomach.

You're not that kid. Not anymore.

The pattern of thoughts was commonly referred to as

imposter syndrome, wherein a person—usually someone in a successful career—attributed their success to external factors rather than their own merit. And when Cassandra considered her journey from abusive foster homes to a position as an assistant U.S. attorney, she sure as hell felt like she didn't belong.

Hell, she was about to walk into a room full of polished, successful federal agents, each of whom had undergone months of grueling training at Quantico. Two of them, Dean Steelman and Amelia Storm, were also veterans of the U.S. Army. Any one of them could drop Cassandra with one arm tied behind their back.

She was just the annoying lawyer who showed up to make sure they'd dotted their *i*'s and crossed their *t*'s. The person who killed their buzz by reminding them to finish up their paperwork.

As she knocked on the closed door of conference room 503, she did her best to bury the lingering doubts. She could doubt her abilities and be irritated with herself later. Right now, there were three innocent people dead, one of whom was a federal judge.

Without waiting for a response, Cassandra let herself into the sunny room. The bright rays of sunshine streaming through the window were a welcome change from the fluorescence of the hallways. Though the temperature outside wasn't predicted to go much past twenty-five, the clear, sunny skies gave the day a deceptively pleasant appearance.

"Good morning, Agents." Cassandra paused inside the doorway to take stock of the incident room.

Three agents sat around an oval table in the center of the space. Standing beside a whiteboard that nearly spanned the length of the wall perpendicular to the window, Amelia tapped a dry-erase marker in the palm of one hand, a contemplative expression on her face.

Dean Steelman stretched both arms in front of himself. "Morning, Counselor. We saw the press conference earlier. How'd everything go after it?"

Cassandra waited to respond until the door was closed. Now that she was entering "work mode" again, she felt the pieces of her composure falling back into place. "It went as well as expected. We kept it short and stuck to the facts. The media hasn't had much time to come up with any crazy conspiracy theories yet, so I'm sure the next one will be more eventful."

"I can imagine." Dean's vivid blue gaze drifted from Cassandra to the whiteboard. Pictures of Anna Denson, her husband, and their two children were taped to one side, along with pertinent information about each.

Before her focus could linger on the image of Anna Denson, Cassandra looked from Agent Steelman to Agent Cowen, who was studying a tablet. At the other end of the table, Zane Palmer's face was buried in his laptop, and Amelia Storm moved to peer over his shoulder.

As Zane straightened, he ran both hands over his face. Cassandra couldn't tell if he was simply focused or if he was tired, irritated, or all three. "Good timing, Counselor." He glanced at her and gestured to the laptop. "We just got the medical examiner's preliminary report back for the autopsies of Stephen and Anna Denson. Kelly Denson's prelim report is being finalized, and we should have it soon. The M.E. said she called in her most senior pathologist, Dr. Adam Francis, to help with the exams."

Amelia waved the dry-erase marker at the whiteboard. "We've also gotten the results back from ballistics. Forensics is still going through everything collected from the scene, so those reports are gradually trickling in. The main takeaway right now is that the killers didn't leave much behind in the way of physical evidence."

Cassandra pulled out a chair beside Sherry Cowen and sat before pulling out the black-rimmed glasses she only wore when her eyes were extra tired. "Do we think there's more than one perpetrator?"

Amelia dropped both hands to her hips as she turned to the board. "There's no physical evidence to indicate one way or another, so right now, we're going with Kate Denson's account that she heard the gunman talking to someone else in the house."

Their case wouldn't be the first time contract killers had doubled up for a large, dangerous job. Setting her bag on the floor by her feet, Cassandra propped her elbows on the table. "I had a meeting with the U.S. Attorney earlier, and the main thing she wants us to rule out right now is a political motive. If we can figure that out one way or another before the next press conference, we'll be able to stave off a media frenzy. Judge Denson wasn't much of a political figure, but we all know how much the press loves to put a political spin on everything."

Drumming his fingers on the table, Dean leaned back in his chair. "We were thinking the same thing. Our first stop was to go through Judge Denson's recent cases and see if there was anything in there that might raise an eyebrow."

Sherry swiped at her tablet. "Nothing on her docket looked all that contentious. Not any more or less than you'd expect from a district judge, anyway. The majority of her recent cases were civil issues, but none of them were controversial, and none really had much of a media following. Same for the criminal cases. From what I've seen so far, she didn't even have any violent crime hearings scheduled for the near future. Definitely none that would've benefitted from her being dead."

The agent's summary was consistent with what Cassandra had learned since the night before. She'd hoped the FBI agents would have somehow uncovered a hotly contested trial Cassandra had missed, something she could lean on when the time came to feed the wolves again.

Alas, here she was. Shooting in the dark to try to piece together a motive. "Okay. We can circle back to her old cases later. What about forensics? Agent Palmer, you said you received the autopsy reports for Judge Denson and her husband?"

Zane tapped a couple keys before turning his attention back to the room. "The M.E. conducted the autopsy of Anna Denson, and the senior-most pathologist did the post-mortem for Stephen Denson. I'll start with Anna since she's the reason this case is in our jurisdiction to begin with." He cleared his throat. "Keep in mind these are preliminary findings so something might change later. Lacerations to her face and head are consistent with blunt force trauma sustained from a fist. The blows weren't heavy enough to knock her unconscious, which means the guy was either holding back on purpose, or they weren't very strong to begin with."

Though an image of Kate Denson came to Cassandra's mind right away, she dismissed the thought. Even mild punches would have left marks on Kate's knuckles, and the girl hadn't had a scratch on her. "They were roughing her up, then." She ran a thumb over her polished nails, her gaze returning to the whiteboard. "It's not that uncommon, even for a hit. What *is* uncommon for a contract killer is what they did to Stephen Denson."

Eyes fixed on the laptop, Zane pulled out a stick of gum, and Cassandra wondered if the reminder of what had happened to the male victim had put a bad taste into the agent's mouth. It sure had left one in hers.

"That's true." Zane popped a piece into his mouth and tossed the container onto the table. "Stephen sustained a blow to the temple, but like Anna, it wasn't enough to knock him out. However, Dr. Francis's report indicates that the laceration is more consistent with the grip of a handgun than a fist."

The image painted in Cassandra's head was grim, and she took Zane up on his silent offer, snatching a stick of gum too. "Could it be a possible defensive wound? He tried to resist, and the perp hit him with the gun to keep him in line?"

"It's possible, yeah." Zane's gaze flicked to the laptop, then back to Cassandra and the two agents from Violent Crimes. "Both vics were double-bound with zip-ties, and their mouths were duct taped. Anna's head was bound to a table and her eyes taped open, ostensibly so that she would be forced to watch our unsub rape her husband."

The mint from the gum replaced the bitterness of stomach acid as bile threatened to escape her mouth. Cassandra pressed her hand to her belly. Poor Anna. Poor Stephen. And their poor daughter. Cassandra wasn't sure who she felt sorrier for.

Either ignoring or oblivious to her distress, Zane went on. "The marks on their wrists indicate they both strained against the binds, but the unsubs knew what they were doing. Without a knife or a blade of some sort, it was doubtful they'd be able to get out of those zip-ties."

Amelia circled around the back of Zane's chair and stood in front of the whiteboard. "Kelly Denson wasn't bound, though."

Anger simmered in Cassandra's chest. "Meaning he probably killed her first. Took her by surprise when she was sleeping. Which also means he knew she was there in the first place."

Dean fiddled with his watchband. "There's no doubt this was premeditated. My question is, how did he miss that Kate wasn't there? Or that she should've been there?"

"She was out with friends." Sherry Cowen lifted a shoulder. "Might not have been a planned outing. If he was watching the area, it's possible he missed her leaving. It could've been an oversight on the unsub's part. I doubt they intended to leave a witness."

And Cassandra doubted the killer would be likely to let that witness live if they knew of her existence. "That's why we kept Kate out of the presser this morning. There's been no mention of her in the news, either. The only people who know she was there are the friends she texted while she was on her way to the hospital."

Sherry adjusted her sleeves. "How on earth did that poor girl have the presence of mind to text anyone in the state she was in? She was nearly catatonic when we interviewed her."

Dean nodded understanding to his partner. "Kids today are inseparable from their devices. Her thumbs may have been doing all the thinking, and she never even realized what she was doing."

Amelia agreed with her fellow agents. "The important thing is she's in a safe house now. As Agent Cowen just noted, we didn't get much out of her when we tried to talk to her last night. She did give us one thing, though. I asked her if she recognized the person who assaulted her father, and she didn't."

Leaning back in her chair, Sherry tapped a pen against her cheek. "Which tells us that, if this was a personal vendetta, then it's one that's exclusive to one of the three people who're dead. Just because Kate didn't recognize the unsub doesn't mean it isn't someone her parents know. For most of the year, she lives in a dorm on the other side of the city. So, it's not a stretch she wouldn't recognize someone her parents associated with."

"That's good, though." Amelia uncapped her marker and strode over to the other side of the whiteboard. "If we come up with any suspects, we can categorize them based on whether or not Kate could recognize them. It rules out close family friends and relatives."

Zane held up a hand. "Or it could mean those people hired a hitman."

Dean rubbed his chin, his expression thoughtful, even a little perplexed. "I'm not as well-versed in hitmen as you two are, but I assume contract killers leave rape off the table because it risks leaving behind physical evidence, right?"

Zane nodded. "Rape is about control, and hitmen already have that. And they don't usually have a personal connection to their target. Rape also adds more time they spend with the vic, thus increasing the likelihood they could be discovered. And, yes, leaving behind DNA evidence is something they meticulously try to avoid."

"Are we sure the target here was Anna Denson?" The entire room's attention shot to Sherry Cowen as she posed the query.

Letting out a heavy breath, Dean unclasped and clasped the silver band of his watch. "She's the judge, so that's what we all thought right off the bat. But she wasn't the one who was sexually assaulted."

Cassandra had considered Sherry's question, but she had to admit she hadn't given it much thought. Then again, they were less than twelve hours into the investigation. There wasn't a lot to which she'd had time to devote brainpower. "Well, we haven't found any case yet that makes us think revenge. It's possible Stephen Denson was the target, and maybe this is a personal grudge that doesn't have anything to do with the district court."

Cassandra was grateful the Denson investigation had been assigned to *these* agents. The four of them clearly respected one another's opinions, even if they ran counter to the current theory. Avoiding tunnel vision was pivotal in their line of work.

"As we suspected, Anna Denson was killed with a single shot to the back of the head." Zane paused to take a drink from a coffee mug. "Ballistics confirmed all three victims were killed with the same .22 caliber handgun. Since no neighbors reported gunshots, the killer likely used a sound suppressor. No shell casings were found on the scene. So far, the CSU hasn't found any prints in the bedroom that didn't belong to the family."

Sherry pressed her lips together. "We should get the BAU involved. Get an opinion from them. This has all the markings of a professional hit, but it's also got all the markings of a deeply personal feud. The sexual assault is what upends the hitman theory, at least as far as I'm concerned."

"I agree it could be beneficial to get a behavioral analyst to weigh in on this." Amelia pointed the tip of the marker at the information scrawled under Anna Denson's picture. "Otherwise, we ought to go check with Judge Denson's peers to see if any of them noticed something unusual going on with her lately. We should do the same for Stephen Denson too."

Steelman began to push to his feet. "Right. Cowen and I can take Stephen's acquaintances. The campus is probably mostly empty for the holiday, but we might get lucky and run into some workaholic professor."

"That leaves us with the courthouse." Zane shot Amelia a sarcastic smile. "Guess we'll be spending the afternoon with a bunch of lawyers and former lawyers."

A flash of excitement surged through Cassandra, and she ignored the tongue-in-cheek remark about dealing with her peers. Not that she truly took any offense to the comment. Even *she* didn't like dealing with attorneys on most days.

However, she was used to interacting with lawyers, judges, and their ilk. This was *her* area of expertise, and she could finally offer some value to the investigative team.

Plus, getting away from the potential of running into Joseph was an added bonus. She picked up her gum wrapper and discarded the piece in her mouth as delicately as she could. "I'll go with you two to the courthouse. Having an attorney there along with your badge might help cut through some of the red tape."

To Cassandra's surprise, Amelia quickly nodded her agreement. "You're right. We might save some time if you can cut through the usual crap."

Zane had refocused back on his laptop. "Since three's a crowd, you two go have your fun. I'll keep looking through Anna and Stephen's personal contacts."

Despite the number of questions Cassandra still had about Amelia's personal and professional relationship with Joseph Larson, she had no hang-ups regarding the woman's capability as a federal agent.

They had bigger fish to fry than Joseph Larson, and there was no reason for Cassandra to mention the prick. She wasn't even dating him anymore.

The mental reminder came with a soothing wave of relief, and the task ahead of her allowed her to bury the nagging voice that insisted she wasn't out of the woods yet.

There were murderers walking freely among the public. They needed to find them before the perps realized they'd left a witness alive.

8

Marlee Hendricks wiped her sweaty forehead with the back of one hand as she surveyed the kitchen. Every surface was spotless, and the floor was so clean it damn near sparkled. It was the perfect place to bake a thousand cookies, busy herself prepping a fancy dinner or any other activity that would keep her mind off Kate and her family.

Tears prickled the corners of Marlee's eyes, but she bit her tongue, refusing to let them fall. She'd cried enough since receiving Kate's series of text messages late the night before.

In an ambulance. I think I'm okay. Not sure what's happening

My parents and Kelly are dead

I should be dead too

But I'm alive.

Why am I alive?

Going to hospital. Not sure what happens after that.

I love u

I don't know what to do. Wish you were here

I'm such a mess. Maybe this is all a dream. None of this feels real. How can it be?

Is this real????

I'll text more later

When she received the first text, Marlee had been in the midst of drifting off during a movie Jared had picked out for them to watch before bed. She'd ignored the message, not sitting up until the fourth or fifth time her phone buzzed.

Her first thought was that Kate was bored and messing with her, but as the messages kept coming, she'd been shook.

Jared had asked if Kate was playing some sort of prank, but Marlee had already dismissed the possibility. Kate wasn't a prankster. Ever since Marlee and Kate were in middle school together, Kate had by far been the more sensitive of the pair. There was no way in hell she'd ever send a text saying her *entire family* was dead just to get a rise out of someone.

Then the two FBI agents had shown up, and reality crashed into Marlee like a cold, unforgiving wave.

So many questions.

Had she noticed anyone at the bars paying extra attention to them when they were out together? Did any strangers follow them? How much had they imbibed that night? Had she heard from Kate? How had Kate acted the last time they'd spoken? Who were her other friends?

The questions seemed endless. But Marlee doubted any of her responses had helped.

Oh, how she wished she could help her friend.

Agents Steelman and Cowen had left her and Jared their cards, bidding them to reach out if they remembered anything. When Marlee had asked the agents if Kate was okay, they'd given her a non-answer. Marlee wasn't sure if they were legally bound to silence or if something terrible had happened to Kate and the agents were waiting for the powers that be to announce her fate.

Not long after the Feds left, Marlee had scrolled through the first of the news reports on her phone.

"Family of Three Found Murdered in Their Home, Perpetrator Unknown."

Even thinking of the headline made Marlee queasy. She'd tried to sleep but hadn't managed more than a few hours. Upon waking, she'd found task after task to occupy herself. She'd started by doing laundry, and then she'd moved on to cleaning every room in the damn apartment. Jared wasn't a slob by any stretch, but his place was now cleaner than when he'd moved in.

The Densons had always been like a second family to Marlee. They'd given her a safe place to stay when her home life had become turbulent, and even though they were a nearly picture-perfect family unit, they'd never judged Marlee for her parents' drama. Anna Denson had even gone out of her way to empathize with Marlee, sharing stories of her own youth. And if Anna could make it through those experiences to become a federal judge, then surely the sky was the limit for Marlee.

Now Anna was dead, and Marlee didn't have the first clue why.

"Hey, hon, do you need help with anything?" Jared's voice cut through her reflections like a light in thick fog. From where he stood at the edge of the dining room, just past the galley kitchen, his worried gaze was fixed on Marlee. He'd stopped asking her if she was okay. He knew she wasn't.

Taking in a shaky breath, she rubbed her eyes and forced herself to focus on the apartment. "Could we, um, go to the store? I was going to make some food. It helps me when..." She trailed off and simply tapped her temple.

Fortunately, Jared spoke Marlee's language. He knew she battled with anxiety on a normal day, and he'd been a blessing ever since she'd received the text messages last night. "Yeah, we can do that."

With as much of a smile as she could manage, Marlee

walked over and wrapped Jared in a tight embrace. "Thank you. I'm sorry you have such a crazy girlfriend."

Jared gave her a slight squeeze and kissed the top of her head. "You're not crazy. You're the strongest woman I know, and I'll help you get through this. I love you."

Words couldn't describe how grateful she was for Jared in that moment, so she just hugged him tighter. "I love you too."

As they donned their coats and shoes, Marlee felt like a fool. Her best friend's family had been murdered, and here she was, about to go to the grocery store so she could make snickerdoodles and an elaborate dinner.

But what else was she supposed to do? Curl up in bed and cry herself back to sleep? That had never been Marlee's style. When she was worried or anxious, she always had to do *some*thing. Anything to keep her mind occupied.

Kate would understand. In fact, Kate did the same damn thing. It was one of many traits she and Marlee had in common.

Tucking her plaid scarf into the top of her coat, Marlee led the way as she and Jared descended to the first floor. The halls still smelled of fresh paint, and coupled with the clean, dark carpets, the old apartment building gave off a welcoming vibe.

As Marlee shoved open the front door, a wall of cold air buffeted them. She clenched her jaw to keep her teeth from chattering and shoved both hands in her pockets.

Side by side, she and Jared traversed the partially snow-covered lot. Halfway to Jared's black Honda Civic, Marlee realized with a start that they weren't alone. That wouldn't have been enough to cause alarm, not during the early afternoon of a weekday, but the man who'd just stepped out of his car was headed toward *them*.

If they hadn't been in the middle of a half-full parking lot in broad daylight, Marlee might have been inclined to turn around and sprint back to the relative safety of the apartment building. She had no real reason to believe that whoever had hurt Kate's family was after her, but paranoia wasn't exactly reasonable.

Stop being ridiculous. He might be a cop. He might have news for you.

She perked up at the thought. After spending most of her youth looking over her shoulder for anyone who resembled law enforcement, she never thought the day would come when she was actually *hoping* to run into anyone wearing a badge.

"Excuse me." The man waved at the two of them and increased his gait to a near jog. "I'm sorry to bother you. Are you Marlee Hendricks?"

Her heart thundered in her chest, and despite the cold, her palms were suddenly clammy. A quick glance at Jared confirmed he was just as curious as Marlee. "I am. Can I help you with something?"

The man's light brown eyes shifted between the two of them. Producing a small notepad from inside his coat, he offered them a slight smile. "You can, actually. My name's Zack Hartman, and I'm a reporter with the Chicago branch of the *National Horizon* online news site. I'm sorry to come across you so unexpectedly, but I was hoping you'd have a moment to talk."

Marlee's mouth went dry. A reporter? How was she supposed to deal with this? Was she even allowed to tell him anything? More importantly, did she even *want* to tell him anything?

She might have only been twenty-one, but she was well aware of how the media liked to spin the stories it produced. Who knew what the *National Horizon* wanted to say about Kate's family. Since Anna Denson was a judge, she was sure the reporters all had plenty of opinions about her.

On the flip side of the same coin, Marlee was an avid supporter of the press and free speech. She just didn't want her words to wind up twisted to fit some agenda.

Straightening her back, Marlee turned to fully face the reporter. "Maybe. Do you have any credentials?"

Hartman shot her a disarming smile that revealed slightly crooked, albeit perfectly white teeth. "I do." Clearly prepared for her question, he produced a wallet from the pocket of his coat, flipped it open, and held the ID card out for Marlee and Jared.

Sure enough, he presented his identification card, commonly referred to as a press pass. Marlee might never have heard of Zackary Hartman, but his credentials appeared legit.

She couldn't find it within herself to return the smile. "Okay. What can we help you with, Mr. Hartman?"

He waved a dismissive hand. "Please, I'm not even forty yet. Just call me Zack." He returned the wallet to his pocket, his expression becoming somber. "First of all, I just wanted to say I'm sorry for your loss. I know how difficult it is to lose a close friend."

Marlee's stomach dropped to the frigid ground. "T-to lose a friend? What…do you mean?"

Jared scooted closer to her and placed a hand on her shoulder, a silent message of reassurance.

The reporter blinked a few times in rapid succession, seeming confused. "I'm sorry. I assumed you'd have been visited by law enforcement before now?"

Marlee took Jared's hand and squeezed, though her attention didn't drift away from Zack Hartman. "We were, but… that was last night. They just asked us about, well, about Kate. They didn't say anything about her being dead."

Hartman's eyebrows scrunched together. "Well, maybe we can start there. I was covering the scene last night, outside the Densons' house. None of the folks I talked to saw anyone other than law enforcement personnel leaving the house, so I assumed..." He left the sentence unfinished, genuine concern deepening the otherwise faint lines on his clean-shaven face.

Mind reeling, Marlee tried desperately to catch up to what the man had just told her. No one had left the house other than law enforcement—that was a statement straight from a person who'd physically been at the scene.

"That doesn't make any sense," Jared said. Marlee was grateful he'd been able to find his voice when she couldn't locate hers. "Kate sent Marlee a text message saying she was alive, but she didn't really know what happened."

Zack Hartman scribbled a few notes on his pad of paper. "Kate Denson was at the scene?"

Jared opened his mouth but closed it and looked to Marlee.

She didn't know what to tell him. The FBI hadn't given them a straight answer about Kate's whereabouts or even whether or not she was alive. Now, a reporter who'd been at the Densons' house in the immediate aftermath was telling them he hadn't witnessed Kate leave the premises.

Had the killer sent the text to them from Kate's phone? Was she really dead? Or had the killer ambushed the ambulance on the way to the hospital? Surely that would have made the news, wouldn't it? Was Kate even alive?

Marlee's head was a mess. "I...I don't know. All I can tell you is what we told the FBI agents last night. We dropped Kate off around ten-thirty, and we didn't see anything weird outside the house. Roughly an hour later, she sent me a message saying she was alive, but her parents and her sister were gone."

Her confusion was echoed in Zack Hartman's expression. "She's a witness, then? Shit, we didn't have any idea there was someone there who *saw* any of this happen." He scrawled furiously on his paper, and when he returned his gaze to Marlee, there was a new, suspicious glint in his eyes. "You're sure you haven't heard from her since? What about the FBI agents you spoke to? Did they say anything about Kate?"

Apparently, Zack trusted Marlee about as much as she trusted him. Which was to say, not much. "No, they didn't. Why? What are you thinking?" A new charge of shock rushed through her veins like an electric jolt. "No way. You can't be thinking Kate had anything to do with that, can you? You can't report that! You can't!"

Taking a step back, Zack held up his hands. "I'm not saying anything, all right? I write the facts and let people figure out the rest for themselves. And the *fact* is that Kate Denson was present when her parents and her sister were murdered, but there's been zero mention of her from the FBI or the police. I'm not sure how familiar you are with the Federal Bureau of Investigation, but they don't exactly have a history of being honest and straightforward with the public."

Well, he wasn't wrong. Marlee was sure the FBI had their reasons for keeping certain details secret, but she didn't know where they drew the line.

But if this reporter was going to make Kate out to be some sort of vengeful, crazed murderer…

As anger seized hold of Marlee, she balled one hand into a fist and jabbed an accusatory finger at Zack Hartman. "You're going to ruin her life if you report that. People are going to think she murdered her family You don't even know Kate. She wouldn't hurt anyone! She hit a squirrel once when we were in high school, and she cried for hours about it!"

Hartman took another step back, his stance stiffening. "Like I said, I report *facts*. I'm not going to slander your friend, okay? But I report the truth, and the truth is the FBI is hiding something. Par for the course with them, but people in this city deserve better."

She could hardly believe this self-righteous ass. With ire flowing freely through her bloodstream, she wanted to grab him by the collar of his coat and shake him until he gained some damn sense. If looks could kill, she'd have vaporized him right then and there.

A gentle tug on the sleeve of her coat reminded her she was in the real world. A world where punching reporters in the face was frowned upon.

"Come on, Marlee." Jared's calm, gentle voice kept any additional anger at bay.

Raging at a reporter wasn't who Marlee was. It wasn't what Kate would want and certainly wasn't what Anna would have wanted.

Zack Hartman touched the notepad to his forehead. "Well, thanks for your time, Ms. Hendricks."

Marlee flipped him off before spinning on her heel to stalk toward the Civic. The idea of grocery shopping wasn't appealing any longer, but she knew herself well enough to realize she'd regret not being able to stay busy by making cookies later this afternoon.

There was no possible way Kate had killed her own family. Marlee knew that much for certain. To think of her best friend's name being dragged through the mud by online tabloids and conspiracy theorists…

As she took her spot in the passenger seat of the Civic, she slumped over and hung her head. How did she fix this? Could she even fix it?

"Hey." Jared's hand was warm on her shoulder as he pulled his door closed. "Those FBI agents left us their cards and said we could contact them any time, right?"

Marlee squeezed her eyes closed to avoid tears. "Yeah. Why?"

"Well, call one of them. I'm sure they'd like to hear about Zack Hartman and the *National Horizon*."

Blinking to clear her vision, she turned to Jared. "I doubt they'd even care."

He turned the key over in the ignition and lifted a shoulder. "Maybe not, but it wouldn't hurt anything."

Marlee sighed. "I don't know. It's the FBI. They probably already know all about it. What if *they* think Kate did it? What if someone's framing her?" A jolt of worry shot through her like an electric charge. "What if they start to think we had something to do with it? Oh my god..."

"Hey, Marlee." Jared leaned in and placed a hand between her shoulder blades. "That's the anxiety talking, okay? Remember what your therapist said?"

Clenching and unclenching her hands, Marlee wished she could curl up into a ball and hide in her coat. All she could picture was the FBI shackling Kate and loading her into the back of a prisoner transport vehicle. And then the two agents from last night breaking down Jared's door and slapping a search warrant in their faces.

"Marlee?"

She gritted her teeth and forced herself to take in a deep breath. It was damn near impossible for her to recall her therapist's words at a time like this, but she'd gotten better about it in the last year. "I remember. My body can only hold this level of anxiety for so long. It'll pass. I know it will."

Seconds ticked away in silence, turning to minutes as Marlee's heart rate gradually began to return to normal.

Jared was right about reaching out to the FBI agents. She didn't understand how telling the FBI about her and Jared's run-in with Zack Hartman would help the investigation, but she wasn't an FBI agent. The best she could do was provide them with the information and let them figure out whether or not it was useful.

"Okay." She straightened in her seat and reached for her seat belt. "Yeah, okay. You're right. I'll call one of them in a little bit."

At Jared's reassuring smile, Marlee wished she could feel any sense of relief. But she couldn't. She wouldn't. Not until the person responsible for killing Kate's family was caught, and that damn reporter was proven wrong.

9

Rubbing the back of his neck, Zane approached the closed door of the incident room. For most of the afternoon, he'd either been staring at a computer screen or talking on the phone while staring at a computer screen. Thirty-four wasn't old, but his eyes and neck sure *felt* positively ancient today. The mug of breakroom coffee in his hand wasn't likely to do him any favors, either.

As he let himself into the room, he was pleasantly surprised to find that BAU Agent Layton Redker had joined Amelia, Dean, and Sherry at the oval table. The man's dark hair, sprinkled with gray, was neatly styled into a toned-down version of a faux hawk. Coupled with a pair of black-rimmed glasses Zane hadn't seen the agent wear before, he could have easily passed for a quiet computer geek like some of his former colleagues in the Bureau's Cyber Crimes Division. But the cunning glint in his brown eyes made Zane believe the man's shrewdness ran deep.

While the three agents and the Assistant U.S. Attorney had been out interviewing colleagues and professional acquaintances of Stephen and Anna Denson, Zane had secured the assistance of a member of the FBI's Behavioral Analysis Unit. One of his eight-million phone calls so far that day.

Not only would the expertise of someone like Agent Redker go a long way in learning more about the motive that had driven the killer, but more manpower meant they could get through more leads in a shorter amount of time. As Cassandra Halcott had warned them, the media loved to put a political spin on just about everything. The sooner they discounted that particular motive, the better off they'd all be.

The silver lining—and really the only good news in such a brutal case—was that when a federal judge and a well-regarded law professor were two of their three victims, the FBI was more than willing to provide the manpower necessary to track down the killer. It wasn't how justice should work, but he didn't have time to ponder the harsh realities of the stilted system he worked within.

Zane blew on his coffee as the door closed behind him. They were one person short, but he was eager to get started. "Where's Halcott? Or is this everyone?"

Amelia rose from her seat and walked over to the window. "She stepped out to update the U.S. Attorney. She said not to wait for her. We can just brief her later. She didn't want to hold anything up."

After Cassandra Halcott had effectively led the charge against Amelia during the Ben Storey case—when Amelia had been framed for the councilman's murder by a fellow FBI agent and a Chicago police officer—Zane was never certain of her and Amelia's standing.

Amelia had told Zane that Cassandra had apologized for her shortsightedness and had revealed that she'd been under a great deal of pressure from her bosses. In their line of work, nagging from the top of the food chain often led to tunnel vision and mistakes.

They'd all been there, he was sure. What Zane found most peculiar about the entire situation was that Cassandra was currently dating the same man who'd tried to blackmail Amelia into sleeping with him—the same man who was apparently buddy-buddy with Brian Kolthoff, *The Shark*. Zane didn't know much about their relationship, but the connection left him with a sense of unease he hadn't quite been able to shake.

Taking a seat beside Amelia's currently vacant chair, Zane focused on the people in the room. "How was everyone's break? Good?"

Dean Steelman tilted his soft drink bottle toward Zane like it was a pint. "Good. Had enough time to go to Herman's and shovel a sandwich into my face."

As Zane pictured the well-dressed man cramming a sub into his mouth like a snake devouring an animal twice its size, he barked out a laugh. "That's good. I swear I think you're on their payroll the way you promote that place. I hope everyone else had as much fun as Steelman did."

Steelman grinned, and Zane could tell the others were as grateful for the moment of humor as he was.

But as the saying went, all good things must come to an end. They had a murderer—a *pair* of murderers, according to Kate Denson—to catch.

Feeling the minutes ticking by, Zane decided to take on the task of getting them back to business. He assumed no one's research had led to any groundbreaking discoveries. Otherwise, they'd have shared the information by now.

Well, that wasn't necessarily true. Zane had come upon a tidbit that had the potential to sway the course of the investigation. He just hadn't had enough time to thoroughly vet the intel.

It was a good starting place.

"Before we get to Agent Redker's analysis so far, I've got

something to throw out there. Something I haven't had a chance to review thoroughly just yet, but I think it's worth a look."

Redker folded both hands atop his closed laptop. "Let's hear it."

Setting aside his tar-black coffee, Zane lifted a manila folder. "It's a case I found through ViCAP. A quadruple homicide from a little over three weeks ago. Scott Graham, Carla Graham, and their two kids." His stomach sank a little as he recalled the kids' names. "Christian and Dane, ages thirteen and nine, respectively."

Sherry Cowen's expression darkened, echoing the grim mood that fell over the room's occupants. "Is it one of ours?"

"No. It's city jurisdiction. It's an active investigation, but currently, the CPD has no leads and no suspects. I talked to the captain of the precinct working it, and she said the detectives have hit a wall. The entire family was killed, execution-style, just like the Densons. Small caliber weapon, no shell casings left on the scene. Different weapons were used in both crimes. A .22 caliber was used in the Graham case, and according to the ballistics report we received this morning, a .22 was also used to kill the Densons. Same weapon was used to kill all three of them, just like the same weapon was used to kill the entire Graham family. But the biggest commonality was the sexual assault."

One of Sherry's eyebrows lifted. "Meaning the husband was sexually assaulted?"

"Correct." Zane held out his hands in an effort to remind his coworkers he hadn't delved into the case yet. "I haven't checked to see if he and Stephen Denson are connected, but I think it's something we should keep in mind. Anna Denson was a federal judge, but she might not have been the target."

Layton Redker's chair squeaked as he scooted closer to the table. "He's right. We've got to keep an open mind. Anna

Denson being a district judge is what landed this case in the FBI's jurisdiction, but that doesn't mean it's linked to the reason she and her family were killed. Based on the commonality of the brutality the men endured, *if* the crimes are connected, we may need to look more closely at the male victims."

Amelia strode away from the window to take her seat beside Zane. "I suppose that brings us to the next order of business. Cassandra Halcott and I talked to Judge Denson's colleagues at the courthouse this afternoon."

"Anything useful?" Zane suspected he knew the answer to his own question but asked anyway.

"Not really." Amelia flipped open the little notepad she always carried to interviews and crime scenes. "Judge Denson didn't have any dramatic dealings with her coworkers. We asked if they knew of any personal upheaval in Anna's life, but none of them did. They said that as far as they knew, Stephen and Anna Denson were a happily married couple with two equally happy, well-adjusted daughters."

Dean nodded. "Cowen and I got the same from Stephen Denson's colleagues at the University of Chicago. He's had a few professional disagreements with some other instructors, but nothing that got contentious. There were zero reports of him ever being inappropriate with a student, and the dean said Stephen always got great reviews when they surveyed his classes at the end of the semester."

That was one strike against the possibility of a student seeking revenge for an affair gone wrong. Usually, if a college professor was sleazy enough to screw his or her students, there was a trail of bad behavior that accompanied it.

Unlike the stories romance novels and Hallmark movies depicted, a professor Stephen Denson's age didn't just up and fall in love with a girl thirty years his junior. And he almost definitely didn't stick to just *one* girl.

At the end of the day, college kids liked to talk. If Stephen Denson truly had been inappropriate with a student, Zane was confident they'd find a trail.

But they hadn't. The guy had been a model professor.

Layton Redker threaded his fingers together. "In my opinion, the likelihood that this stems from an affair with a student is slim. The killers used a silencer for their weapon and policed their brass. That's not indicative of a college student to me."

The man had a point. Still, they'd be loath not to explore every possible avenue. "It seems more like a mob hit, except…" this was the part Zane still couldn't wrap his mind around, "for the sexual assault." That was the wrench in his theory. "Of course, a college student with money and the right connections could've *hired* people to do the deed, but even if that was our current theory, there are plenty of holes in it."

"I agree." Redker opened his laptop. "The sexual assault doesn't align with a classic mafia execution scenario, especially with the similarities in the case you found."

Bingo.

"I'd been thinking the same thing." Zane turned to the profiler. "What's your take on the whole scenario, Redker? Have you had a chance to go through everything we've gotten so far?"

"I did." Drumming his fingers on the table, Redker leaned back in his chair, a contemplative expression on his face. "Like I said, it's certainly not your typical mob hit, if there is such a thing. There are elements of the crime that are methodical and precise, such as the killers' ability to disarm the Densons' home alarm system. That level of skill indicates our killers are familiar with technology and that despite the rage they display, they've got the foresight to plan for almost every aspect of their crime."

Another thorough psychopath. Great. Zane kept the sarcastic comment to himself.

Dean Steelman pushed his plastic bottle around in a circle. "What do we think about the level of anger? Are we sure it's our unsub's primary motivation?"

"Or unsubs," Amelia added from her position at the murder board, tapping her marker on the second question mark.

Dean lifted the bottle in a silent toast. "True."

"That's something I asked myself, actually." Redker glanced at the dry-erase board. "Kelly Denson was killed with a single shot to the head, and the M.E. found zero evidence of defensive wounds on her body. It's likely she was killed in her sleep."

Amelia turned the marker over and over in her hands. "If that's the case, our unsub was being careful to eliminate a potential witness."

"More than likely." Redker tapped a few keys on his laptop. "We all know rapists don't assault their victims for sexual gratification. They do it for a feeling of power and control. As we already discussed, the fact that Anna Denson is a federal judge is the main reason this case was given to the Bureau. However," he swept his gaze over the agents gathered at the table, reminding Zane briefly of a schoolteacher in the middle of a lecture, "we have to keep in mind she might not be the killer's primary target."

"Right." Amelia picked up a red folder and scanned the page. "The M.E. confirmed her on-scene analysis that Stephen Denson was sexually assaulted, but no semen was found. He may have been penetrated with an object the unsub took with him. Or a condom could have been used and the unsub took that with him, just like the shell casings.

Dr. Ackerly will go over Mr. Denson's body more thoroughly back in her lab just to be certain nothing was left behind."

Zane still wasn't sure what in the hell a squeaky-clean law professor like Stephen Denson could have done to warrant such a brutal response, but if he'd learned anything in this job, it was that people were unpredictable. There were plenty of accounts of seemingly normal folks flying into a violent rage due to a slight inconvenience. It was possible Stephen Denson had simply happened across someone whose fuse had burned down to nothing.

As Redker tapped the laptop's track pad a few times, he rubbed his chin. "Palmer, if you could send me the case you found today, I'd like to compare that with the Denson case."

Moving the case files to the side, Zane reached to the center of the table for his laptop.

Dean Steelman leaned back in his chair and took a long drink. "What about the possibility that our guy is targeting entire families? That we're dealing with a serial killer?"

Redker's jaw tightened, though only for a split second. "It's possible. That's part of why I want to go through the Graham murders. It sounds like there are several similarities, but we need to verify the MO is the same. Palmer, what did the Grahams do for a living? Did they work in the legal system too?"

Without pulling his gaze away from the laptop, Zane shook his head. "No, none of them did. Scott Graham was a plumber, and Carla was a manager at a grocery store. They were about as far from a courtroom as you can get."

The crease between Redker's eyebrows deepened. "All right. We'll have to dig a little deeper to find a connection between the two families. We're obviously dealing with a male, or two males, according to Kate Denson's statement so far. These two men are meticulous and thorough, indicating they have a good deal of life experience. Mid-thirties to forties, but at least one of them has kept up with technology pretty well. That one could work in a tech-related field, which would make bypassing a home security system somewhat easier."

Amelia turned from where she'd been writing the names of the Graham family on the board. "Forensics said the alarm system was knocked offline on-site and not through the internet, and Agent Steelman was able to obtain the security logs. Those logs show that the time the system was disengaged aligns with the rough time frame we've constructed based on the victims' times of death and the statements we got from Kate and her friends Marlee and Jared."

Redker nodded. "If the unsub knocked the system offline on-site, that means he had the right tech to get past it. If the Grahams had an alarm system, that could be another clue as to whether or not we're dealing with the same unsub. Since we're potentially dealing with two, I think they're either both motivated by the same thing, or the dominant one has a motivation that overrides any reservations the more submissive one might have. Whether it's a personal vendetta or something else remains to be seen."

Zane mentally grimaced. A pair of vengeful, tech-savvy mass murderers. Just what the city of Chicago needed. "What do you think about the contract killer angle?"

"I obviously don't know as much about organized crime in this city as the two of you." Redker gestured to Amelia and Zane. "And contract killers can be difficult to profile since killing is essentially just a job for them. For the Denson case, I wouldn't completely rule it out. But if we are dealing with a hitman, then we're dealing with one that's taken on murder for hire to satiate a great deal of repressed anger."

Zane knew the higher-tier criminal enterprises in Chicago wouldn't want to throw in with a hitman who had anger issues. If the Leónes, D'Amatos, or the cartels wanted someone dead, they wanted the deed done with surgical precision.

Not to mention, most of the cartels or crime families were traditional, stuck in an old-fashioned mentality filled with sexism and homophobia. If one of their contract killers was found to have sexually assaulted a *man*, he'd be effectively exiled from future work with the organization.

The murders could have been ordered by a more small-time operation, maybe one that was newer and wasn't stuck in the same draconian ideals as the Leónes or the D'Amatos. They could be dealing with the inception of a brand-new criminal empire.

Was that better or worse than their suspect being a serial killer? If Zane and Amelia's previous case, James Amsdell, was any indication, he wasn't sure.

Unease crept down Zane's spine at the memory. Amsdell, also known as The New Moon Killer, had murdered two people in the city of Chicago and numerous others in other parts of the Midwest. He'd come damn close to ending the life of a third Chicago resident, and if Zane hadn't lost his shit and dove into the frigid waters of Lake Michigan, Amsdell's final tally would have been higher.

All because the young woman Amsdell had kidnapped from the streets of Washington Park had reminded Zane so starkly of a ghost from his past.

Katya. He still didn't know her last name, but he'd never forget her emerald eyes and strawberry blonde, corkscrew curls.

At the beginning of his tenure with the CIA, he'd been tasked with infiltrating a Russian mob operation located on the shore of the Sea of Okhotsk. They'd dealt in the illegal seafood trade, but smuggling crab to the States was only one layer in a much more sinister business.

Human trafficking was the bulk of what occurred in the

Okhotsk location, but the Russians had also dabbled in arms dealing and drugs.

That was the thing about guns and heroin, though. He could stand by as a mountain of heroin was smuggled through an American port, but human beings who were treated like cattle? No, the girls had been treated worse than livestock.

Standing idly by and watching those pricks inflict suffering and misery onto innocent young women was far from one of Zane's crowning achievements in the CIA. There were too many unsavory deeds to count, but Katya stuck in his memory the clearest.

In a way, diving into Lake Michigan to rescue Paige Milling had given him a sense of vindication for failing to save Katya. He was well aware he was a day late and more than a few dollars short, but at least he'd been able to do something. Even if it had taken him more than a decade.

The icy venture had nearly killed Paige, and Zane's fate hadn't been far behind. If they hadn't been whisked away to a hospital when they were, he'd have likely suffered lasting damage, and Paige would have died.

Before Zane's brain could spiral too far down the memory rabbit hole, a knock jerked their collective attention to the door. "It's unlocked."

He hadn't even finished the words when Cassandra Halcott appeared. Her cheeks were slightly flushed, and her expression made Zane's stomach sink a couple feet closer to the floor.

Whatever she had to tell them, it wasn't good.

Waving her phone in the air, she shoved the door closed. "Kate Denson's in the news. I just found a mobile article stating she was present at the crime scene. The author didn't directly write that he thought Kate might've been involved in her family's murder, but the comments are full of exactly that."

"Shit." Dean Steelman spat the word like it had been a foul taste on his tongue. "When? How long has it been out? Who wrote the damn thing?"

"It was published less than an hour ago by the *National Horizon*. They used to be a print operation but recently went digital. The author is a reporter named Zack Hartman. According to his bio, he's been working for the *Horizon* for more than a decade."

"Shit." Dean picked at the label of the plastic bottle. "So, he's not just some chucklehead who's trying to put out click-bait. He's an actual reporter, and people *actually* listen to him."

Cassandra's grim expression echoed the sudden mood shift in the room. "Exactly."

A jolt of irritability ran through Zane, and he gritted his teeth to keep a slew of four-letter words at bay. "How in the hell did he get that information? Or is a ten-year veteran reporter suddenly keen on pulling this kind of speculative bullshit out of thin air?"

Cassandra held up her hands in a stance that implored him not to shoot the messenger. "I don't know where he got the information. He doesn't cite much in the article, just says he learned this from a source 'close to' Kate."

Rubbing his forehead, Dean muttered a handful of curses. "Her friends. Jared Olsen and Marlee Hendricks. Cowen and I took their statements last night while you two were working the scene. We didn't tell them anything about Kate being a witness."

To his side, Sherry Cowen opened a tin of mints. "Kate could've told them herself…before we took her phone and ordered the hospital staff not to confirm her presence to an outside source." She tossed a mint into her mouth and crunched it hard between her teeth. "Can't blame the kid for wanting to reach out to someone after what she went through."

For a fraction of a second, Cassandra's face softened with something that might have been sympathy, leaving Zane to wonder what types of secrets she harbored beneath her polished veneer. "Maybe not, but we need to do damage control immediately. If the person, or people, who killed three members of the Denson family realize Kate was there to witness it, they'll set their sights on her. They didn't have any problem killing Kelly, so I doubt they'll hesitate to do the same to Kate."

Sherry pushed herself away from the table, turning to her partner as she stood. "We currently have Kate in a safe house. Steelman and I will go check on Kate's security detail and give them an update. While we're there, we'll check to see if she's more responsive or better able to provide a statement today."

With a nod, Steelman followed his partner's lead and shoved to his feet.

Cassandra's expectant gaze, along with Layton Redker's, fell on Amelia and Zane.

Zane crushed his empty paper mug. "Agent Storm and I will pay a visit with Zack Hartman just in case there's anything else he learned that he might not have yet published."

Amelia tossed the marker onto the table and headed toward the door. Zane followed suit. They didn't stick around to exchange lengthy farewells. There was work to do.

The public loved nothing more than a macabre tale of death and destruction. If word began to make its way around less-reputable press circles that Kate Denson had been involved in murdering her entire family, she'd become an overnight media sensation.

And extensive public attention would muddy the waters of their investigation and potentially render Kate's safety more difficult to maintain. If they lost their only witness to a triple homicide—not to mention the fact that the man who killed Kate's family might have killed four other people—their investigation would be in dire straits.

Whether it was misinformation about Kate's involvement in her family's murders or alerting the killers to her presence at the crime scene, that young woman now had a giant target on her back. They needed to put out these flames or prepare to weather one hell of a firestorm.

10

As Dean Steelman slid out from behind the wheel of his nondescript work car, he glanced to the shrinking sliver of daylight beneath the garage door. Not every FBI safe house sported a two-car garage like this one, but the howl of the cold December wind made him grateful for the amenity.

Before departing the field office, Sherry had alerted the security team of their impending, albeit unscheduled, visit. Dean figured the forty-five-minute drive through rush hour traffic had allotted plenty of time for the agents to prepare. He'd spent an additional fifteen minutes making sure they weren't being followed, not heading directly to the safe house until he was certain no one was on their tail.

To the side of his and Sherry's ride was another equally inconspicuous sedan that belonged to the agents overseeing the location. The cars didn't look like anything special, but they'd been reinforced to withstand a limited number of gunshots. Otherwise, the garage was tidy and minimalistic. Yard work equipment, such as a shovel and rake, hung on the wall, and a lawn mower sat beside the storage area. The place was run by the FBI, sure, but it wasn't exempt from basic upkeep.

The neighbors would grow suspicious if the "homeowners" let the grass grow wild in the spring and summer or if they didn't rake leaves in the fall and shovel the sidewalk during the winter. Even the generous space between lots in this part of town didn't shield the safe house from the eyes of middle-aged men who judged everyone they met by the status of their lawn.

Pausing to wait for Sherry, Dean took a moment to send out a quick prayer of thanks that he never wound up like one of those guys. At thirty-seven, he was coming close to the age where lawn upkeep began to define many men.

I'll just keep living in an apartment or a condo. That way, I won't have a lawn to be proud of.

As Sherry strode over to him, he shook off the thoughts and rapped his knuckles against the door in the specific pattern of knocks they'd been provided by the security detail. Sherry and Dean each brandished their badges in front of the peephole in the door. The metallic *click* of the deadbolt followed almost immediately, and the door swung inward to reveal a vaguely familiar woman, Special Agent Lacey Spaulding.

With Lacey's casual, plaid button-down and dark-wash skinny jeans, she could easily pass for any other inhabitant of the neighborhood. Her reddish-brown hair hung a few inches past her shoulders, part of it pinned back to keep the strands out of her face.

Agent Spaulding's gaze shifted from Sherry to Dean before she stepped aside and ushered them forward. "Afternoon, Agents. I'm Agent Spaulding. My partner, Agent Reeves, is monitoring the security cameras."

The confidence with which the agent spoke was reassuring, a reminder to Dean that the security specialists knew what they were doing.

Sherry unraveled the black scarf around her neck. "I'm sure you've gotten the news already. Kate was the subject of an article published a couple hours ago by the Chicago outlet of the *National Horizon*. We'd intended to keep her role as a witness a secret for as long as possible, but well..." She gave a hapless shrug.

"We're aware of it." Spaulding's jaw tightened, her face a mask of determination. "We'd considered moving her to a new safe house just to get ahead of things in case anyone knew she was here. But we've had her here for fewer than twenty-four hours, and our contact in intelligence hasn't come across anything that indicates this location has been compromised."

Sherry draped her scarf over a wall-mounted hook. "So, right now, the risk of moving her to a different safe house would be greater than staying here since we have no reason to believe this location is compromised."

"Exactly. We're taking some extra precautions around here, and our intelligence contact will let us know the second she's got any information that might mean we're vulnerable. In an hour or two, we'll have surveillance set up at the end of the block to monitor traffic in the area."

Dean shrugged out of his coat as he mulled over the words. Beefing up security while maintaining a nonchalant appearance was a fine line to walk. "It's just you and Agent Reeves in the house with Kate, isn't it?"

"For now, yes. The house is big enough that we could comfortably double-up on security, though."

"Perfect." That solved one problem, at least. "Aside from the security cameras and the surveillance team, what other security measures do you have around the house?"

The agent started down the hall leading out of the mudroom, Sherry and Dean following close behind. "The windows in the house are all sealed shut. We've also got the windows and doors fixed with a silent alarm that'll alert us, as well as the field office, if they're broken or tampered with in some way. The system has a battery backup in case of a power outage, as do the security cameras. They record to a cloud-based server that we can access on a computer or a mobile device."

High-tech was good, but in Dean's experience, most modern technologies had at least one exploitable weakness. Of course, that's what Agents Spaulding and Reeves were for —they were the backup in the event technology failed.

Sherry tucked both hands into the pockets of her knit cardigan. "Do you have a backup generator?"

"We do, yes. It's out back. We even had a special casing built around it, almost a mini room if you will, so that it would be virtually tamper-proof." Spaulding chuckled. "Probably the only house in the damn neighborhood that has one, and its presence probably makes us look like doomsday preppers."

Dean was glad to hear the safe house wouldn't lose power due to a grid failure, or worse, a targeted attack. "You said the cameras record to a cloud-based server. Is there any form of backup if the internet or cable line is cut?"

The agent didn't miss a beat. "Yes. It would take a few minutes for everything to migrate over, but that's just the nature of the beast. Better to only lose a few minutes than to lose the entire system, you know?"

Sherry offered Spaulding a quick smile. "True. I don't have great luck with technology, so I like to hear when there's a backup plan for everything."

Dean couldn't help a chortle at the comment. Sherry was grossly understating her near-constant war with technology.

A few years back, she'd gone as far as taking a broken printer to a shooting range to use as target practice.

Clearing his throat, Dean set aside the amusing memory. He was satisfied with the rundown of the safe house's security, but now it was time to move on to the reason they were all here in the first place. "How's Kate doing? Any improvement?"

As they entered a spacious, eat-in kitchen, Spaulding dropped her hands to her hips. "Some improvement, yeah. She hasn't said much to either of us, but she's been occupying herself instead of just staring off into space like she did when she first got here. She's in the living room right now, watching TV. I'm no psychologist, but I'd say she's doing as well as can be expected."

If television was one of Kate's coping mechanisms, then she and Dean had something in common.

Sherry perked up at the news. "Speaking of psychologist, has she spoken to a therapist at all?"

Agent Spaulding leaned against a counter. "She has, earlier today. We had one of the therapists from the Bureau come try to talk with her and perform an assessment."

Dean didn't have much experience with the FBI's on-staff counselors, but he was sure the Bureau hadn't skimped. "We need to speak to Kate today, but we should also work out a time to interview her when the therapist is on-site."

Spaulding shot him an approving glance. "We can do that. And I agree, I think that would be the best approach."

As his gaze drifted over to the doorway, Dean was struck by a rare pang of anxiety.

He didn't often experience nervousness when interviewing witnesses, but Kate Denson was...fragile. Dean's approach to questions was straightforward, but such a tactic might be detrimental to Kate's mental state. The last thing he wanted was to be the dumbass who asked the wrong question and sent their only witness into another period of catatonia.

Sherry's good with people. Let her ask the questions, and just follow her lead. She talked to Kate last night.

He turned to his partner. They'd worked together long enough for Sherry to understand his weak spots and for him to understand hers. The reason they were paired together so often was because they complemented one another's investigative styles.

Rubbing her hands together, Sherry tilted her head toward the doorway. "All right. Let's see how she's doing."

Despite his mental hesitancy, Dean started for the living room like talking to traumatized young women was a part of his everyday life.

He'd half-expected the space to be as sterile as a hospital or as dull and professional as the FBI office. As he glanced around, however, he felt like he was in someone's home. All they were missing were family photos on the walls, but in their places were photos of sunsets and other visually appealing landscapes. Impersonal, sure, but still comforting. While it was true the décor provided hiding places for listening devices or tiny cameras, the house was swept for such devices every day.

The cream area rug beneath the couch and coffee table was decorated with blue and green swirls that matched the throw pillows and blankets on the overstuffed sectional. Dean was almost certain the furniture was nicer than his.

From where she was curled in the corner of the U-shaped couch, Kate Denson's gaze snapped over to Sherry and Dean. For a beat, her posture stiffened, her hand tightening on the fleece blanket covering her lap. Recognition swept across her face as she spotted Sherry, and her body quickly relaxed.

"Hello, Kate. Do you remember me from the other night?

My name is Sherry, and this is my partner Dean. Mind if we sit?"

Sitting up straighter, Kate pressed a button to pause the program on the television screen. "Yeah. That's fine."

Dean was relieved to hear the kid speak. The night before, she'd been so traumatized, she only nodded or shook her head in response to Sherry and Amelia's questions.

As he took his spot beside Sherry, far enough from Kate to give her space but close enough to feel like they could have an actual conversation, he permitted himself a moment of cautious optimism.

After an affirmative glance to confirm he and Sherry were on the same page, Dean leaned forward to prop his elbows on his knees. Sherry would ask the questions, and Dean would provide the information. "Kate, you know why we're keeping you here at a safe house, right?"

She swallowed but dipped her chin. "Yes. Because you think the person who...did *that* to my mom and dad, and my sister, might come for me because I saw them."

Dean met the poor girl's gaze and softened his tone. "That's right. Agents Spaulding and Reeves are constantly monitoring the area around the house. You're in very good hands, and I want to make sure you know that, okay?"

Her eyes turned glassy. "Okay."

Though none of the day's events were his fault, Dean was still struck by a twinge of guilt for what he was about to tell her. But there was no reason for him to beat around the bush. Traumatized or not, Kate deserved to know what type of danger she was in.

"We'd been keeping you out of the news, making sure reporters didn't know you were a witness. But we've run into a problem with that. We don't know how the information got out, but an article was published earlier today stating you were at the crime scene."

Kate's knuckles turned white from her grasp on the blanket. "W-what does that mean? Am I in danger…I mean, *more* danger?"

The hint of sarcasm in her voice almost made Dean smile. Kate was smart. Neither he nor Sherry had to spell the situation out for her. Being the daughter of a district court judge had undoubtedly prepared her, on some level at least, for a worst-case scenario.

And now, she was living it.

"It does." Sherry picked up the dialogue as they prepared to wade into their questions. "But like Agent Steelman said, you're in very good hands. We'll be stepping up security here, and we'll have another agent staying in the house with the three of you." She paused to tilt her chin at Dean. "My partner and I will take turns providing additional security, as well as two other agents who are working the case."

"Okay." Kate's voice was small, the moment of near normalcy slipping away.

Sherry scooted forward, partially obscuring Dean's view of Kate. The couch was comfortable but not quite made for a couple of FBI agents to talk to a witness. "I know this is a very difficult time for you, and we'll do our best to help as much as we can. However, we need your help too."

Fear radiated off Kate in waves. Licking her lips, she shifted in her seat and nodded once. "O-okay."

Sherry clasped both hands together on her knees. "Before your phone was taken as evidence, you contacted your friends, Marlee Hendricks and Jared Olsen, to tell them about what happened to your family, right?"

Another nod, this one almost sheepish.

"Did you reach out to anyone else? Any other family members, friends, classmates?"

Kate shook her head. "No. Just Marlee and Jared."

Dean considered the assurance. If she hadn't alerted

anyone else, then the couple *had* to be the source of information for Zack Hartman. Either unwittingly or otherwise, Marlee and Jared had spilled the beans to Hartman, and Hartman had spilled them to the entire world.

It was possible there was a leak in the Chicago PD or even in the FBI, but Dean had learned years ago in this job that the simplest explanation was usually correct. More often than not, there was no grand conspiracy behind an unfortunate event.

But when there was...

He swatted away the thought like it was a bug. If there was an intricate plot to kill Anna Denson due to her work as a district court judge, then they'd cross that bridge when the evidence indicated. Right now, the evidence suggested a deeply personal grudge with Stephen Denson.

"Now, you shook your head when Agent Storm and I asked you if you recognized the voice of the person who was speaking in your parents' room. You didn't recognize them, is that correct?" Sherry's question returned Dean's focus to the room.

"Uh-huh." Kate swallowed, her hands busy smoothing out the blanket. "I'd never heard him before. I don't know who he was."

As Dean pulled out a small notepad and a pen, Sherry forged ahead.

"That's helpful, Kate. Thank you. Your responses also indicated there was more than one person in the house. Can you tell us if you've remembered anything about the second person?"

From the rise and fall of Kate's chest, Dean could tell her breathing and heart rate had accelerated. "I...I heard the first man talking to someone else. I couldn't really hear the other person, but I think it was a man."

Dean scribbled his notes, remaining silent as Sherry

paused. "Could you recognize the first man's voice if you heard it again?"

Her head was bobbing before Sherry even finished the question. "Yes. I'll never forget it."

A positive voice identification was huge…if they had a suspect.

Sherry didn't let the excitement Dean knew she was feeling show. She wouldn't want to give the girl any false hope. "Did you get a good look at him?"

Kate's posture grew even more rigid, her shoulders rising and falling with each labored breath. Her wet eyes were fixed on the distance, and her stare was vacant.

Shit, she's about to have a panic attack.

Dean held up a hand. "If this is too much for you right now, just let us know. We can pick up the interview later on if we need to."

Sherry shot him an appreciative glance. "Dean is right."

Swiping her cheeks, Kate hung her head and sniffled. "Every time I try to think of what he looked like, I just see that room again. I see my mom tied up with her mouth duct taped shut, crying. And…and my dad." The recollection ended in a sob.

Though Dean wished he could press her for more details about the picture in her head, her visceral reaction told him they'd best not press their luck. The case was urgent, sure, but Kate's memory was the only real piece of evidence they had right now.

Clicking his pen closed, Dean nudged Sherry's arm. As she turned to him, he slowly shook his head. Not that *he* needed to tell Sherry when to go easy on a witness, but he'd rather be safe than sorry.

Dean was no therapist, but he'd dealt with plenty of post-traumatic stress responses during and after his time with the military. If they pushed her for a more thorough statement now, they might reap some short-term benefit, but in the long run, they'd do more harm than good.

"It's okay, Kate." He kept his tone calm and even, as if he was speaking to a frightened animal. "You don't have to think about that anymore. Just breathe, all right? Focus on your breathing."

Her head bobbed, but she didn't look up at them as she inhaled deeply.

"We have a few more questions, but we won't ask you to go back to that memory again, okay?"

Brushing the strands of hair from her face, Kate finally met Dean's gaze. Her lower lip still quivered, but her ragged breathing had improved. "Yeah. I'm…I'm sorry. I want to help. It's just…"

Dean offered her a smile he hoped was reassuring. "You don't need to be sorry. You've already been a big help to us. Just a few standard questions to wrap things up for today, yeah?"

Her nod was more resolute, and her pallid cheeks had started to regain some color. "Yeah. Go ahead."

"Did you notice anything out of the ordinary over the past couple weeks in your parents' neighborhood while you were home from college? Any people lingering nearby you hadn't seen before? Strange vehicles parked in front of the house, things like that?"

Kate chewed on her bottom lip, but the nervous tic wasn't anywhere near as extreme as her reaction a few moments earlier. "No, I don't think so. I stay on campus for most of the year, so I don't really know the neighborhood as well as I used to. It's not a real close-knit neighborhood, just sort of nosy and a little snooty. But none of it seemed out of the ordinary to me."

Dean scrawled away in the notepad, silently passing the dialogue to Sherry.

"Were there any visitors around the house while you were there? Any salespeople or maintenance personnel?"

"No, not that I remember. We didn't have any problems with the house, and as far as I know, my parents didn't call for services or anything. It was just us, for the most part. Aside from my aunt, pretty much all our family lives outside the state, so we usually just stay home for Christmas. Marlee and Jared were there this year, but I think they were the only visitors we had for the entire time I was home."

As he wrote down Kate's responses, Dean fought the urge to sigh. Whoever had killed Anna, Stephen, and Kelly had been prepared. They'd known the type of alarm system the family used, and they'd known how to circumvent it.

Not only that, but they'd managed to get to and from the house without any of the neighbors noticing. And based on how rubbernecked those people had become the second the crime scene tape went up, that alone had to have been a feat. Not much got past nosy neighbors. Maybe they'd need to canvass the area again but ask different questions.

Or maybe the killer had just been that damn stealthy.

Killers. Two of them had to get in and out unnoticed.

There was no way the suspects had come and gone often enough to study the details of the Denson house without *someone* noticing. Problem was, whoever had seen them likely didn't have the first clue what they had truly witnessed.

Sherry's question about salespeople and maintenance personnel was precisely the type of query they needed to pose around the neighborhood.

"I'm sorry." Kate's quiet apology tugged at his heart. "I wish I could be more helpful."

Dean pocketed the notepad and pen. "You have nothing to apologize for. We're here to help *you* and to find the person responsible. You have my word. We'll do everything we can."

He wished he could assure her they'd catch the sick bastard responsible, but one of the first lessons he'd learned in the FBI was never to promise anything he couldn't deliver. Catching killers was never guaranteed, not even with the funding and expertise the Bureau possessed.

What he *could* promise was his best. He could give that, and he would.

Whoever had killed Kate's family would almost definitely hurt other people. Someone capable of murdering a teenager while she slept, of sexually assaulting a person in front of their spouse...those people didn't magically return to being productive members of society.

Dean would do his damnedest to find these pricks before they had the chance to wreak havoc on another family.

11

Amelia held out her hands to let her icy fingers soak up the heat from the air vent of Zane's car. The temperature outside had dropped at least ten degrees since lunch, and they were still a half hour away from sunset. As warm as the interior of Zane's Acura stayed on their trip to the edge of downtown, Amelia had been busy swiping through a tablet for most of the trip to the *National Horizon*'s Chicago office, leaving her fingers cold and achy.

Rather than the towering skyscrapers of nearby downtown, *National Horizon* had set up shop in a business center that resembled a strip mall. Across the street were a grocery store, a fast-food joint, and a gas station. Not quite the glamorous world of journalism depicted by Hollywood.

As Zane pulled into a parking stall in front of *National Horizon*'s suite, he turned to flash her a curious glance. "How do you think we ought to play this? There's not much we can do as far as the published article is concerned. This is a base we *need* to cover, but covering it seems…" He made a show of balancing his hands. "I don't know. It seems like it isn't going to get us far."

Another press-related incident popped into Amelia's head at the mention of covering bases.

Only a few short months ago, Zane, in the company of Cassandra Halcott, had visited a so-called "news" agency called *Real Chicago News*.

Where the *Horizon* was regarded as a legitimate source for information on current events, *RCN* had been much closer to a tabloid. Their only goal was to entice readers to click on their articles so they could earn ad revenue.

It was a scam, and Amelia hated almost everything about the operation. Sensationalist publications like *RCN* were ruining legitimate news outlets by taking over their spaces in the press, as was evidenced by the fact that *RCN* had been located in the rented offices of a skyscraper downtown, whereas the *Horizon* was here in a strip mall.

During the Ben Storey investigation, part of Glenn Kantowski's effort to frame Amelia for the councilman's murder was to share fake, explicit photos of Amelia and Ben. Kantowski had likely known such images wouldn't fly with a reputable outlet like the *Horizon*, so she'd sent them to *RCN*. *RCN* had barely vetted the source before publishing the photos on their website.

At the memory, Amelia clenched her jaw, a surge of anger burning through her veins.

This isn't the same. The Horizon *is an actual journalistic operation. They have locations all over the country. Hell, I've read their articles before.*

She didn't want to walk into Hartman's office with a chip on her shoulder. There were no lies or exaggerations in his piece about the Denson case, and he had a history of fairly covering high-profile murders in the past.

You catch more flies with honey. That's the saying, right? In other words, don't be an ass, and Hartman won't be an ass in return. Maybe.

Amelia held her hands up to the vents, reveling in the heat warming her frozen fingers. "We know reporters don't like to give their sources, so we'll have to get creative in how we can get Hartman to confirm that his sources for that article were Jared Olsen and Marlee Hendricks."

"True. You said he worked for *The Chicago Standard* before he moved over to the *Horizon*?"

"Yeah, that's where he started out." Amelia recalled another *Chicago Standard* journalist she and Zane had worked with, a woman named Vivian Kell.

Vivian had helped them take down a nasty León̈e human trafficking ring being run on a Kankakee County farm. Not only had the Leóne men in charge of the farm dealt in forced labor trafficking—a form of trafficking that equated to modern-day slavery—they'd also kidnapped and exploited underaged girls from their point of operation in the basement of a warehouse.

Though Amelia, Zane, and the FBI were able to shut down the disgusting operation, Vivian had paid the ultimate price. She'd been tortured, sexually assaulted, and murdered by Carlo Enrico.

"Do you think he knew Vivian?"

Amelia blinked a few times as her focus returned to the car. She hadn't expected such a poignant trip down memory lane during her and Zane's trip to the *Horizon*.

"He might have. I didn't see anything about the two of them specifically when I was researching Hartman on the way over here. But." She looked to Zane and lifted a shoulder. "Half an hour of research does not a complete profile make."

He killed the engine and, to Amelia's dismay, the heater. "You could have worded that less weird, but yes, you have a point. It's almost five now, and their office closes to the public at five-thirty."

His sarcastic comment made her smile. "We're not the public, honey."

Hand on the lever of his door, Zane shot her a smarmy grin. "We can at least *try* to have some manners, okay?"

She rolled her eyes in feigned indignation. "Whatever you say. Let's go have a chat with Mr. Hartman."

With a smile, Zane shoved open the driver's side door. A wave of cold air rolled through the car's interior, but Amelia tried to ignore it as she stepped out into the waning sunlight. Teeth chattering from the sudden temperature drop, she elbowed her door closed and stuffed both hands in her pockets.

In silence, they hurried to the entrance of the *Horizon*'s Chicago office. The silvery bell of a Christmas wreath jingled as they pushed through a second interior door. Apparently, the FBI wasn't the only one that left their holiday décor up into the new year.

The man seated behind a sturdy wooden desk at the back of the small waiting area perked up at the two visitors, a smile slowly creasing the corners of his eyes. His kind expression seemed genuine to Amelia, and she figured his demeanor was the reason he'd been staffed at the front desk.

"Hello. Can I help you two with something?"

She returned his smile as she produced her badge. "Evening, sir. I'm Special Agent Amelia Storm with the Federal Bureau of Investigation, and this is my partner, Special Agent Zane Palmer. We're here to talk to one of the *Horizon*'s reporters, Zack Hartman."

"No need to call me sir. I'm not even fifty yet. You can just call me Abe." If the presence of two federal agents set him on edge, the man didn't show it. His fatherly vibe didn't dissipate in the slightest as he glanced over to his computer monitor. With a slight nod, he turned back to Amelia and

Zane. "He's still here, yes. Can I ask what this visit is about so I can let him know?"

"The Denson case. He published an article covering it a few hours ago, and we need to talk to him about it." Amelia had expected more pushback like Zane and Cassandra had received during their trip to *RCN*.

She had to remind herself the *Horizon* was a reputable source for news, and they received visits from law enforcement on a regular basis. More than likely, reporters like Zack Hartman had valid points of contact in the Chicago Police Department, and maybe even with the public affairs sect of the FBI.

Abe's fingers flew over the keyboard. "I have to ask, do you have a warrant?"

A flicker of annoyance passed over Zane's face at the question, and Amelia jumped in to respond before him. "No, we don't. We're hoping we won't need to get one."

Abe chuckled quietly. "Of course. I pinged him, and he should be out shortly." He waved at the small waiting area. "Have a seat in the meantime. Could I get you anything to drink? Water, coffee, or soda?"

Amelia returned the man's smile but shook her head. "No, thank you. I think I've had enough coffee to supply a small continent today."

Abe threw back his head and laughed. Rather than polite or uptight, his laugh was hearty and genuine. "I've had plenty of those days myself, Agent."

A sense of cautious optimism made Amelia's heart a little lighter. From what Zane had told her of his visit to *RCN* during the Storey case, the atmosphere of the *Horizon* was a night and day difference.

As she dropped into the chair closest to the reception desk, she waited for Zane to take his seat before turning her attention back to Abe. "This might be a weird question, but

I'm curious. Do you guys here at the *Horizon* deal with *Real Chicago News* at all?"

Abe made a sound in his throat that best resembled an unflattering snort. "I wouldn't say we 'deal' with them, but we're familiar. They're just a tabloid garbage can, not a single real reporter in the whole damn office. But I guess there're enough people who click on their website to keep them afloat."

The obvious contention toward the tabloid gave Amelia another shot of hope. Good reporters weren't their enemy. *Bad* reporters were.

Before she could ask more about the *Horizon*'s history with *RCN*, a door in the back corner of the waiting area swung open, revealing a man she assumed was Zack Hartman.

His astute gaze shifted from Amelia to Zane, no shortage of uncertainty in his stance. "Agents. You're here to see me?"

Amelia glanced to Zane as they both pushed to their feet. For the second time, they each produced their badges and introduced themselves, though Hartman was already aware of their identities.

"Mr. Hartman, we're here to talk to you about the article you recently published regarding the Denson case. It shouldn't take too long." Though Zane's tone was calm and even, the underlying mistrust matched Hartman's skepticism.

As the reporter's light brown eyes moved back and forth between her and Zane, Amelia thought the man intended to tell them no, or to come back with a warrant. Not that his refusal would make any damn sense.

What did he have to hide? Unless...

No, she was just being paranoid. They had no reason to suspect Hartman was connected in any way to Stephen Denson.

Did they?

Would a reporter commit a heinous crime in order to draw fame from reporting it?

She'd keep the question in the back of her mind.

Blowing out a long breath, Hartman finally moved to the side and beckoned them forward. "Yeah, all right. Come on back to my office."

An awkward silence followed Amelia and Zane as they strode down the carpeted hall behind the reporter. They passed a handful of closed doors, as well as the entrance to a cozy break area.

From the exterior, the place hadn't seemed like much—just another suite in a strip mall built in the eighties. Inside, however, a mix of modern and classic fixtures gave a professional yet homey feel. Not to mention the sheer size of the place.

Hartman finally paused at the second from the last door in the hall, sparing only a fleeting glance at Amelia and Zane before opening it. Without speaking, they followed him into the office.

A window behind Hartman's L-shaped desk sported partially open blinds that gave an unobstructed vantage point of the grocery store, as well as the cars zipping up and down the street.

Well, the atmosphere and square footage of the office was comfortable, but the view left a little to be desired.

As Hartman took his spot behind the desk, he gestured to a pair of cushioned armchairs. "All right, Agents. What can I help you with?"

No pleasantries, no small talk. Hartman wanted to get right down to business, presumably so he could get them the hell out of his office.

Amelia was glad to return the favor. "We're here about the Denson case. Your article from just a few hours ago states

Kate Denson, Anna and Stephen Denson's oldest daughter, was present at the house right after, and potentially *during* her family's murder."

Hartman propped an elbow on the armrest of his chair. "And? Is that inaccurate?" When neither agent answered his question, the reporter was the first to break the silence. "No one said even a peep about Kate Denson. Not whether she was alive, whether she was a witness, whether she was vacationing in the Swiss Alps, or whether she was a suspect." He shrugged, looking pretty pleased with himself. "I figured it out and printed it."

Thanks, smartass.

Amelia swallowed the knee-jerk comment and offered him a wooden smile instead. There was no reason to try to deny Kate was present for the triple homicide—Hartman had already told the city and the entire damn world that much.

"Clearly, it isn't inaccurate." Amelia held up a hand to stave off an immediate response. "However, there's more at play here than you realize. There was a reason we hadn't mentioned Kate in any of our updates to the press."

Amelia could have sworn the man's ears had perked up like an antenna. "And? What might that be?"

As much as Amelia disliked the wary edge in Hartman's voice, she had to remind herself he was a reputable journalist. Asking questions and remaining critical was literally in his job description, just as it was in hers.

"You know we can't tell you all of that." Zane threaded his fingers together, his attention fixed on Hartman. "It'd compromise our investigation if too much information fell into the public's hands."

"Of course it would," Hartman deadpanned. "It's like this whenever a judge or a politician is killed. You Feds keep everything close to the vest, like you don't want the commoners to know what's going on with the man behind the curtain."

Amelia could sense Zane's impending snarky response like it was an electric charge in the air.

His temperament was almost always even keeled, but the calm didn't stop him from lobbing backhanded remarks when a person was getting on his nerves. She didn't need to survey Zack Hartman to acknowledge the reporter wouldn't take such a slight kindly.

She cleared her throat. Loudly. "We didn't mention Kate Denson's whereabouts or involvement because we were trying to keep her safe. You seem like a sharp guy, Mr. Hartman, so I know you have to have realized we'd have paraded her out in front of the entire world if we honestly considered her a suspect. The longer this case goes on *without* a suspect, the more difficult it'll become for us to manage the media response."

Aside from the tic of a muscle in Hartman's jaw, the man didn't respond, verbally or otherwise. His silence confirmed what she had suspected. He wasn't dumb enough to genuinely consider Kate Denson a suspect.

Amelia took the cue to continue. She had to be careful not to give Hartman too much information, but they weren't going to get him on their side if they didn't give him *something*.

"The evidence we've collected so far indicates the Densons were targeted. Specifically, they were targeted by someone who knew the family's comings and goings. If the unsub realizes there was a witness, no matter how much or little she might have seen, they're going to come for her, and they're going to try to kill her."

Hartman shifted in his chair, his stony expression softening into something more malleable. "Kate Denson *witnessed* her family's murder?"

"We don't know what she witnessed. She's too traumatized to talk about what happened that night."

Rubbing his temple, Hartman offered a solemn nod. "Poor kid. You're right. I didn't honestly think she was a suspect. I've been covering high-profile murders for long enough to know law enforcement won't hesitate to display a suspect if they have one. Which, to be clear, you don't have one right now?"

Amelia narrowed her eyes, silently warning the man not to press his luck.

He held up his hands in surrender. "All right, all right. Can't blame me for asking, can you? It's what I do. Is that why you're here? To make sure I don't think Kate Denson is a suspect in her parents' murder?"

"Not quite." Amelia mentally prepared herself for another round of obstinance. "We need to know your source for that article. Who told you Kate was present at the house?"

The reporter made a show of appearing both stunned and insulted. "Agent Storm, you ought to know better than to ask a reporter for their sources. I don't have to give you that information, and if that's what you're here for, then I'm sorry you wasted your time."

Pinning the man with a scrutinizing stare, Amelia leaned forward in her chair. Her pulse rushed in her ears and reining in her irritability felt akin to dragging a boulder up a hill. "If your *source* is someone who was present at the crime scene before the CPD arrived, then yes, it's something we need to know."

Hartman shook his head. "No, it's not like that. They didn't have anything to do with those murders."

One of Zane's eyebrows quirked up. "They? I don't suppose you're referring to Jared Olsen and Marlee Hendricks, are you?"

A flush darkened Hartman's cheeks, and for a beat, he

appeared as if he'd be happier crawling into a hole than sitting where he was. "If you knew that, then why the hell did you come here?"

Amelia wanted to laugh at how quickly he'd reneged on his assurance to protect the identities of his source, but part of her also empathized with his embarrassment. They'd all been there.

"We're not leaving a stone unturned, Mr. Hartman. We wanted to verify your source was Jared and Marlee because, if it wasn't, then that would have meant you'd spoken with someone *else* who'd been at the scene. Catch my drift?"

He groaned and rubbed his eyes. "Yeah, I get it. Seems like a lot of work just to check that off your list, though, doesn't it?"

Amelia lifted a shoulder. She'd thought the same initially, but all she had to do was imagine the fallout if Hartman had interacted with a suspect and the FBI *hadn't* followed up on it. "Maybe. But...I think you might be able to help us a little bit."

Hartman turned his incredulous gaze directly to Amelia. "Help you? With what?"

On the drive to the *Horizon*'s office, Amelia and Zane had decided—based on the outcome of the conversation, of course—to enlist Hartman as a potential resource for their investigation. There was only a limited amount of information they could give him right now, but at least if *they* were his source of updates, then they had a better chance of him reporting the truth.

They'd worked with a reporter in the past, and she'd been a huge part of their victory over a Leóne trafficking ring. As much as Amelia often detested the media, they were sometimes a great deal of help.

"This is unrelated, but I've got another question for you." Both Amelia and Hartman turned to Zane as he spoke. "You started out at *The Chicago Standard*, right? Did you ever work with Vivian Kell?"

Hartman's response was immediate. "Vivian? Yeah. She was new there at the time. We both were. We kept in touch after I moved over to the *Horizon*. We'd help each other out every now and then, and I'd say we were friends. She was a damn fine reporter. What happened to her was…" He looked away and shook his head. "The Leónes are a bunch of fucking animals."

At the comment, Amelia's opinion of Zack Hartman ratcheted up a few notches. Hartman had been covering murders in Chicago for more than a decade, so he knew how the Leóne family operated. Did that mean he was privy to the same knowledge as Vivian? Had he known about the exposé she'd been writing?

Excitement rushed through her veins, prickling the hairs on the back of her neck.

Did Hartman have information about the Leónes? About their connection with Stan Young or with Brian Kolthoff?

With *Joseph*?

Stop it, Amelia. You're not here about the damn Leónes. Just because Hartman was friends with Vivian doesn't mean she'd told him anything about the exposé on Happy Harvest Farms. There's a traumatized girl in an FBI safe house who just lost her entire family. That's why you're here.

Picking Hartman's brain about his experiences with the Leónes was an activity she'd have to save for another day.

"We worked with Vivian before she died," Zane said. "She brought us information about the Leónes' trafficking ring in Kankakee County. She's a big part of why we were able to take that place off the map. She trusted us enough to help, for whatever that's worth to you right now."

Hartman pressed his lips together, his distant stare turning thoughtful. "So, you want my help? With what, exactly?" He finally met Amelia and Zane's expectant gazes. "And what do I get out of it?"

Amelia tempered a sudden bout of eagerness. "You were the first to publish an article mentioning the possibility Kate was at the scene of her family's murder. Once the bastard realizes there was a witness, they're going to want to try to tie up that loose end. We think they might try to reach out to you for information."

Hartman tapped a finger against the desk. "Okay. So, what's my role?"

"Just keep an eye out on any communication you get asking for information about Kate. If anyone seems a little overeager to figure out who your source was, send them our way. No matter who they claim to be."

"Yeah, I can do that."

"In return, we'll make sure you're the first person to get details as this case unfolds. We can't give you anything we aren't able to give to anyone else, but we *can* make sure you get it first." At the least, Amelia figured Zack Hartman scoring the big headlines would be preferable to shining the spotlight on some shithouse like *Real Chicago News*.

Hartman scooted closer to his desk. "Is there anything you can give me right now? Any new developments?"

Amelia suppressed a sigh. Not because she didn't want to give Hartman an update, but because they didn't have much to give him in the first place. "It's still developing, but so far, our evidence indicates there was no political motive at play. Everything points to a personal vendetta."

"I've covered cases that were tried in Anna Denson's courtroom." Hartman drummed his fingers against the desk. "She always struck me as the type of person who *ought* to be a judge, you know? Someone level-headed and fair, who made her decisions based on the evidence in front of her and the law. And she was never like a machine about it, either. When she handed down a sentence, you could see on her face there was always a human element to what she did."

During Amelia and Cassandra's trip to the courthouse earlier, Anna Denson's colleagues had given a similar account. Still, hearing the words again was a stark reminder that the justice system, and the people of Illinois for that matter, had lost a valuable asset.

Zane rubbed his chin before propping his elbow on the arm rest. "That bolsters the theory that our guy had a personal vendetta. Anna Denson's work hadn't ruffled any political feathers on either side of the fence, and considering she mostly dealt with criminal cases, a political motive just doesn't seem likely."

"That's true." Hartman held up a finger. "And that's good. I can publish that. Get it out there before all the garbage tabloids start spewing their conspiracy theories."

Halcott sure will be relieved when she hears that.

The lawyer's goal earlier in the day had been to rule out a political motive, and now that they'd done so, Zack Hartman would spread the good word. Two birds, one stone. Everyone was a winner.

Everyone except for the Denson and Graham families.

The solemn reminder overshadowed the brief satisfaction of Amelia and Zane's small victory.

They'd taken a step in the right direction, but the real journey had only just begun.

12

Squinting at my computer monitor like it would somehow enhance the image in front of me, I used the wireless mouse to pan the screen a little farther to the right. The fisheye lens of the neighbor's security camera captured a larger image than my screen could display. The sun had gone down a couple hours earlier, and the Osbornes' motion sensor light only lit up a section of the front porch and part of their front walk.

Shoulders hunched, Cyrus took one last drag off his cigarette before depositing the stub in an ash tray. He spared one last glance at the neighborhood before pulling open the front door and disappearing from view. Stray snowflakes whipped in front of the lens, reminding me how glad I was to be warm and comfortable inside my apartment's home office.

I'd assumed—wrongly, as I'd recently learned—that Cyrus Osborne was one of those bougie types who'd have security cameras set up every three feet as part of his home's security system. Hell, I'd cracked open his household's wireless network like a can of soda. Shouldn't the rest of it be just as easy?

The answer to that question was a resounding "no."

With Carla Graham and her family, I'd been able to tap into the home's computers to monitor their movements *inside* the house. It had helped ensure I was prepared and thorough when the day finally came for Carla to meet her fate.

The Osbornes, on the other hand, didn't have a single connected webcam in their entire house. I was familiar with the company that produced their home's alarm system, but even that wasn't connected to a camera.

I had no eyes on the interior of their house, and I'd been forced to settle for the next best thing—the neighbor's outdoor security camera. At the very least, this allowed me to monitor the family's comings and goings without physically being present in the area.

After standing in line behind Cyrus, his wife, Mabel, and their daughter, Julie, at the grocery store earlier in the day, I had a better understanding of their current family dynamic, as well as their opinions of their plans for the next few days. Julie wasn't thrilled about being relegated to spending New Year's Eve with her parents, but she'd broken her curfew for two nights in a row and had been grounded for a week.

Maybe the knowledge of Julie's tendency to stay out with her friends too late didn't *seem* pertinent, but every little piece of information was valuable to me.

If I hadn't overheard the dialogue in the store this afternoon, I might have been inclined to think Julie was out with a friend. I could have the time of my life with her parents, kill them, and wind up with a witness to the whole damn thing.

Just like I'd done with Kate Denson.

The embers of anger burned to life in my chest.

How could I have been so careless? So *sloppy*? Kate had

been in the damn house, and I didn't even notice. I still wasn't sure what exactly she'd witnessed or whether she'd be able to identify me or my brother.

It wasn't supposed to have gone down like that.

I'd been just as careful monitoring the Densons as I was with everything else, and I'd learned through text messages that Kate wasn't supposed to return until after midnight at the earliest. The idea of a family member walking in and discovering their family's dead bodies had been thrilling. It would have been a death in a very different way.

Young Kate found the bodies, all right. What else she'd seen, I still didn't know.

As if on cue, the creak of footsteps turned my attention to the hall. My brother's broad-shouldered frame took up most of the doorway as he stopped to fix me with an expectant stare.

I knew that look. I'd come face-to-face with that expression more times growing up than I cared to count. My brother was unhappy. Specifically, he was unhappy with *me*.

Before he could speak, I threw both hands up in the air. "You were there too! You didn't know she was in the house, either. You can't blame me for this."

Crossing his arms, my brother leaned against the doorway. "There's a witness who probably saw us kill those three people. What're we going to do about it?"

His use of the word *we* sent little tingles of excitement through my veins. My brother was five years my senior, and I'd looked up to him since I was a little kid. Back then, I'd just been the little brother trying to tag along with Evan and his friends, but now...

Now things were different.

I shook off the memories and refocused on the present. "We don't know that. The Feds haven't said anything about what she did or didn't see, and they haven't come breaking down the door. Don't you think they'd have busted in here by now if she'd actually *seen* anything?"

My brother snorted. "Doesn't mean we need to sit around and wait for them to show up. What's the plan?"

I'd been trying to answer that exact question for the last hour. "If Kate's a witness, then we need to deal with her. I know I didn't leave anything at that crime scene. She's the only loose end. If we can get rid of her, then there's no way—"

"No way, what?" My brother snapped, an unmistakable fire in his eyes. "No way you'll go to prison? These people tried to ruin my life! Did you forget about that? Why are you being such a damn coward all of a sudden?"

I winced as if he'd dealt me a physical blow. "I know they tried to ruin your life. They tried to put you away, and they ruined everything. We'll get them, but I just...*we* need to be careful."

My brother waved a hand. "Careful? Careful isn't going to get the job done, little brother. Besides, you threw caution to the wind when you had your fun with Stephen Denson, didn't you? Yeah, you might've picked up all them shell casings, but with all that sweating you did?" He let out a derisive chuckle. "Not just Stephen either, but the other guy, Scott. How're you going to tell me you want to be careful after that?"

No way was I going to let my brother berate me for *that*. "You're the one who suggested it in the first place! You sure as hell liked watching, didn't you?"

The condescending smile vanished from his face like a part of a magician's act.

"I did it just like you taught me." I added the reminder before my brother could speak again. "When we were kids, remember?"

He snapped up a hand. "That wasn't the same. Dad always

thought you were a little too...*feminine*. You always liked that artsy shit, you know? Painting, singing, shit like that. You're lucky you had me there to show you how to be a real man."

My brother was right. Our mother had died before I turned two, and our father had never remarried. He'd focused all his energy on raising two sons who would carry on his legacy, who'd truly be men in an age when masculinity was constantly under attack.

I'd never tell a soul, but the late-night visits from my brother back then were some of the only times I'd ever felt loved or appreciated. Expressing affection was strictly off-limits in our household, so when my father had walked into the room and caught us in the middle of the act, I'd expected him to lash out with all the fire and fury he could muster.

Instead, he'd done the opposite. Sure, he was surprised at first, and he'd called us a few choice names. Mostly me, because my brother had always been his favorite son. However, the next day, he'd suggested setting up a camera to record our nights together.

I'd only been twelve at the time, and I hadn't grasped his intent until a few years later, after my brother had moved out of the house to join the military.

He'd recorded those videos so he could sell them. When the realization dawned on me, I'd been livid. That time with my brother had been special, and for my father to record it and sell it to some creep in another part of the world?

Clenching my hands into fists, I glanced to the feed on the monitor and then back to my brother. "I'm doing all this to avenge you and to get back at the people who tried to ruin your life." My brother was the only family I had left, and deep down, I wasn't sure how I'd navigate the world alone. I knew better than to vocalize the sentiment, though.

He sighed. "That's not the point. The point is, why are we going to be cautious suddenly? Why're we going to go out of our way to take care of this Kate Denson kid when we've got bigger fish to fry?"

I gritted my teeth. He had a point. We were still working our way up the food chain to deal with those responsible for trying to put my brother away for the rest of his life. "You're right. We can't just stop now. If we stop now and get caught, then we'll never get the opportunity to take care of the worst ones. The ones we're saving for last."

His face reddened with an anger barely contained. "Exactly. The lawyers. The assistant prosecutor and the lead prosecutor. You remember all the shit they said about me in that courtroom, don't you? They *have* to pay for it. We have to make them suffer."

A renewed sense of purpose energized me as I sat up straighter, needing to reassure him. "We do. We will. I've been monitoring the Osbornes' house. They're all home tonight, and they don't have guests. Cyrus's planner didn't say anything about plans until sometime tomorrow."

"Perfect. We have a wide window of opportunity. Once we've crossed Cyrus Osborne off the list, then we can move on to the final one. The lead prosecutor."

Just thinking about that damn lawyer put a foul taste on my tongue. "The prosecutor will pay dearly." My methods so far had remained largely the same—efficiency, efficiency, efficiency. A small-caliber handgun, single shot to the back of the head. After I'd had my fun, of course.

But for the lead prosecutor, the person who arguably shouldered the most responsibility for trying to put my brother behind bars for his entire life, I had different plans. Better, grander plans.

Soon, I'd revel in the sweet suffering of those who tried to take away my family.

13

Mabel Osborne carefully placed the egg casserole she'd assembled in the deli drawer of their side-by-side stainless refrigerator. A small bowl filled with crepe batter perched precariously on the top shelf. Sighing, she realized Cyrus and Julie would need to eat some of the left-overs, or she'd have to pitch them to make room for the rest of the feast's elements. Mabel surveyed her granite counter and chuckled to herself. There was no room for the straw-berry puree that would go inside the crepes. No room for the pitcher of fresh-squeezed orange juice. And definitely no room for the fruit platter.

Cyrus approached his wife from behind and wrapped his arms around her midriff, resting his chin on her shoulder. "You've outdone yourself again. Are you expecting a small army?" Mabel turned in his arms and gazed into his kind blue eyes before sniffing the air around him.

"You were outside smoking." It wasn't a question, and the look in Cyrus's eyes answered Mabel's question. She shook her head with a trace of a smile. "New Year's resolution?"

"Sure." He kissed the tip of her nose. "I'll try. But seriously, what's all this?"

Mabel allowed him to change the subject. "You know nothing brings me more joy than cooking for you and Julie. And with all of us off for the holidays, I wanted to do something extra special. There's more in the fridge, but I don't have room for any of this." She gestured at the abundance of platters and bowls.

"Well, dinner was its own feast." Cyrus patted his dad-bod belly and laughed. "But if you need me to tuck into those leftovers to clear some space, I'm happy to oblige, ma'am." They laughed before sharing a tender kiss.

A tear caught in the corner of Mabel's eye, and concern clouded her husband's features. "What is it?"

"I'm fine." She hastily wiped away the tear before meeting his worried eyes. "Really. I'm better than fine. You know I always get sentimental at the holidays. My childhood was… forgettable. Well, not *forgettable* so much as scarring." Cyrus went to kiss his wife, but she gently placed a hand on his chest. She knew he'd heard this story before, but she needed to get it out of her system again. "I used to hate the holidays. We had no money, and my dad…"

Mabel swallowed a few times, and Cyrus stroked his hands up and down her back, his face the perfect mixture of caring and concern. "It's okay, sweetheart. You can say it."

How had she been so lucky to be married to this man for twenty years?

"The abuse I endured from my dad…it made me hate men and the concept of 'family' and especially the holidays. He drank our meager finances away, so 'Santa' never made an appearance in our home. Then he took out his anger over his own shortcomings on my mom and me."

Cyrus growled low in his throat. "The bastard."

She wrapped her arms around her husband and clenched

her eyes tightly closed while reliving her past. "I never thought I'd find love. Find true happiness. You showed me how wonderful a man can be, the profound unconditional love a parent can show a child. Your love saved me."

Cyrus gently held her at arm's length. "Honey, I didn't save you. You saved yourself. *You* are the one who overcame all those things long before our paths ever crossed. I'm sure you know all the appropriate psychiatric terminology better, but I don't need ten-dollar words to know you healed all on your own. I don't know how, but you did. And I love you for the strong woman that you are, for the loving wife you have been these past twenty years, and for the compassionate mother and role model you have been to Julie."

As Mabel's eyes cast downward, Cyrus gently lifted her chin to meet her tear-filled eyes. "Julie adores you, even when you're strict. You have already molded her into a strong, independent woman. You two may butt heads from time to time, but I can see how much admiration and love she has for you." He leaned forward and pressed his lips to her forehead. "Your love binds this family together, and we would be lost without you."

Mabel squeezed her husband tightly, thanking God for the millionth time for allowing her to have this life. It seemed like only yesterday she was cursing that very same God for her father's disgusting nightly visits and his repeated beatings of her and her mother.

Yes, she had pushed past all of that. She *did* feel healed, something she never thought possible. And while she had been the first person in her family to attend college and then put herself through grad school, achieving her Ph.D. in Child Psychiatry, those accomplishments paled in comparison to the accomplishment she felt as a wife and mother.

Silently berating herself for her highly nonfeminist views, she adjusted her mindset—a habit she had adapted over the years to give space to her thoughts without judgment. Her years of schooling and her dysfunctional childhood had taught her that her thoughts were not facts. Ruminating could be unhealthy, but if the thoughts weren't overanalyzed and simply given space to float away like clouds on a sunny day, the thoughts held no power.

Mabel gazed again at the counter before a burst of giggles escaped her lips. "I suppose I did overdo it a bit, huh?"

Her husband barked out the belly-shaking laugh she adored so much. "No such thing when I'm around. Drop some leftovers on the counter, and I'll eat them right out of the container. We need to make space for the fabulous breakfast you've prepared." After pausing a moment for effect, her *Monty Python* movie-loving husband uttered a phrase she'd heard countless times during their marriage. "It's only a wafer-thin mint."

The two dissolved into laughter as Mabel cleared the fridge, and Cyrus pulled up a stool to sit at the counter. Wielding a fork in a clenched fist, he tried to calm down before doing his best to waste none of their leftovers.

"I swear, if you vomit all over the kitchen, you'll be the one to clean it up."

"What's going on?" The Osbornes' fourteen-year-old daughter stepped into the kitchen, eyeing both parents suspiciously.

"Are you hungry? Your mother has once again prepared more food than is possible to consume in one sitting, so we need to clear room in the fridge."

Julie grabbed a second barstool and plucked a fork from the appropriate drawer before sitting next to her dad. "Wow, Mom, you've really gone nuts this time. Did you forget? Noodle said it was a 'no bones' day."

The trio shared a laugh over the pug guru who had become the barometer for the mood and activity levels of many millennials. His social media account was checked daily by Julie, and she eagerly announced Noodle's prognostication about whether or not it was a "bones" or "no bones" day.

Mabel had too much schooling to put any stock in the thirteen-year-old pug, but his owner's message was positive and upbeat. After working with so many troubled youths in her job as a child psychologist, Mabel couldn't argue against the nonjudgmental messaging Noodle's owner provided.

After stowing the rest of the breakfast feast in their fridge, Mabel left her husband and daughter in the kitchen while she tended to the laundry and turned down the bed for the night. The sound of their shared laughter warmed Mabel to her soul.

When Cyrus later found her in their walk-in closet hanging up clean clothes, he leaned against the doorframe, folded his arms across his chest, and simply smiled.

"What?" Mabel eyed him as she continued to hang the various items on their respective sides of the closet.

"Nothing. I just, well, I just love you so much. Are you okay? You seemed sad earlier when you brought up your past."

Hanging up the final item from the laundry basket, Mabel moved to her husband and placed her hand on his bicep. "I couldn't be better. Honestly. I have more than I could ev—"

Cyrus ducked almost into a crouch, lifting a finger to Mabel's lips. "Did you hear that?" His words were barely louder than a breath.

"Yeah." The word was muffled as she attempted to speak around his finger. "It's probably just Julie."

"No." His mouth was close to her ear. "She told me she was going to Snapchat Cheryl before saying goodnight and dashing off to her bedroom with a small plate of leftovers."

A creak of the floorboards outside their bedroom seemed to echo through the unnaturally quiet home.

Cyrus's unease had shifted over to Mabel, and her voice was barely audible as she clutched her husband's arm with a death grip. They both stared at their partially closed bedroom door. "How long ago did she go upstairs?"

"I don't know. She left the kitchen shortly after you. Maybe thirty minutes or so?"

"Shit. My phone is charging in the kitchen. Do you have yours?"

"No. Honey, relax." The tension in his body told Mabel the extent of his worry. "I'm sure this is nothing. This old house likes to creak and moan to remind us of its age."

Another creak came from the staircase to the second floor.

The sound triggered a flood of memories, and all her training as a psychologist dissipated like a wisp of smoke over a dying fire. Replacing the logic and reason were the images of her father stealing his way to her room. The unique creaking sound of the hardwood floor outside her bedroom door under his inebriated weight. How she willed the doorknob not to turn while knowing it would anyway. As she prayed to a God who never heeded her prayers, she disassociated from the vile things her father did to her each night, leaving her bleeding and bruised and ashamed.

Was she overreacting? These noises felt different somehow. She'd learned to trust her instincts, and the hairs on the back of her neck were telling her to run, get help. With every pore of her being, Mabel believed evil was lurking in their house. It was the same feeling she'd felt as a child. She would not dismiss it so easily.

"I think someone is in the house." Her heart was pounding so hard she barely heard her own words. "We need to get to Julie. Need to get to a phone. We need hel—"

Before the word could leave Mabel's mouth, the room went dark, and the distinctive sound of the door pushing across the carpet sent chills down her spine.

While she could not see an intruder, she knew he was there. Paralyzed with terror, she unconsciously held her breath. When the room burst with light, the air rushed from her lungs.

Standing before her was a stranger. A man wearing a black hoodie. And pointed at her—no, at Cyrus—was a gun with a weird attachment at the end. Before her mind could ponder what it was, the intruder spoke.

"Well, hello, Cyrus. Hey there, Mabel."

He knew their names! How did this stranger know their names?

The intruder smiled. "Getting ready for bed so soon? I think we need to have a little chat before that happens." He waved the gun at Cyrus while staring directly at Mabel. "I just want to talk, but I don't trust either of you. So, here's what we're going to do. Cyrus, you're going to lie down on your stomach on the bed and put your hands behind your back."

Gesturing with the gun again, through clenched teeth the madman ordered Mabel to sit on the floor. Once she was seated, he produced a roll of duct tape and quickly bound Cyrus's hands behind his back, his eyes barely leaving Mabel where she cowered. He then placed another piece of tape over Cyrus's mouth. With wild eyes, he turned on Mabel.

"I'll ask them the questions in a minute. Let me do my business first." The man swatted at the air by his head as if flies were talking to him. Although her professional focus was on children, Mabel's schooling had taught her about all forms of mental illness, and it was clear this man was unhinged, although that wouldn't be his official diagnosis.

She racked her brain, wondering if reasoning with the man would prove useful.

"What can I do to—"

The gun rising to press into her forehead was all that was needed to silence the rest of Mabel's question. The lunatic ordered Mabel to turn around and put her hands behind her back. "Don't make a sound. I know Julie is home." Mabel's heart seemed to stop as the madman continued his speech while he bound her wrists. "If you cooperate, I won't hurt her. She doesn't need to suffer for her father's sins."

Sins? What the hell was he talking about? Was this because of Cyrus's job? If he was here for vengeance...

No. He said he just wanted to talk. If we cooperate, he won't hurt Julie. I have to protect my daughter the way my mother failed to protect me.

"What do you want with us?" Mabel hated how weak she sounded.

After securing her hands behind her, the intruder roughly turned Mabel around until she was seated on the floor facing the bed. "I don't want anything with *you*. It's your husband who needs to provide some answers. And I can't have you interrupting with your questions." He tore off another piece of duct tape and pressed it firmly over Mabel's mouth.

Finally, as hope seemed to ebb from her body, he secured her to the leg of the bulky table resting beneath their curtained picture window. To her horror, he secured her head the same way, the tape wrapping several times around her head while the wood dug in the back of her skull.

Mabel closed her eyes, but the man made a tutting sound. "Open your eyes. You need to watch. You need to see everything."

His voice sent another wave of shivers down her spine, but she managed to do what she was told. Before she could even blink, he'd secured tape on her upper eyelashes.

"No." At least that was what she'd tried to say, but the word came out as a muffled scream.

He ignored her, and she wasn't even able to yank her head away as he taped her other eye open.

Heart beating out of her chest and her breathing shallow and erratic, Mabel feared she was having a panic attack.

Breathe. Calm down. If the opportunity presents itself, kick the man and try to break free.

But what happened next was too horrific for Mabel's mind to grasp.

Standing over Cyrus, the man worked to remove her husband's pants.

No! No. This can't be happening.

Her husband's muffled pleas and ineffective struggle told another story. His cries of pain were evidence that what was unfolding in front of her was very real.

As if viewing a movie with no soundtrack, Mabel was stunned by the horror before her. As the bastard repeatedly penetrated her husband, Mabel was torn between the present and the past. For a moment, this stranger wore her father's face, and she struggled to understand why her father was brutalizing her husband.

It seemed to go on and on and on.

Once he was finished, the rapist stood over Cyrus's prone, unmoving form. Was he dead?

Please, god, let him be alive.

With sweat pouring down his face, the man stepped back and removed his condom. He's done this before, she realized as she was forced to watch him peel one of the blue gloves he was wearing from his hand, turning it inside out, and effectively trapping the used condom and its wrapper inside the latex. With that done, he fastened his jeans and tucked all the waste inside his pocket before pulling on fresh gloves.

He's not done with us yet.

"Yeah, yeah, I'm coming." The stranger swatted at his imaginary flies again and then produced a haunting laugh. "Get it? I'm *coming*. Give me a sec. Almost through here."

The stranger spun, and with a calm, almost sad expression, moved over next to Mabel and crouched down. Leaning in close to her, he offered a trace of explanation. More explanation than she'd ever received from her own father.

"I'm sorry you got caught up in this. Your husband wronged my family, and we came to even the score."

Mabel's eyes darted around the room. *We? Who was with him? Oh god, was Julie okay?*

"Sshhh. It's all going to be okay. Julie's already dead. I killed her in her room before coming here to visit with you and ole Cyrus there." A muffled groan and sob came from the bed. "She didn't suffer. Young girls aren't my type." He rose to his full height and glanced between Mabel's bound body and that of her violated husband.

"I read up on you, you know. You've overcome a lot. I think you and I actually have a lot in common." His expression seemed to be genuinely sad. "But Cyrus had to pay for his sins. And I can't leave any witnesses."

He stood and produced a gun from his back, and Mabel instinctively knew what would happen next.

Now I lay me down to sleep...

Though she'd intended to pray, the children's rhyme was all that came into her mind, and Mabel longed to close her eyes as the man moved behind her.

I pray the Lord my soul to keep...

Cyrus moaned again, and Mabel focused all her attention on her husband's face.

If I should die before I wake...

The click of metal made her jump.

I pray the Lord my soul—

14

The squawk of an officer's radio drew Zane's attention away from the crowd that had begun to form in front of the Osborne residence. He and the others who were investigating the Denson murders had received a call from the Chicago Police Department less than an hour after they'd all convened in the incident room.

His brief scan of bystanders at the site of the Denson murders hadn't been enough to commit any faces to memory, but he made a mental note to compare footage from both scenes. If they caught a familiar face from each location—one who wasn't associated with the press or law enforcement—that would be a person of interest.

After another radio squawk, he turned from the crowd and hurried to follow Dean Steelman to the pair of officers stationed at the front porch. Sometime overnight, another family had been killed. Zane and the rest of the team had hoped the murder of the Denson family was a one-time, isolated incident. Despite the similarities to the Graham case, Zane had held onto a sliver of hope that the slayings weren't connected.

He'd *hoped* they wouldn't be hunting for a serial killer who targeted entire families, but there were plenty of sayings for him to pick from when it came to hope.

After providing their credentials to the officers by the porch, Zane and Dean made their way into the house. They were quickly provided gloves and booties from the tech stationed in the small study that adjoined an even smaller foyer. Once they were signed in via a tablet at the tech's table —a necessity to ensure the crime scene unit knew exactly who had come and gone from the house—they headed to the living room.

A handful of evidence markers dotted the floor leading in the direction of a brightly lit hallway, and Zane assumed, the site of Cyrus and Mabel Osborne's final moments. The yellow triangles had been placed next to what appeared to be melted snow mixed with dirt. There was also a framed photo shattered on the floor.

Turning to the pair of officers standing beside the brick fireplace, he noted the sergeant's insignia on the shoulder of the woman's uniform, as well as her shiny name plate. "Sergeant Carpenter. You and one of your officers were the first to respond to the scene, right?"

With a crisp nod, Carpenter gestured to the younger man at her side. "That's right. Officer Brewer and I responded to a 911 call our precinct received this morning."

Dean Steelman took a step back as he checked his notepad before glancing around the room. "That call came from Cheryl Davila after she woke up. She'd been SnapChatting with Julie Osborne last night when Julie's messages just stopped. Cheryl stated the Osborne daughter had fallen asleep before while the two messaged, so she thought nothing of it. However, when she awoke this morning and didn't find a gushing apology from her friend as she usually did, she thought something might be wrong and called Julie.

When she received no answer, she told her parents, and they'd tried calling both Julie's mom and dad. When they got no response from anyone, they decided to call 911 and have someone stop by the home."

"Correct." Carpenter lifted a shoulder, suddenly seeming much more tired than she had at the start of the conversation. "We didn't know what to expect, but it sure as hell wasn't *this*. Brewer's been on the force for…how long has it been?"

The young man's Adam's apple bobbed as he swallowed. "Three weeks and a couple days."

Zane was struck by a pang of sympathy at Officer Brewer's obvious discomfort. The guy was barely old enough to be allowed into a nightclub, but here he was at the site of a gruesome triple homicide.

Carpenter dropped both hands to her duty belt, the moment of weariness gone. "We figured it'd just be a welfare check to start with. Thought maybe the friend was overreacting. You know how kids are, right? But when both cars were in the driveway and no one answered the door, we had probable cause to enter the house."

Dean Steelman produced a pen from his black peacoat, and Zane took the cue to continue. "Was the door locked when you got here?"

Carpenter's posture stiffened. "That's the weird thing. It was."

Zane bit his tongue to keep from swearing. The Densons' door had been locked when officers arrived at the scene, and so had the Grahams'. Who in the hell broke into a place to commit a triple or quadruple homicide and then locked the door on their way out?

Someone with OCD?

A very organized and methodical killer?

He filed the question away to ask Layton Redker when

they returned to the field office. "Were there any suspicious vehicles parked in the area? Anything strange you noticed on your way into the house?" The inquiries were a long shot, but at this point, Zane and Dean were grasping at straws.

Glancing to Officer Brewer, the sergeant shook her head. "No. Nothing out of the ordinary. The girls had been messaging until around ten-thirty before Julie's messages just stopped."

"Okay, thanks." Zane swallowed a sigh. "Just making sure we cover all our bases." He gestured toward the hall. "Is that the master bedroom?"

"Yeah. That's where Mabel and Cyrus Osborne were... well, that's where they are, I guess. Their daughter, Julie, is upstairs." Sergeant Carpenter pointed to the hallway. "The stairs are down that hall. The forensic pathologist is up there. He said to tell you where to find him when you arrived."

"All right." Zane resisted the urge to extend a hand to the pair of officers and contaminate his fresh pair of gloves. "Thanks again. Sergeant, do you have officers out canvassing the neighborhood yet?"

"Sure do. Brewer and I are about to head out there to help them. Just wanted to make sure we touched base with the FBI before we got to it."

Zane offered the duo an appreciative smile. "Sounds good. Stay warm out there." Though he and Dean would stop at the nearest houses before they went back to the office, the Bureau didn't have the manpower to sift through an entire neighborhood. He was grateful they had the Chicago Police to help them.

As the two officers departed, Steelman pocketed his notepad. "Parents are dead in their room, and the daughter is dead upstairs. So far, it's the same as the Denson case."

Sadness tugged on Zane's heart as he recalled the research he'd done on the couple while Dean drove them to the house. Mabel Osborne was the product of an upbringing marked by abuse and abject poverty, but she'd pulled herself out of the muck. Not only was she the first person in her family to attend college, she'd gone a step further and put herself through grad school to become a child psychiatrist.

He rolled his shoulders and turned his attention back to Dean Steelman. "We've got another common thread. Cyrus Osborne was a federal prosecutor. There could be a link between him and Stephen Denson, since Denson was a law professor."

"Or between him and Anna Denson." Steelman frowned as they started for the stairs. "The water starts to get muddier when we add in the Graham family. We'll have to dig into this some more back at the office. There's got to be something we're missing."

Zane couldn't agree more, and he wondered if he'd drive himself insane trying to find the common thread between the three families.

There were no evidence markers on the stairs, but Zane kept his attention fixed on the floor just in case. The dark railing was covered in a fine, gray powder from where the CSU dusted for prints. Zane and Dean would have to check with the lead forensic tech to find out if they'd obtained anything promising.

As the two agents picked their way to the second-story hallway, the snapping of a camera shutter drew them to a bedroom off the hall. A familiar forensic pathologist glanced up from where he was stooped over the body of a teenage girl lying on her bed. The man's goatee was just as neatly trimmed as it had been when Zane first met the man during the Lars Poteracki case, and his dark brown eyes were shrewd and observant but still kind. Standing a few feet behind him was a woman Zane recognized as the pathologist's assistant, Shanti Patel.

Dr. Adam Francis rose to his full height, raising a hand in greeting. "Morning, Agents."

"Morning. Where's Dr. Ackerly?" Zane's curiosity got the better of him, and he posed the question before he could stop to think of how it might come across. Quickly, he held up a hand. "Since she was at the Denson scene, I just figured she'd be here too."

To his relief, Dr. Francis only chuckled. "Even the M.E. has to sleep sometimes. She was up all night finishing the Denson autopsies, getting all the blood work and tissue samples sent to the right places. It's a lot of work when you've got one victim, but three at the same time, from the same scene is a different story. You've got me this morning instead."

Zane returned Dr. Francis's chortle, hoping the moment of awkwardness wouldn't stick in anyone else's memory. If worse came to worst, he could always blame a lack of caffeine and sleep deprivation. "Very glad you're here. What've you got so far?"

The pathologist's expression sobered, and he gestured for Zane and Dean to move closer to the still form on the bed. The form Zane had avoided thus far.

Even his years in the CIA and FBI never quite prepared him to experience the death of a kid who'd been murdered in cold blood. Julie Osborne's black hair fanned out along her pillow, darkened by dried blood and chunks of brain matter.

Dr. Francis stooped over one side of Julie Osborne's bed, allowing room for Zane and Dean to stand over the body and face the pathologist. Though the bedroom was not small, the presence of four grown people hovering over the twin bed reminded Zane of mourners peeking into a casket.

With a gloved finger, Dr. Francis pointed to the bullet hole in the back of Julie's head. "This is consistent with the manner in which the other children in the other families were killed. One gunshot to the back of the head."

To Zane, the news wasn't comforting. "She'd been messaging a friend of hers over an app, then the messages just stopped. Her friend thought she'd fallen asleep, which she'd apparently done a few times in the past. Any sign of her phone?"

Dr. Francis nodded to Shanti Patel.

"The forensic team found it on the floor just under her bed. They bagged it for evidence. Took her cord too. Apparently, the phone had died overnight since it wasn't plugged into a charger."

Steelman nodded. A succinct recollection of the final moments of a life that had been cut far too short. "We're operating under the assumption that Julie's time of death matches up with the messages she sent to her friend. How does that line up with what you've found so far, Doc?"

Dr. Francis lifted one of Julie's arms, and her wrist and fingers remained frozen in place. "From what I've seen so far, I think that's accurate. Rigor's set in completely, and that usually happens around six to eight hours after death." He returned the girl's hand to her bed. "But we've also got her liver temperature to get a more accurate gauge. Ms. Patel?"

Shanti tapped a pen against the clipboard in her hand. "A body's internal temperature drops by about one-and-a-half degrees per hour, depending on the temp of the environment around it. Based on that, we can put Julie Osborne's TOD at about ten-thirty p.m."

Zane didn't miss how Shanti specified *Julie's* time of death, not her parents. His stomach sank, and he suspected he already knew the answer to his next question. "Is that consistent with Cyrus and Mabel's TOD?"

"Not quite." Dr. Francis leaned back on his heels. "With the variation in each person's normal body temperature, it can get a little tricky to measure exact times of death, especially when we're narrowing it down to the hour. That being said, the temperature of our other vics' bodies indicate they were both killed after Julie."

"How long after?"

Dr. Francis pushed to his feet. "This is all strictly based on body temperatures, but it appears Julie was killed first, and then the adult Osbornes were both killed within an hour of that."

Zane checked his notes. "There were no reports of gunshots, so we're pretty sure the killer used a suppressor. It doesn't appear Julie was aware that anyone was in the home."

"Do you suspect Cyrus Osborne was killed before or after Mabel?" Dean's question redirected the conversation back to Dr. Francis's area of expertise.

Dr. Francis pulled off his gloves with a snap. "Time of death isn't an exact science. It certainly seems Mabel and Cyrus were killed roughly at the same time. And that time, we're estimating to be roughly less than an hour after Julie was shot. All three vics were killed with a single shot to the head. Small caliber, no shell casings left behind. Aside from a few minor lacerations on Mabel Osborne's hands and arms, neither she nor Julie appear to have sustained any other injuries."

Zane hated like hell to ask the next question, but he needed to know. "And Cyrus?"

Dr. Francis dropped both hands to his hips. "I'll know more when I get him on my table, but from what I've observed so far, he was beaten pretty severely. It appears he was lying on the bed and took several severe blows to his head and back. And, like Stephen Denson, he was sexually assaulted."

Zane tightened his jaw. They might have had some doubt about who the real target had been at the Denson house—

whether the killer had wanted Anna or Stephen dead—but there was no second-guessing who the target had been last night. Mabel had hardly been touched, but her husband had been beaten and brutalized. Anna Denson had also been beaten pretty badly, so perhaps their focus needed to be there when it came to who the targets were.

At least they had a clue to point them in the right direction. Knowing who the killer, or killers, had targeted could potentially enable them to establish the relationship between victims. The realization left a bitter taste in Zane's mouth, but right now, more than at any point in the investigation so far, they *needed* to head in the right direction.

Though Cyrus Osborne hadn't been a federal agent, he'd been a prosecutor for the U.S. Attorney's office. Osborne had been one of them. To some extent, even Anna Denson had been one of them.

The killers' blows were striking closer and closer to home, growing more brazen as each damn minute passed.

Zane and his fellow agents needed to find and stop these madmen before they could terrorize any more families.

15

Amelia departed the forensics lab with a renewed purpose in her step. She'd practically flown down to the lab when she'd been notified about a new piece of evidence from the scene of the Denson murders.

At nearly three p.m., Zane and Dean were finally headed back to the office from the scene of the most recent triple-homicide, and Sherry Cowen was still on duty at Kate Denson's safe house. Amelia, on the other hand, had used the day to do research and behind-the-scenes work. She'd called so many people, she worried she was becoming one of those automated bots that incessantly nagged about extended car warranties.

The tasks weren't glamorous, but they were necessary, and Amelia was a practical person. Just because she wasn't on the front lines of the investigation didn't mean the work she did was any less pertinent. Tedious, but important.

To start with, while she waited for more information to roll in about the Osborne family, she'd reached out to the colleagues of Anna and Stephen Denson, who she and Cassandra hadn't gotten to talk to the day before. Afterward, she'd pulled security camera footage to double- and triple-check that Kate's friends weren't suspects.

While she was at it, she'd also gone over the notes of the officers who'd canvassed the Densons' neighborhood. Included in the notes were surveillance recordings from a handful of private security cameras, but nothing in the film jumped out at Amelia. Lastly, she'd reviewed all the threats Anna Denson received dating back to when she was an assistant U.S. attorney.

Though marking items off the to-do list gave Amelia a sense of productivity, she still felt like a greyhound chasing a stuffed rabbit in circles. There were answers out there *some*where, but Amelia wasn't sure her jam-packed afternoon had led her any closer to them.

So, when she'd received a call from one of the lead forensic techs, Bailey Howison, she hadn't hesitated to jump out of her seat and head down to the lab.

News from forensics was almost always good, and Bailey's rundown of the analyses from the Denson house thus far had indeed been a breath of fresh air in an investigation that grew more stifling with each passing hour.

Now, as she stepped into an elevator to head back to the fifth floor, Amelia was off to await the return of Dean and Zane so she could update them on everything she'd done that day. After reviewing the crime scene, the two men had set out to interview the Osbornes' neighbors. Amelia hadn't received an update in a few hours, so she assumed they were still busy. Hopefully, busy meant good news for their investigation. Armed with the new forensic information, she wondered if they might finally be turning a corner in this case.

The murder of Cyrus Osborne had hit a bit closer to home for Cassandra than the rest of them since she'd worked directly with the man in the past. Amelia had met Cyrus, exchanging a handful of case notes and files with him when they were making an attempt to bring Brian Kolthoff to trial.

Had Kolthoff's expensive lawyers not shut the case down after it had barely started, Amelia might have wound up working more closely with Cyrus. Alas, her interactions with him had been minimal.

Regardless of Amelia's affiliation—or lack thereof—with Cyrus, the murder of one of their own was unnerving. An eerie shroud of paranoia had settled over the entire field office. Cyrus had worked *with* the FBI.

As the elevator came to a halt and the doors slid open, a chill skittered down her spine. The sooner they discerned a connection between the victims, the sooner the dark fog would lift. Hopefully, Cassandra had some insight about Cyrus Osborne that would help connect the dots.

Amelia hurried down the hall to the incident room and let herself inside. To her pleasant surprise, Dean Steelman and Zane were both in the process of removing their coats. They'd been in the middle of a discussion about pickles, but the dialogue ceased as their gazes both snapped to Amelia.

Dean draped his black peacoat over the back of an office chair. "Welcome back, Storm. You were just down in the lab, right? Did forensics have anything for us?"

Amelia held up a manila folder as she closed the door behind her. "Some good news."

Dropping down to sit, Zane rubbed his hands together. "We'll take whatever you can give us."

Offering him a slight smile, Amelia returned to her seat at the oval table. In another case—a normal case, if there was such a thing—the comment would have likely elicited a laugh from both Amelia and Dean. However, the somber atmosphere snuffed out any semblance of humor like a lack of oxygen extinguished a flame.

Down to business. The sooner they made headway on the

Osborne and Denson cases, the sooner they'd be able to eliminate the foreboding shadow looming over them.

Amelia flipped open the folder and pushed it to the center of the table. "A hair was found on Stephen Denson's body. Visual comparison indicated it didn't belong to him or Anna, so the lab is doing a full DNA analysis. We've put a rush on it, so we ought to have the results within the next day or two."

Steelman leaned forward, his sapphire eyes fixed on the top photo.

As Steelman sifted through the documents, Zane offered Amelia an approving nod. "That's good. There were a couple hairs recovered from the scene of the Graham murders too. The DNA wasn't usable in either of them since there weren't follicles, but we could get a visual comparison to let us know if we're on the right track with thinking their murders are connected."

Amelia returned his nod. "Already done. Well, not done yet, but the lab is on it. They're pulling the old trace evidence and will be making a comparison this afternoon."

Steelman closed the folder and slid it back to Amelia. "Hopefully, we'll get lucky and learn something. It's a huge step in the right direction, especially if we can get a hit in the national database."

With as thorough as the killers had been at each crime scene, the potential DNA evidence was a good reminder there was no such thing as the perfect crime. Every criminal left behind *some*thing. A hair, a partial fingerprint, a speck of glitter...

Amelia almost smiled at the memory of the Gifford case, but the case in front of her didn't allow for even a moment of gaiety. "Otherwise, everything else is still processing. The hair is our most promising trace evidence so far." From there, Amelia went on to give the two men a rundown of what she'd accomplished since they'd departed that morning.

As she wrapped up the recap, Steelman let out a low whistle. "Productive day."

"I guess." Amelia wished her efforts had been more fruitful. "I checked a lot of possible leads off the list, but none of it panned out. Except for the news from forensics, I suppose. What about you two?"

"We've got a little something. Just need to follow up on it and see if we've *actually* got something." Dean grabbed his laptop from the center of the table.

Zane rubbed his chin. "You already know that the MO was the same. Cyrus Osborne was sexually assaulted, then shot in the back of the head. His wife and daughter were both killed with a single shot to the head. There were minor injuries on Mabel Osborne, potentially from being duct taped to a table, and Julie, the daughter, had been messaging with a friend before her life was cut short."

Amelia's heart clenched in sympathy for the family. She couldn't imagine how horrific their final moments must have been.

The grim expression on Zane's face matched Amelia's thoughts. "Forensics was still combing through the place when we left. If there's any trace left behind, they'll find it. The CPD canvassed the neighborhood, asking folks if they'd noticed anything out of the ordinary."

Dean gave the mouse a couple clicks before turning the laptop to face Amelia. "I have the notes from the officers who went door to door." He minimized the document and opened another. "Turns out that everyone in the near vicinity of the Osbornes' house reported trouble with their outside cameras during the time of the murders."

Amelia narrowed her eyes. "Please tell me that someone has contacted Ring and the other camera companies to see if there was an outage issue."

Zane smiled. "Of course we did. And guess what we found."

Amelia didn't have to guess. "There was no systemwide outage issues. No electric outage, either."

Zane touched his nose. "Exactly, but we got lucky."

Amelia would take lucky seven days a week. "Tell me."

Zane scooted closer and gestured to the screen. "This is from the Osbornes' next-door neighbors. They had an issue with their Amazon deliveries going missing from the front porch, so they installed this security system so they could watch and catch their thief."

With a snort, Dean maximized the image to fill the screen. "Turns out they'd forgotten to update their address after they'd moved, but they didn't figure that out until after they installed this."

Amelia was confused, but only for a moment. She snapped her fingers, anticipation flooding her veins. "That means our unsub scanned for cameras by digital location instead of searching for them door to door, and since no camera data was provided for that particular address, our unsub missed it." She put her hands together in a prayer position. "Did it catch something?"

"Maybe." Steelman pressed play, then hit another button to accelerate the video speed.

Cars zoomed past the house at Mach speed, the fast pace giving the illusion the Osbornes lived in a far busier area. Another click slowed the pace, and after several moments, a white Midwest Communications van pulled up across the street. What appeared to be a man stepped out, wearing a cap pulled low over his face. Dean paused the video, zooming in for a closer look. In slow motion, they watched the man walk out of the frame.

Amelia cursed under her breath. "I can't see his face."

Steelman reversed, and they watched it again. Still nothing.

In silence, Amelia, Zane, and Dean watched as more vehicles zipped by the camera's field of view. According to the timestamp in the bottom left of the screen, the van remained parked for a total of four hours before the man returned—his face still completely hidden under his cap—and drove out of sight.

A lengthy appointment with the cable guy, but Amelia had heard of longer. Before she could make a comment about her skepticism, she bit her tongue. Dean Steelman had asked for her opinion. She needed to wait to share her observations.

Sure enough, not long after day two rolled around, the van was back. No one emerged from the vehicle this time, piquing Amelia's suspicion. After another three hours, it left.

Prying her focus away from the video, Amelia rubbed her eyes. "Um…did it actually catch anything?"

Dean dragged the scroll bar at the bottom of the screen before pressing play again. "Keep an eye on the far right. You can see the side of the Osbornes' porch."

Amelia leaned in closer, just in time to catch a shadowy figure emerge at the very edge of the screen. The hairs on the back of her neck stood on end as Dean tapped the space bar to pause the footage.

The creak of Zane's chair drew Amelia's gaze to him as he propped his elbows on the table. "The forensic pathologist estimated the family's TOD ranging from ten-thirty to possibly midnight. Timestamp here puts us at ten-fifteen."

"That's him, then." Amelia squinted at the screen, struggling to make out even the slightest detail of the figure as it strode up to the Osbornes' porch. To her dismay, the person was dressed in all dark colors, including a hood shrouding their face. "We think we're dealing with two unsubs, right? Where's the second?"

After exchanging a glance with Zane, Dean pressed his lips together. "Could've gone around the back. Come at the place from both entrances to make sure no one freaks out and runs. It'd fit in with the thorough approach they've been using so far."

"Yeah." Zane dropped his chin into one hand. "That would make the most sense. There were no signs of forced entry at either door, so that means we'd be dealing with two men who, among other things, know how to pick locks."

There were videos online that could teach a damn toddler to pick a lock. Amelia was less impressed with the idea that both unsubs were familiar with lock-picking than she was them knowing how to access camera and security software.

Dean pulled the laptop back to himself. "The owners gave us full permission to access the archived video footage, and we've sent everything over to Cyber. It's all stored on a cloud, so the couple who live there can check it from an app on their phones. We'll probably have to issue a subpoena to obtain details such as IP addresses, cookies, or other trackers, but then Cyber will be able to sift through login records of the other neighbors' cameras to see if anyone accessed them. If so, that access might possibly provide some type of link to our unsub."

Considering how many layers a criminal could hide behind online, Amelia doubted they'd get far with the information. Despite the slim likelihood, they'd ensure this base was covered.

"So, what've we got from this scene so far?" Zane's chair creaked in protest as he leaned back, holding up a finger. "First, there's that van. Midwest Communications is a pretty sizable internet and cable provider in this part of the country. I don't use their services, but I'm willing to bet plenty of people in this office do."

"They suck." Dean frowned. "But they're the only ISP offered where I live."

"That's a conversation for a different day." Zane raised a second finger. "Second, we've got the next-door neighbors, who apparently installed a camera on their front porch but forgot to change their address on Amazon. That singular camera caught someone going into the Osbornes' house at ten-fifteen, but there're absolutely no details visible. The person doesn't even *look* at the camera."

Though Amelia had held onto a sliver of hope that the security camera footage would blow their case wide open, the weight of disappointment dropped in her lap like an anchor. Even if Cyber Crimes managed to manipulate the image of the man on the Osbornes' porch into something usable, the guy had never even glanced in that direction.

"Any chance the guy was careless on his way out of the house? Does the video show him leaving?" Amelia searched her colleagues' faces and knew the answer.

Steelman slapped the table. "Nope. My guess is he went out the back door and around the house. The camera never captures him again."

Zane added a final observation. "We also have the time that Julie's messages to her friend stopped. That, plus the M.E.'s analyses should provide us with a solid approximation for time of death."

Save the potential breakthrough of the hair found at the Denson scene, they were right back where they'd started at the beginning of the day.

No, we're not. We've got a whole new crime scene. New victims and new information that might help us find a pattern.

She straightened her backbone as well as her resolve. "We should try to figure out how these victims are connected."

Dean ran a hand through his hair. "Agreed. We've got a dead district court judge and a dead federal prosecutor. Each of them and their families murdered in similar fashion within little more than twenty-four hours of one another. There's no way these *aren't* connected."

He was right. A federal lawyer and a federal judge. Husbands sexually assaulted. Everyone shot with a small caliber bullet to the head. Casings policed at each scene. Security systems disarmed.

Since Dean was the only one with an open laptop, Amelia turned to him. "Can you pull up Anna Denson's case record? Let's see if we can find any cases Cyrus tried in her courtroom."

Dean's fingers flew across the keyboard.

As Zane fished in his pocket, his eyes met hers. A shadow of foreboding passed over his unshaven face, setting Amelia's nerves back on edge. "Cyrus Osborne was overseeing the charges pressed against Brian Kolthoff, wasn't he?"

"Yeah." A split second of paranoia whirled through Amelia's head. There was no way Kolthoff was behind all these deaths.

Was there?

The Shark was a billionaire—a venture capitalist turned D.C. lobbyist. Only God knew how many companies had placed him on their executive board or how many others still consulted him. A man like that didn't get to his status by murdering district court judges and lawyers just for *trying* to bring him to trial.

Amelia doubted Kolthoff would have any moral hang-ups about murdering an entire family, but killing someone as high-profile as a judge and then offing a federal prosecutor twenty-four hours later? It didn't fit the profile they had of the man.

Typing and scrolling, Dean barely turned away from his

laptop. "Kolthoff? He was one of the suspects tried for Leila Jackson's abduction and forced prostitution, wasn't he?"

If they'd been outside, Amelia would have spat on the ground to show her distaste. "He was never tried. His expensive prick lawyers threw motion after motion at the prosecutors. They gradually whittled the charges down from sex trafficking of a minor to solicitation, and then to nothing at all."

"Money talks and bullshit walks." Dean spat the words. "If you've got as much money as that guy, you damn near rule the world. But..." his expression transformed from anger to confusion, "Anna Denson didn't have anything to do with that case. Cyrus Osborne was the lead prosecutor, and Cassandra Halcott helped him with it. What little action they saw was in Eldon Caldwell's courtroom."

The room lapsed back into silence, Dean Steelman's keystrokes the only sound as Amelia digested the information they'd gathered so far.

"All right." Dean snapped his fingers like he was a parent trying to wake his children. "All right. Here. Here. Shit, check this out. We've got something."

Rather than scoot closer, Amelia sprang out of her chair, followed closely by Zane. Like a pair of sentinels, they each took a spot to either side of Dean.

Steelman circled the cursor around Anna Denson's name. "November of last year, thirteen months ago. *U.S.A. v Evan MacMillan*. Anna Denson's courtroom. The lead prosecutor was Cassandra Halcott."

Amelia connected the dots, and a flurry of excitement rushed through her veins. "Who was her assistant?"

But she already knew the answer before Steelman met her gaze and confirmed it. "Cyrus Osborne."

Zane cursed and leaned in closer. "Can you pull up the jury?"

Steelman was already clicking away. "Got it."

The name seemed to jump off the screen at Amelia. "Carla Graham was the jury foreperson."

Zane straightened to his full height. "Are these guys planning to take out the entire courtroom? Jesus, the foreperson of the jury is just a civilian. Who's next, the fucking stenographer?"

Dread settled low and heavy in Amelia's stomach. All day, she'd felt the unnerving presence of a dark cloud hanging over the FBI office. When one of their own was harmed, the shockwave always rippled through the entire office. "No. Cassandra is."

This time, it was Dean's turn to swear. "Storm's right. They're going to be after Halcott next. We need to look this case over front, back, and side to side." The agent shut his laptop, rose from his seat, and grabbed his coat in one swift motion. "We need to see if there's anyone else involved that might be at risk here. But first..."

"First, we need to get to Cassandra." Amelia glanced down at her watch, a timepiece given to her by her beloved sister-in-law. A sister-in-law she'd seen less and less of lately. "I've got forty-five minutes before I'm scheduled to be at Kate Denson's safe house."

Dean snatched up his phone. "I'll call her now, see where she is."

"Okay. Amelia, can you keep diving into the case file a bit? If you find anything of interest, give us a shout." Zane pulled his coat off the back of his chair. "Once you head to the safe house, maybe you and Sherry can talk to Kate, get something more from her. Now that we've got this new lead, it might help. Steelman and I can head to Cassandra's place right now. We'll get her to a safe house ASAP, then I'll get in touch with the cable company and get a list of their employees and their schedules. See if we can determine who was in that van."

"All right. That sounds like a plan." Despite her confident tone, a rare pang of trepidation tightened Amelia's chest.

She and Cassandra Halcott hadn't started on the best of terms during the Ben Storey investigation, but Amelia had started to warm up to the lawyer over their past couple cases.

The woman was abrasive, but she was excellent at her job. She and Amelia might not be going out for best friend lattes any time soon, but Amelia was glad to have Cassandra on their team when they were working to take down assholes.

They just had to get to this bad guy—or bad *guys*—before he could strike again.

Before he could get to Cassandra.

16

As the redhead came into view, I tapped the keyboard to pause the recording. Resting both elbows on the armrests of my chair, I leaned in until I could make out the individual pixels of the frozen image.

She was it.

The last and most important name on my list. I'd always been keen on saving the best for last, even when it came to something as simple as eating dinner. If I'd taken out the lead prosecutor in my brother's trial before anyone else, the others would have felt like a chore. This work was too important for me to lose interest, so I'd held off on going after her.

Plus, there was the added bonus that watching the others drop around her would make her squirm. She needed to squirm, just like she made my brother sweat.

I realized my decision came with its share of hazards. By waiting to take out Cassandra Halcott until after the other three, I left the potential open for the Feds to catch up to me. With that in mind, I'd done my best to mitigate the risk.

I'd read as much about modern forensics as possible, and

though I was very familiar with home alarm systems, I'd spent weeks educating myself on the newest ones on the market and how to circumvent them. Coupled with the knowledge I already had regarding technology, I was confident I'd covered all my bases.

They might catch up to me eventually, but not until after I'd dealt with this lawyer bitch. If anyone, federal agent or otherwise, tried to stand in my way, I'd make them pay too.

As long as I got to the attorney bitch first, I didn't much care what happened to me after that.

Refocusing on the redhead, hate and rage burned in my chest. In the image on the screen, a pair of sunglasses covered her eyes, and her gray coat obscured most of her hourglass figure.

It was a shame that a woman so pretty wound up so terrible. Not only a bitch but a whore too. When I'd started monitoring her, a man had made fairly regular visits to her apartment. In the last few weeks, I'd only spotted him a couple times.

Seemed likely to me he'd realized what kind of snooty whore he'd been screwing. I doubted he'd pose a problem, but if he tried to get in my way, I'd be more than happy to add him to my plans. Women were okay, but I preferred the men. And a man who looked like *him*...

Desire stirred within me. If I wasn't so determined to finish my task, I'd do my damnedest to catch them both together.

Maybe when I was finished with her, I'd set my sights on him. Couldn't hurt. The guy was a Fed, but his job title only seemed like another reason to take him out.

What else would I do when Cassandra Halcott was dead? Go back to my usual work schedule at the cable company? Get back to the grind after what I'd experienced over the past month?

Was that even possible?

No. I didn't have to give that much thought. I knew I'd never be able to return to "normalcy" when I was finished with this bitch. Perhaps that was my calling. I'd spent my time in the military working in communications and technology, and when I'd gone back to the civilian world, I'd done the same.

Deep in the back of my mind, I'd always known my work had a purpose greater than simply restoring internet connections. I'd learned so much from the job, and all that knowledge was put directly toward my ultimate goal.

The mission to avenge my brother, to eliminate the people who'd tried to take away the last member of my family.

"That's her. Cassandra Halcott." My brother's voice made me jump. "What's your plan for her?"

I turned to where Evan stood in the doorway, both arms crossed over his broad chest. "I've been tracking her for the last few weeks. Right after I took out Carla Graham. I had an appointment in Cassandra's apartment building, so I went in and damaged the coaxial cable leading to her condo."

Evan snorted. "People these days can't go a day without their damn internet."

I ignored the comment. Evan knew about my affinity for technology, and he always liked to find ways to slip in a derisive remark about my vocation. That's what brothers did, though. They gave one another grief. I was man enough to take Evan's occasional ribbing.

"She made an appointment the next day, just like I figured she would. I took it, and the boss didn't think much of it since I'd just been in that building the day before. Probably assumed it was something related to the work I'd done that day." I laughed at people's foolishness.

"Tell me you did more than fix her internet connection."

I ignored Evan's mocking tone. "Of course I did. While she sat all high and mighty in her home office, I found her keys by the door. I just needed a few seconds to pop open the key fob and plant a tracker inside."

Evan's eyes narrowed. "Why her keys? You already had the tracker on her phone."

"BECAUSE IF SOMETHING happens and she decides to run, she'll know to toss her phone but—"

"She'll keep hold of her keys." As a grin spread over Evan's face, pride swelled in my chest. "Smart thinking, little bro."

I dug a fingernail into my palm to keep my expression as neutral as possible. My brother's compliment wasn't a reason for me to start gushing like a little schoolgirl. "We've got to play this carefully, though. Kate Denson's still out there, and I don't know where the hell she is."

"We can deal with her after we get this lawyer bitch out of the way."

Of course, the lawyer came first. If I got caught and arrested after I'd eliminated Cassandra Halcott, then so be it. My mission would be complete, and my brother's vengeance would be satiated. At this point, I had nothing to lose.

"We need to lay low until then. For all we know, the Denson girl already talked to a sketch artist. They might have my face hanging up all over the damn FBI office."

Evan toed the duffel bag beside my desk. "That's why you're packing up shop, yeah?"

"Yeah." I exited the recording of Cassandra Halcott's parking garage and shut down the computer. "I don't know how close the Feds might be, but we've got to prepare for the worst."

I didn't have the time to lug all the components out to my car, but fortunately, all I really needed was the hard drive. I'd cleaned up the rest of the apartment, and in the event of a search warrant, the Feds would be hard-pressed to find anything remotely incriminating.

I'd taken trophies from each family…their house keys. But I wasn't stupid enough to leave those behind. The keys would stay with me no matter where I went.

Rubbing one key with an imprint of the Chicago Bears logo, I recalled the look on Scott Graham's tormented face as I had my way with him. That bitch wife of his could do nothing but watch. Her horror and grief when her husband submitted to me was the last thing she saw.

I couldn't suppress a grin as I stroked the key faster. I could never part with my mementos.

As if aware of my thoughts, Evan lifted a sarcastic eyebrow. "When are we leaving?"

Collecting myself, I popped the hard drive out of my computer and grabbed the duffel bag. "Now. This was the last thing I needed. I've got everything else packed in the car. We've got an RV waiting. We'll stay there for a few days, or however long it takes to finish that bitch."

Clapping me on the shoulder, Evan laughed. "You'll have her on her knees before you know it."

I would. When I was finished with her, the possibilities for me would be endless.

17

Cassandra hadn't stopped moving since she'd received the call from Dean Steelman thirty-seven minutes ago. Her focus had bounced from the clock to the front door, then to the bare necessities she'd been instructed to pack to bring to the safe house. Movements twitchy, like those of an addict suffering from withdrawals, Cassandra jammed a handful of underwear into her suitcase.

The agents at the Bureau would go through the contents, and despite Cassandra's experience with FBI procedures, she wasn't sure what exactly she was permitted to bring. Clothes, sure. That was a given. But how was she supposed to do her damn job from a safe house? Would the U.S. Attorney assign the Denson and Osborne cases to someone else?

Anger seared through her veins.

No. This was *her* case. Just because the psychopath who'd murdered Cyrus, Mabel, and their poor daughter was after her too didn't mean she would bow to the sick bastard's will.

"I won't." Her voice sounded bizarre after spending so long in silence. Clenching and unclenching her hands, she shook her head. "This is my case. I'm going to make sure whoever did this to Cyrus and his family is buried under the jail."

Beneath the rage for her colleague and his wife and daughter, a persistent shadow of unease lurked. Cassandra stood a whole five-foot-four and weighed a whopping one-hundred-twenty pounds soaking wet and with her keys in her pocket.

She wasn't skinny or overweight, but she also wasn't in the best shape. For most of an average day, she sat on her ass, her eyes glued to a computer screen. When she ascended a flight of stairs too quickly, she wound up out of breath, and carrying groceries up to her condo was the closest she got to exercising.

She could throw down in a courtroom, but to her chagrin, that was about the extent of her combat prowess.

Plunking the suitcase down beside the coffee table, she closed her eyes and took a deep breath.

That's why mankind invented guns and knives. I go to the range every damn week, and I can hit a gnat from two hundred yards away.

Firearms were the great equalizer. If it came down to it, she couldn't put someone like Joseph in a headlock, nor could she land a solid blow that would incapacitate him.

She *could* pull a trigger and blow his guts out his ass, though.

To emphasize the point to herself, she picked up a wood and steel finished .40 cal from the stone surface of the coffee table. She'd been more than a little out of place at the gun show where she'd bought the weapon. All around her had been men and boys clad in denim, camo, and the occasional plaid. The few women at the place had been dressed much the same as their male counterparts, though there were splashes of pink in their attire.

Then, there'd been Cassandra. Fresh off work for the day,

wearing a chevron pencil skirt, ivory Chanel blouse, and Louboutin pumps that added five inches to her height.

A chuckle slipped from her lips as she recalled the strange looks she'd received. She'd had to work hard to maintain a neutral expression and to keep herself from bursting into laughter every thirty seconds.

The memory lessened the tension in her tired muscles, a merciful reprieve from the near-constant anxiety of the past half hour.

With a sigh, she dropped down to the center cushion of her overstuffed couch. As much as she always wished she had a pet, she was glad she didn't have to worry about a cat or a dog right now. The guilt of leaving a furry companion behind would have been overwhelming.

Most people could ask a friend to check on their pet, but Cassandra wasn't most people. She didn't have any damn friends in this city. Cyrus and his wife had been the closest thing she'd had to friends in Chicago, and she hadn't known them particularly well. Work friends just weren't the same as real friends.

After the initial call from Agent Steelman, he'd called again with an update. Apparently, Amelia had been digging into the MacMillan case file and learned a great deal.

Fewer than six months after he was sentenced to life in prison without the possibility for parole, Evan MacMillan had been stabbed to death in a prison yard brawl. Evan had been smuggling in drugs for a biker gang called the Iron Wolves, and he'd tried to take what he believed was "his share" of the product.

Before he could take a beating for the transgression, Evan had marched up to one of the gang's ring leaders and tried to cut his throat.

According to the guards' accounts of the altercation, Evan had proclaimed his intent was to prove his dominance. To throw out the weaklings and take over the biker gang himself.

Amelia had stated there was no record of who had landed the killing blow on Evan. With no one willing to testify, and any video evidence conveniently going missing, the murder of Evan MacMillan went cold and remained unsolved.

Agent Storm had reasoned that Kenny MacMillan's inability to get to the men who'd actually murdered his brother had driven his decision to instead go after those who'd convicted Evan. To Kenny, the people who'd worked to put Evan behind bars were just as culpable as the bikers who'd stabbed him thirty-four times.

Since the investigation into Evan MacMillan had primarily revolved around drugs, the case had fallen under the DEA's jurisdiction. Amelia had notified both agents who'd been responsible for it, and the DEA was taking the necessary steps to keep them safe.

A heavy knock ripped her away from thoughts like a gardener pulling a weed from the dirt.

Blood pounded in Cassandra's ears, the temperature in the room suddenly stifling. Reaching a trembling hand to her phone, she checked for new messages. Agent Steelman had assured her he'd send a text once he and Palmer arrived, but there were no notifications.

When she'd picked up the .40 cal, she hadn't actually expected to contemplate *using* the weapon. The gesture had solely been to give her a sliver of comfort in the midst of what a psychologist would likely deem a panic attack.

Tightening her hand around the grip of the handgun, her muscles creaked as she rose to stand. Each step slow and measured, as if moving too quickly would somehow allow the unexpected visitor to enter, Cassandra picked her way toward the door. She doubted someone coming to kill her would knock, but with the way this case had been going, she couldn't rule out anything.

At the edge of the foyer, she cleared her throat. "Who is it?"

"It's me. It's Joseph."

Cassandra's stomach flip-flopped with fresh anxiety.

Well, at least it's not the guy who wants to kill me, right?

She wasn't sure how *right* the thought was. With each hour that went by after her and Joseph's breakup, the more convinced she became there was darkness in him. Something truly evil.

Licking her lips, Cassandra carefully watched the doorknob, half-expecting Joseph to try to pick the damn lock. "What do you want?"

Through the heavy door, his sigh was muffled. "I just want to talk. You haven't responded to any of my texts, and we never finished our conversation last night."

You mean the one where I dumped your ass?

She gritted her teeth and kept the callous remark to herself. Joseph had indeed sent her a slew of text messages, the contents of which ranged from sappy to passive aggressive. She'd deleted them all as they'd been received.

It had become increasingly clear to her that he wasn't going to go away until he got in his final word. Cassandra had no desire to schedule a time for them to meet in public, and she damn sure wasn't going to let him inside when she was home alone, and no one knew what was happening.

However, Agents Dean Steelman and Zane Palmer were due to show up at her condo at any moment. If she wanted to get this over with, she wasn't going to get a better, safer opportunity.

"Fine. Just a second."

Tucking the .40 into the waistband of her skinny jeans, Cassandra shrugged into a zip-up hoodie to fully conceal the weapon. She stuffed her phone in her pocket, rolled her shoulders, and returned to the entryway.

Stay strong.

Jaw tight, she threw the deadbolt, undid the chain lock, and pulled open the door. Joseph lifted his head from where he'd been gazing at one of his dress shoes.

A day's worth of stubble darkened his cheeks, leaving Cassandra to wonder if he was trying to play the part of a man grieving for a lost relationship. Aside from the facial hair, his tailored slacks were crisp and pressed, and his peacoat-scarf combination made him look every bit the part of a Fed.

Wordlessly, she stepped to the side, gesturing for Joseph to go to the living room.

His shoes better not leave wet spots on the damn floor.

She reached for the deadbolt but stopped short of flicking it. No, she'd leave the damn thing unlocked. If the lunatic who wanted to kill her showed up, maybe he'd do her a solid and take out Joseph.

She snorted quietly at the thought, turning to make her way back to the living room. It was time to finish this nonsense.

Her chest tightened as a voice in the back of her head told her she'd never be finished with Joseph until *he* was finished.

Hadn't he found a new piece of ass, though? What the hell happened to the woman he'd been taking out to expensive dinners and screwing before he came over to Cassandra's place?

If there was even such a woman. Cassandra didn't even care. That excuse simply gave her a good reason to get rid of him since telling him that her gut had judged him as evil would only make her look like a lunatic.

Joseph nudged her suitcase with the toe of one shoe. "You going somewhere, babe?"

Cassandra's pulse spiked, anger burning in her gut. "Don't call me that. Say what you want to say, *Joseph*."

The corner of his mouth twitched in a ghost of a smirk. "You're so hot when you're mad, you know that?"

She kept her face carefully blank. He was trying to piss her off or trying to give her a reminder of their respective positions of power. Either way, she wouldn't grant him the satisfaction, even if she did want to rip off his damn head.

"I'm not mad. I'm impatient." She jutted her chin at the suitcase. "As you can see, I've got somewhere to be. So, spit it out, Larson."

He rubbed the back of his neck. "Where're you headed? Taking a vacation?"

Managing anger had long been a challenge for Cassandra, and knowing she had a semiautomatic handgun within reach wasn't helping. If she shot Joseph in the foot, maybe he'd finally get the picture.

Then again, a close-range shot from a .40 caliber would effectively *destroy* that particular body part. She wasn't going to jail for anyone.

She heaved a sigh, making no effort to conceal her exasperation. "Is that why you're here? You want to know my travel plans for the next week? I thought you were a federal agent, not a damn travel agent."

He held up both hands as if to surrender. "All right, I'm sorry. You're right. That's not why I'm here. You're a grown woman, and you can go on vacation whenever you want."

Didn't need your permission, but thanks. She bit her tongue and remained silent.

Raking his fingers through his sandy-blond hair, he turned his gaze to the floor. "I guess...I just wanted to know why. I thought things were going okay. That we were solid, you know? I really care about you, Cassandra. I thought that maybe, well...I think I'm falling in love with you." He turned puppy dog eyes on her. "It's been a long time since I had these thoughts about someone, and I didn't really know what to do about them. That's why I was acting so, well…" He lifted his chin, his pale blue eyes meeting hers. "Weird. I'm sorry."

Ten years ago, or perhaps even five years ago, Cassandra would've been liable to buy his explanation, hook, line, and sinker.

Not today. She'd heard this bullshit before. She'd been through this whole song and dance—the manipulative, cheating ex who tried to smooth-talk his way back into her good graces, who convinced her *she* was the problem. That if she'd only opened her heart more, their relationship would have been fine.

Cassandra shifted her weight from one foot to the other but didn't move from her closed-off stance. "Hm." The sound was more of a grunt than an actual word. She cocked her head, pretending to genuinely consider his declaration.

Whether he bought the fake concern or just wanted to listen to himself talk some more, Joseph took the opportunity to forge on in his explanation. "Look, it's been more than six years since my second divorce. I haven't exactly been looking for anything serious in all that time. There's sex, sometimes, but never anything that seems…*real,* you know? When we met, I wasn't really sure what I was doing. I knew you were sort of off-limits, since you work for the U.S. Attorney's office, but…"

For a beat, she almost thought the pained expression on his face was real, that his hushed, albeit strained tone was genuine.

Only for a beat, until she pictured the unopened condom she'd found in his wallet or the receipt to an upscale restaurant. More than any of that, she remembered the sense of unease she got while in the man's presence.

There was nothing genuine about Joseph Larson. He was every negative stereotype about men, all rolled into one.

Morbid curiosity—the same type of compulsion that drew a person to stare at a car crash—niggled at the back of Cassandra's mind.

She arched an eyebrow, feigning interest in Joseph's story. "But?"

He took a swift step forward, and Cassandra barely kept herself from flinching. Instead, she took a single step backward.

The unmistakable fires of ire flickered in Joseph's eyes, albeit only briefly. His expression of anger was replaced almost immediately by the same strain and sadness he'd displayed since his arrival.

His slipup was so quick, so subtle, Cassandra doubted she'd have noticed if she hadn't already suspected he was full of shit. The prick should have been an actor. By now, he'd have at least seven Oscars on his shelf.

Gesturing back and forth between the two of them, he blew out a weary sigh. "But there was something between us. Something that just made sense, you know? With you, I felt like I was on the right track somehow. I mean, I know my job is important too, and it's what I always wanted to do. But outside of the FBI, I always felt like I was just aimlessly wandering through life. Until…you."

Wow. That speech was so cheesy it might make me lactose intolerant.

If the man she was facing wasn't dangerous and unpredictable, Cassandra would have let the bitter remark fly.

But she knew what Joseph was doing. She knew why he'd resorted to pleading with her and laying bare his alleged feelings.

He wanted her to change her mind, to take him back so *he* would be in control, and not her. The idea that Cassandra had ended their relationship on her terms didn't sit well with men like Joseph. Men who had to control every aspect of their lives.

Guys like that, like Joseph, would beg, cheat, and steal to retain even a semblance of power. A shred. Even a morsel.

They were pathetic, but oftentimes, they were dangerous.

Lifting her chin, Cassandra met his gaze, her expression carefully blank. Rather than go for a personal attack, she decided to stick with the story about him cheating. It was safer that way. "You've been fucking another woman for the past three weeks. You can't tell me I was *that* special to you when you've been sticking your dick in someone else for almost a month."

He tensed. At his side, one hand curled into a fist.

Cassandra's heart slammed against her chest, sweat beading along her spine. Shit, she'd grabbed the .40 for protection to make herself feel better, but she hadn't expected to need to *use* the damn thing.

She'd never shot someone before. Aside from a couple scuffles at college parties, she'd never even *hit* another person. All her fights were fought and won with words.

Joseph's a battle you can't win with words. You know that. If you didn't know it before, you sure as hell do now.

Her thoughts had entered a tailspin.

What did she do? Brandish the weapon and scare him off?

Yeah, right. He'll just overpower you and take the damn thing right out of your hand. If you pull out that weapon, you'd damn well better be prepared to pull the trigger.

Just when she was certain Joseph intended to advance on her, he tilted his head back and rubbed his eyes with one hand. "That receipt, that condom, it's not what you think. The condom has just been there, and I never thought to take it out. The receipt was from dinner I had with a friend. You know how the Bears lost a few weeks ago? Well, I lost a bet. With Green Bay's best wide receiver on the bench, I thought the Bears had it in the bag. So," he dropped his hand and let out a self-deprecating chuckle, "I bet on 'em, and it turned out to be a mistake."

Was he telling the truth? Had she imagined all the mannerisms she'd been so sure indicated there was a darkness within him? The anger she'd spotted in his eyes...was it a manifestation of her past trauma? A projection?

Was she losing her damn mind?

No. Stop it, Cassandra. Trust your instincts. You know what you saw. You know what he is. Don't let an elaborate lie fool you. He's had a full day to come up with this shit. Hell, he might even be telling the truth. It doesn't mean he wasn't screwing someone else too.

None of it mattered, though. She just needed out of this relationship.

When she swallowed, her throat seemed as if it was coated with sandpaper. She had to hold her ground and stay committed to the cheating excuse to get rid of him. "That doesn't explain the showers. Don't lie to me. I *know* you've been sleeping with someone else. Besides, we just aren't compatible, we—"

"Compatible? What the hell are you talking about?" He advanced another step, raising a hand to jab his index finger in her direction.

Cassandra couldn't help it this time. Her entire body tensed as adrenaline rushed into her bloodstream, preparing her to fight or flee. As she shrank away from the highly trained, physically fit man with both military and FBI experience, she wanted to curl up into a ball and cry.

The entire scenario was too familiar. Her foster father, her college boyfriend, her ex-fiancé...and now, Joseph.

"What the hell was that?" Joseph's vehement question

sounded tinny and distant over the thundering of Cassandra's heart.

You aren't a kid or a dumb twenty-year-old anymore. You're a federal prosecutor.

"Did you just flinch?" He raked a hand through his hair, clucking his tongue. "Wow, Cassandra. Just...wow. Have I *ever* done anything that was remotely threatening to you? I've never hit you! Now you're acting like I'm some wife-beating piece of shit, flinching away from me when I'm trying to have a damn conversation like an adult!"

You need to leave.

She wanted to say the words, but they were stuck. Somewhere between her pounding heart and clammy palms, she'd lost the ability to assert herself.

In her mind's eye, she saw the hulking figure of her foster father. A sliver of his gut was visible from beneath his white tank-top, but the belly concealed a mass of muscle that could easily overtake her slight frame. Even from five feet away, the stench of whiskey and sweat was nearly overwhelming.

He'd yell at her for a while, berate her for whatever perceived slight she'd committed that day. Then, he'd pull her onto his lap. She'd never felt a man's erection before living in that god-forsaken house. Once, in seventh grade, she'd kissed Dominick Santiago on the cheek after he'd walked her home. That had been the extent of her experience with males at the time.

"Now what?" Joseph's irritable tone sliced through the memory. "Now you're going to just stop talking? Really? No. No, that's not how this is going to go, all right? Look at me!"

She did and immediately regretted it.

The feral gleam in his eyes told her everything she needed to know.

Not only was he enjoying himself, but he'd done this

before. Manipulation, combined with a sprinkling of intimidation, was nothing new to FBI Special Agent Joseph Larson.

Her stomach sank as the gravity of the situation dawned on her.

As long as Joseph was fixated on her, she'd never be done with him.

She'd made a terrible mistake by ever letting him into her life.

18

As Dean approached Cassandra Halcott's door, he permitted himself a mental sigh of relief. As quickly as the Osbornes had been killed after the Denson murders, he'd been genuinely concerned the killer would beat them to Cassandra's place.

Zane Palmer had stayed behind to monitor the entrance to the building and the street. They knew their suspect had conducted a stakeout of the Osborne house, so it stood to reason that he'd do the same for his next target. Unless, of course, he couldn't find his next target.

Armed with the details Amelia had dug up after he and Palmer had left, it was clear they were dealing with an unstable individual—*one* individual—and needed to get Cassandra to safety as quickly as possible.

Dean raised his hand to knock on the door, but a muffled voice stopped him short. He couldn't quite make out the words, but he was certain the speaker was a male.

Slowly, Dean reached for the Glock. Glancing up and down the hall, he leaned in, held his breath, and strained his hearing. He didn't want to kick down the door to the federal prosecutor's home and barrel in, gun first, to find she was simply watching television.

"You don't get to pull this shit while I'm talking to you. *Look* at me, for god's sake!"

Dean's grasp tightened on the Glock.

That sure as hell wasn't a voice from a movie. Someone—some *man*—was in Cassandra Halcott's condo. And based on the vitriol in his tone, their conversation wasn't a pleasant one.

Rolling his shoulders to loosen the muscles, Dean unholstered his service weapon and reached for the doorknob. There was no time to call for backup. If the suspect was in Cassandra's home, then Dean needed to act *now*.

As he twisted the knob, he was surprised to find it was unlocked. He shoved the door open as quickly as he dared, grateful when the hinges made little sound. A short hall led away from the foyer, but not much of the living room was visible from his vantage point.

"You need to leave, Joseph." Cassandra sounded…small, even scared.

Dean froze in place. Joseph? Who the hell was *Joseph*, and better yet, why was he here?

Wait. Halcott's dating someone at the Bureau, isn't she? Joseph...Larson? From Organized Crime?

"I'm not leaving until you cut this shit out and listen to what I'm saying to you. You hear me?"

Though Dean had only met Joseph Larson in passing, the venomous, commanding tone with which he spoke told him the agent wasn't here with good intentions. As he started to tuck the Glock back in its holster, he hesitated. The last thing he wanted was to start an armed standoff with another federal agent, but there was an edge in Joseph's tone Dean didn't like.

An edge he'd heard before. A long, long time ago.

He shook off the memory, but not before a shudder worked its way down his back.

You don't go pointing guns at other agents just because they're taking a tone you don't like. Maybe the guy just had a bad day. You don't know.

Deep down, Dean didn't believe the half-assed excuse for a second.

He gritted his teeth and holstered the nine-mil. Now, he had to figure out how to approach the two of them without coming across like an eavesdropping moron.

Don't think. Just do it.

Acting without thinking in social situations was a Dean Steelman specialty. He'd always hoped that he'd outgrow the awkwardness, but instead, he'd merely learned to embrace it. To not care if other people thought his commentary was weird.

Clearing his throat, he took the few remaining steps into the living area.

Just in time to catch the predatory glimmer in Joseph Larson's eyes as he towered over Cassandra. The glimpse was so fleeting, Dean almost wondered if he'd imagined the expression on Larson's face.

Almost.

The agent's stance changed before Dean even opened his mouth. From threatening to relaxed, Joseph Larson underwent a full metamorphosis in a fraction of a second.

Who in the hell *was* this guy?

Cassandra appeared as if she'd just witnessed her own death. All color had drained from her already pale cheeks, accentuating the shadows beneath her eyes. Meanwhile, Joseph Larson was either plotting to kill them both or take them out for ice cream. Dean honestly wasn't sure which, though he strongly suspected the former.

"Excuse me. Sorry to barge in, but the door was unlocked, and this is pretty important."

Larson raised an eyebrow. "And who are you, exactly?"

Fighting an eye roll, Dean retrieved his badge and flipped it open. "Special Agent Dean Steelman, Violent Crimes. And you're Agent Larson from Organized Crime, yeah?"

"I am." He gestured to Cassandra. "You're here for her? Why?"

Dean wasn't sure why the guy cared. "I'm not at liberty to say."

As Agent Larson looked from Dean to Cassandra and then back, Dean wondered what was going through the man's head.

Would he protest, or worse, would he use his position as a special agent to insist he accompany them?

Weariness weighed on Dean's bones. He'd been chasing after a mass murderer for the past twenty-four hours and was operating on only a few hours of sleep. He didn't have the energy to deal with a controlling ass like Joseph Larson.

"With all due respect, Agent Larson." Dean kept his voice stern but noncombative. "Time is of the essence right now."

Larson perked up as if he'd roused from a trance. Like a chameleon changing colors, his stance changed from nearly hostile to amiable. "Of course. I won't keep you, Agent Steelman. Have a good night."

"Yeah. You too."

After a couple steps backward, Larson turned around and strode down the short hall. Dean watched the agent disappear and didn't break his attention away until the door latched closed.

"Sorry about that, Agent. He showed up unannounced. We had a...well, we were dating, and I ended it last night." Cassandra Halcott's strained tone was a direct match for the sudden weariness weighing on Dean.

He brushed the stray strands of hair away from his forehead, holding in a sigh as he glanced at the lawyer. Office romances almost always ended in disaster, and this one was no exception. "No problem. And I apologize for not texting that Agent Palmer and I had arrived. I was going to text but then heard the voices, and, well...we really do need to leave. As you know, we've had some major developments in the case, and there's a lot of work that needs to be done."

Cassandra straightened, and the fear Dean had spotted only moments ago vanished with the movement. "Right. The MacMillan case that links all three sets of victims together. And Evan MacMillan's brother, Kenny. You'll need a search warrant. I'd offer to help with obtaining one, but I don't want any involvement by me to come under scrutiny down the road. But I can make a call and at least get the ball moving."

Ever the professional, he admired her ability to push past her own problems and work toward making sure any conviction obtained was beyond reproach. "Thanks. That's much appreciated. Let's head out."

Cassandra held up her phone. "What do you want me to do with this?"

"Leave it here, connected to the charger."

The attorney didn't hesitate to do as he requested. It was best that their unsub believed she was home...unless the asshole was already listening to every word they said, which was possible.

They were covered either way. An agent would be staying in Halcott's apartment in case the unsub appeared. And if he didn't, they'd have Cassandra safely tucked away.

Back in the living room, Cassandra picked up her suitcase. "I'm ready." She looked pale and shaken.

Dean studied her closely. "You okay?"

She lifted her chin. "Yep."

He had a feeling she was less concerned by the knowledge

that a murderer was targeting her than she was by her encounter with her ex. His gut told him whatever in the hell had transpired between Cassandra Halcott and Joseph Larson was only the tip of a much larger iceberg.

Something wasn't right with Larson. Though Dean wanted to tell himself the entire situation was none of his business, such a saying was the mantra of the ignorant.

Whether he liked it or not, he was part of this mess now.

He shot her a reassuring smile. "Let's get you to safety."

Cassandra strode to the door. "Sounds good. Just let me grab my keys."

19

The sun had set a couple hours ago, not that Amelia could tell the difference when every window in the safe house sported blackout curtains. Leaning against the granite counter beside the sink, she sipped tentatively from a fresh mug of steaming coffee she'd badly needed before filling Sherry in on everything they'd learned so far. The house might have been more suited to vampires than human beings, but at least the place had a well-stocked pantry.

As Sherry Cowen appeared in the arched doorway leading to the dining room, Amelia raised two fingers from her mug in a greeting. "Hey, how's Kate doing?"

Offering Amelia a slight smile, Sherry made her way to the cabinet above the coffee maker. "She's good, I guess. The psychiatrist mentioned that Kate needs to be permitted to do as many of her coping strategies as she can. Apparently, when anxious, Kate and her friend both cope by keeping busy with cooking or cleaning." Sherry nodded at the cabinet behind Amelia. "That's why the pantry is so well-stocked. Kate's asked to have some of her recipes provided. Said she can't really cook without them."

Amelia knew how that felt. She could barely cook *with* a recipe and was completely lost without the step-by-step guidance. "How is she otherwise?"

"I'd say having the psychiatrist here for that interview made a huge difference. I figured I'd give them a little space, in case Kate would feel more comfortable without law enforcement in her face."

"That's good. Did she happen to remember anything new?"

Sherry's expression told Amelia her answer before she said it. "No, nothing helpful to the case."

When Amelia had arrived at the safe house, she'd pulled Sherry aside to fill her in on what she'd learned about Evan and Kenny MacMillan. Kenny would certainly be a focus of their investigation going forward, but they couldn't get tunnel vision and assume he'd been working alone. That was why Kate's fuller account of that evening loomed large.

The clatter of the coffee pot returned Amelia's focus to the kitchen as Sherry poured herself a cup. "What're your thoughts on all of this? Kate's full statement seems to cast doubt on there being two suspects involved in the Denson murders."

"Yeah. It might explain why the video footage Dean got only showed one person entering the Osborne house." Amelia was glad to be dealing with a single suspect and not a pair or a group, but the idea that one man was capable of methodically murdering ten people was disconcerting. "Kate said it sounded like he was talking to someone, but she didn't hear the other person, and there was only one set of footsteps. It could be that the unsub was talking to himself, or maybe someone on an earpiece."

"Considering only a single weapon was used at each scene, I'd say that's a fair assessment. One gunman at each scene. Radio communication during something like that is risky, though. The frequency could've been intercepted, and if it was a phone call, they'd risk a digital trail." Sherry blew on her coffee, her expression thoughtful. "Plus, Evan MacMillan only had one living relative. His brother, Kenny. Other than Kenny, it doesn't seem like Evan was very well liked."

Amelia recalled some of the notes from the MacMillan trial. "No, it doesn't. He picked fights with all the wrong people as soon as he was in jail."

Though Evan had made plenty of enemies before he was locked up, the number wasn't enough to warrant protective custody. Once he'd entered prison, his list of foes had grown quickly—too quickly for the Bureau of Prisons to intervene.

Leaning against the counter, Sherry heaved a sigh. "Right. Evan MacMillan wasn't someone who had a horde of fans ready to avenge him. The only ally he'd have had was his brother. Of course, Kenny MacMillan could have hired someone to work with him."

Amelia knew better than most that hiring a hitman wasn't as simple as walking down to a convenience store for a pack of gum. "The problem with that is, in order to reach a competent contract killer—and from what we've seen in the Denson, Graham, and Osborne cases, Kenny's accomplice is most definitely competent—he'd need a criminal connection. Not just any connection, but a good connection."

Sherry nodded her understanding. "As in one of the cartels or another operation that generates a lot of money, right?"

"Right. Now, I'm not saying for sure that Evan's antics with the Iron Wolves would've blacklisted the MacMillan name in the world of organized crime, but it would have made it markedly more difficult for Kenny to get to the right people. Plus, the idea of a seasoned contract killer working with the person who hired them?" She weighed her hands. "Hitman don't like being recognized and tend to work alone."

Sherry drummed her fingers on her mug. "That makes sense."

"It all makes logical sense. But logic is about all we've got so far, at least until the DNA analysis on that hair comes back. We need to interview Kenny MacMillan."

"We've got enough to establish MacMillan as the prime suspect, but you're right. Our evidence against him is circumstantial. All we need for a warrant is probable cause, not proof beyond a reasonable doubt, but..."

"We're not quite there yet," Amelia finished for her. "But we're getting closer. Zane called Midwest Communications earlier and learned that MacMillan works for them, so that's another connection since Midwest was the logo on the van we saw outside the Osbornes' house. Zane also learned that Kenny had called his boss this morning, saying he had a family emergency and needed to take two weeks off."

Sherry pressed her lips together. "Interesting."

Amelia nodded. "Very. Even more interesting is that Kenny joined the military when he was eighteen, and his specialty was electronics and communications. That skillset fits with the killer's ability to easily disarm security systems."

"Any idea on MacMillan's current location?"

Amelia opened a box of blueberry muffins that had been tempting her since she first sat down. "No. Since that phone call to his boss earlier, no one has been able to get in touch with him, and both his work phone and personal cell appear to be powered off."

Sherry shook her head when Amelia offered her a muffin. "If he learned about the inquiry at his workplace, he probably ditched one or both."

Amelia had thought the same thing. "Yeah. That, or he

might have taken out the SIM cards in case he needed them later."

"What about his house?"

Amelia dunked a section of muffin into her coffee. "After securing Cassandra at the safe house, Palmer and Steelman stopped by his only known residence. He wasn't home, and his personal car was gone."

Kenny MacMillan was currently the FBI's prime suspect, and they were close to procuring a search warrant for his residence. An all-points bulletin was out for Kenny, advising officers throughout Cook County that the man was considered armed and extremely dangerous. In the event Kenny was responsible for the murder of Cyrus Osborne and all the others, the FBI wanted to ensure he was approached with caution.

Layton Redker had suggested that, if their man was Kenny MacMillan, then the victims indicated he was fixated on the courtroom. In Kenny's mind, his brother's demise had started with the guilty verdict. Though the circumstantial evidence strongly suggested Kenny was the killer, Amelia kept reminding herself there was still the possibility the killer was someone else.

A member of the Iron Wolves, perhaps, or the street gang Evan MacMillan had pissed off during his drug-dealing heyday. The Asphalt Knights weren't a big-time operation like the Leónes or the D'Amatos, but the street gang was known for their particularly brutal treatment of rivals. She wasn't sure why the Asphalt Knights would want to avenge Evan MacMillan, but stranger things had been known to happen. It didn't help the theory that street gangs typically didn't sexually assault men, let alone consort with someone who did.

For the time being, however, their main focus was to find Kenny MacMillan. One way or another, guilty or innocent, they had to interview Kenny to get the answers they needed.

Sherry stood and began to pace. "Speaking of Kenny, any update on where we're at with the warrant? I think being able to look at where he lives might help us determine if he had an accomplice or not."

Amelia finished chewing and swallowed before answering. "We're getting close. There's so much there. We just need one thing that's more than circumstantial, and it'll all fall in place. Palmer and Steelman are going through the crime scene photos again to see if there's anything we missed. They'll also go through the crowd that was gathered outside each scene to check if Kenny MacMillan was there. If he was there, or if they can find someone else who was present at both scenes, then I think we can get a judge to sign a warrant."

The fact that they were within spitting distance of the next huge step in the investigation made Amelia want to rip out her hair. To either confirm their suspicions about Kenny or eliminate him as a suspect, they needed more information. A sliver of information, a single missing puzzle piece.

"It's too bad Kate didn't get a look at his face or a tattoo. Something that'd give us an ID." Amelia was about to make a comment about how the silver lining to Kate not coming face-to-face with Kenny was that he didn't see her, but she stopped short. "She didn't see him, but she *heard* him."

Sherry's eyes popped open a little wider. "You're right. When Steelman and I were here to talk to her yesterday, she said she'd never forget his voice. Are you thinking what I'm thinking?"

"I am." Amelia set down her coffee and pulled her cell from a pocket. "And I know exactly where we can get a sample of Kenny's voice." She held up the phone for emphasis. "His voicemail. Palmer tried to call him when he didn't answer the door, and he said it went straight to voicemail. A personalized voicemail that included details to contact him at work."

Sherry smiled. "Great idea."

The bone-deep weariness from moments earlier was a thing of the past as a new wave of energy overtook Amelia. "All right. So, we get Kenny's voicemail, and then we get a few guys from the Bureau to read the same words and record them. Then we can do a voice lineup with Kate, and it'll be admissible in court."

Sherry snapped her fingers. "I'll let the D.A. assigned to the case know. That way, we make sure we cover all our bases."

As she dialed Zane's number, Amelia flashed Sherry a thumbs-up. "Let's do it. Let's get that damn warrant."

20

Zane flicked on the light switch in the hallway of Kenny MacMillan's apartment, blinking as his eyes adjusted to the bright bulb. Though faint, the scent of bleach lingered in the air, just as it had near the kitchen and the second bathroom.

Kenny was nowhere to be found, but he'd done some major cleaning before taking off.

Using Kate Denson's positive identification of Kenny's voice in a legally approved lineup, Zane and Dean had obtained a warrant to search Kenny's apartment. Along with two crime scene techs, they'd used the property manager's spare key to enter.

Zane silently cursed that they'd had to ask Kate Denson to listen to the voice of the man who killed her whole family. He hoped it hadn't further traumatized the young woman.

With as shifty as Kenny had been so far, and with as high-profile as his targets were, Zane had half-expected a series of booby traps in the man's apartment.

Much to his surprise, they'd found none.

The place was spotless. A crime scene cleaning service couldn't have scrubbed the place down better.

As Zane peered into the open doorway of the main bedroom, he was reminded of the model unit he'd walked through before signing the lease for his own place. Décor was minimal but coordinated.

Had Kenny MacMillan wanted to fool them into thinking they'd wandered into the wrong apartment? Because he'd damn near succeeded.

"What the hell?"

Dean Steelman's quiet exclamation snapped Zane's attention to where the agent stood a few feet behind him. "What?"

Steelman's gaze was fixed on a collage-style frame of four-by-six photos hanging at the start of the hall. A crease formed between his eyebrows as he gestured to the pictures. "Check this out."

A twinge of unease crawled down Zane's neck like an insect. As he moved toward the frame, Steelman stepped aside.

In the first photo, a teenage boy smiled awkwardly at the camera for what had to have been a school photo. While he resembled Kenny MacMillan, the blue hue of his irises indicated he was the older MacMillan brother, Evan. In the second picture...

"Wait." Zane glanced to Steelman and then back to the collage, the crawling sensation returning to his neck. "This is six of the same picture. Pictures of his brother. What the hell?"

Dean replied with a hapless shrug. "I don't know, man. It's weird as shit."

Turning on his heel, Zane noted the presence of a second collage on the opposite wall. Like the first, this one comprised six photo slots.

And like the first, each of those slots was filled with a

school photo of Evan MacMillan. "This," he shook an index finger at the pictures, "this isn't normal. This is some haunted house shit."

"I'm not going to disagree with that." Steelman held up his hands. "If there's a puzzle box or a weird looking cube in here anywhere, don't open it."

Zane chuckled at the *Hellraiser* reference, but the sound was more akin to a cough. He shouldn't have expected much different in the home of someone who'd murdered three families over the past month, but the bizarre collection of school photos gave him the creeps.

Can't wait to see what's in the bedroom.

As Steelman flagged down one of the forensic techs, Zane made his way to the shadowy doorway of the main bedroom. Holding his breath, he switched on the light.

A nightstand flanked either side of a neatly made bed, the faux driftwood matching the simple headboard. The beige walls were bare, but Zane noted an eight-by-ten photo beside the digital clock on one nightstand.

Another school picture. In this one, Evan's cheeks were darkened with stubble. Rather than the strained smile he'd worn in the other two, his jaw was set in a hardened expression. Zane hadn't smiled for most of his high school photos either, but he sure as hell hadn't worn a look that gave the impression he was ready to jump through the camera and throttle someone.

Kenny MacMillan looked at that mean glare before he fell asleep every night?

Ignoring Evan's intent stare, Zane gingerly pulled open the top drawer of the nightstand with his gloved hand. Aside from a blank notepad and a handful of pens, it was empty. Not that Zane had expected to find one of the murder weapons in such an obvious location. Regardless, a part of him was disappointed.

The bottom drawer contained socks, and the second nightstand was completely empty. How much of the apartment had Kenny cleared before he left? Or had he always lived such a minimalist lifestyle?

"Find anything?" Dean clicked his flashlight a couple times as he entered the room.

"Nothing. And that's what's weird. It's like he knew we were coming." Zane doubted anyone in their department, not even Joseph Larson, would help a lunatic like Kenny MacMillan. Which meant this man was methodical and calculating. He'd planned for this exact moment. The knowledge sent shards of ice through his veins.

Had Kenny MacMillan gone into his mission for vengeance expecting to die? God, he hoped not.

A mass murderer who was scared of death was enough of a threat, but a mass murderer who wasn't afraid to die?

They needed to find this guy.

As Steelman knelt to shine his light beneath the bed, Zane started for the bathroom. "With the place as clean as it is, where do you suppose we'll find DNA?"

Steelman snorted. "Not really sure. Sheets, maybe? Hey, Odgers! I've got a question for you."

Zane only half paid attention as the lead forensic tech entered the room.

When he switched on the light, the bathroom practically sparkled. Hand soap, a bottle of cologne, and an unburnt candle adorned the vanity, but there was no sign of a comb or toothbrush—items that would contain even the tiniest bit of DNA. That was all they needed.

Holding back a sigh, Zane opened the medicine cabinet. The top shelf held band-aids, antibiotic ointment, Q-tips, and a few other bathroom essentials. His hopes had begun to fall when he caught sight of the first prescription bottle on the second shelf.

Curiosity piqued, he pulled out the orange container. Pills rattled as he turned the bottle to read the label.

"Clozapine." The medication was vaguely familiar, but he couldn't recall what exactly it did. Pressing his lips together, he stepped back into the doorway. "Hey, do either of you know what clozapine is prescribed for?"

Like a meerkat, Dean Steelman rose from where he'd been crouched behind the bed. "Clozapine? That's a pretty powerful antipsychotic if I remember right. This ain't the first time I've run into it, I know that."

The shutter of Norman's camera clicked. "Yeah. Typically prescribed for schizophrenia. It's a second-generation antipsychotic, meaning it has fewer side effects than the old antipsychotics. But it's still got some nasty side effects. Long-term users can experience permanent muscle tics, almost like Parkinson's."

"Shit." Zane checked the label closer. "These pills have been expired for more than six months, and this thing's almost full. They're prescribed to Kenny, and the script was filled back in...Jesus, a year ago. Evan MacMillan went to trial thirteen months ago."

"Shit." Steelman's face darkened. "I don't think that's a coincidence. Who prescribed it?"

"Dr. Tom Ferguson."

"You think it's too late to get ahold of the doctor? It's only seven-thirty."

Zane set the bottle on the vanity, snapped off one glove, and pulled out his phone. "Probably. What doctor works this late? Let's see if we can reach him. It'd be nice to speak to someone who might provide a little more insight about how this guy operates. I know the doctor can't violate HIPAA, but maybe we can get more of an idea of his general demeanor."

Steelman stepped to the side as Norman Odgers pulled

back the gray and green comforter. "Yeah. That's true. Any information is good information at this point."

Zane typed "Tom Ferguson, Chicago Psychiatrist" into a search bar. As the results populated, he did a double take. "What the hell? Really?"

Steelman headed his way. "What?"

Raising his cell like Steelman could read the screen, Zane sighed. "Tom Ferguson was all over local headlines six months ago for selling fraudulent prescriptions."

Steelman snorted. "Sounds like a good dude."

"There's a number listed for his practice. I can't imagine he kept his license, though."

"It's worth a shot, I guess."

"Yeah. True." Zane punched in the number and raised the phone to his ear. The soft buzz of a dial tone started, and Zane let his gaze drift back to the queen-sized bed, fully expecting to receive the obnoxious notification that he'd received a disconnected line.

"Jonesy's Pizza Palace, Justine speaking. How can I help you?"

As the young woman chirped out the greeting, Zane bit his tongue to keep himself from swearing. "Hi, Justine. Could I ask how long this number has belonged to Jonesy's Pizza Palace? I understand it used to belong to a Dr. Tom Ferguson."

Justine hesitated before responding. "The psychiatrist? Yeah, we still get calls for him sometimes. This Pizza Palace location has only been open for three months, and this is a mobile number. We assume the carrier recycled the digits."

"Yeah, it must be. All right. Thanks, Justine. Have a good night."

"You're welcome, and you too."

Swiping the screen to end the call, he let out the sigh he'd been holding back for half the day. Nothing in this damn investigation was straightforward. "The number for Dr. Ferguson's office is now the number for Jonesy's Pizza Palace. Suffice it to say, I don't think the good doctor is practicing anymore. I'll read through some more of these articles and see if I can figure out what happened to him."

"Good plan." Dean lifted a pillow, shaking his head slightly. "These sheets look clean. Like he washed them before he left."

"Sure does." Norman Odgers studied the bed before he turned to Zane. "Anything promising in there? Toothbrush, used towel, anything?"

"Nothing. Towel racks are empty. The whole room smells like bleach, and it's as clean as the rest of this damn place."

Norman readjusted the camera around his neck. "For what it's worth, Agents, there's no way in hell someone could scrub every piece of themselves from somewhere they've lived for any period of time longer than a day or two. This guy did his damnedest, I'll give him that, but we'll find something. In the drains, a hair stuck in the baseboard of the bathroom. *Something.*"

Zane didn't doubt the forensic tech. Records indicated Kenny had called this place home for more than two years. One way or another, they'd find the DNA evidence they needed.

But what then? What did a DNA analysis grant them at this point?

Alleles wouldn't tell them where Kenny had gone, or how he planned to lash out at his next victim. The information would be critical when it came time for trial, but they had to *get* to the trial first. Preferably without any more bodies.

Easier said than done.

As confident as he was that Kenny's next intended victim was Cassandra, Zane couldn't say how MacMillan would react when he realized he couldn't get to the prosecutor.

Would he find a different target?

Zane didn't want to find out. They needed to get to Kenny MacMillan before he could make his next move.

"BINGO. You can run, you traitorous bitch, but you can't hide."

Not from me.

The boards beneath the old RV's only bed creaked as I crawled beneath the heavy blankets. After growing accustomed to the constant hustle and bustle of Chicago, the silence of the campground outside the city was deafening.

I'd monitored the lawyer's location until the GPS tracker had stopped moving. It didn't matter if the feebs took away her keys with the tracker inside once they arrived at their destination. All I needed was her location, and I had that now. A quick search through satellite imagery online had revealed she was in a residential neighborhood, as I'd anticipated. I'd made my best effort to cover my tracks, but I was smart enough not to underestimate the Federal Bureau of Investigation.

They'd taken her to a safe house, but I wasn't worried about that. Unlike in the movies, typical safe houses weren't made of steel, and they didn't hold a horde of automatic weapons.

Safe houses were supposed to blend in, so no bars on the windows or razor wire over fences. And once a safe house had been compromised, the Feds bailed. Why fancy up a place they might not have access to for very long?

After locating the blueprints for the house, I studied them closely. A basement with an odd little attached building much too small for a storage shed or garage. Three bedrooms and two baths. Very unassuming. Very blendable. Very safe.

Not for long.

Now, I just needed to plan. I had a target on my back and needed to be careful so that my own target didn't get away.

In their eyes, I'd killed one of them. I figured they'd find the link between Anna Denson and Cyrus Osborne, and they hadn't let me down. My home security system—a basic motion sensor setup—had alerted me to intruders. I could only assume, based on the short video my surveillance camera had captured, that my visitors were law enforcement agents sent to execute a warrant.

They wouldn't find anything. Not without a fair amount of elbow grease and a sprinkle of creativity. I'd cleaned the apartment from top to bottom the night before I'd taken out Anna Denson, and I'd kept up with the obsessive cleaning since then.

I was confident I hadn't left behind DNA at any of the crime scenes since I'd taken the precaution of putting on a rubber before I had my fun. Discovering a hair or two of mine at my apartment wouldn't be the end of the world. They'd have nothing from the crime scenes to use for a comparison.

Even if they did…

I shifted to lay on my side. I had a singular purpose now, and even the FBI wouldn't stop me. Between the squeaky-clean apartment and my secret RV getaway, I'd bought myself plenty of time to formulate a plan that would bring me face-to-face with that bitch lawyer.

The lawyer who'd taken away my only remaining family. That woman had led the charge to lock up my brother without granting him any form of protection against the enemies he'd made in the drug trade.

For god's sake, Evan had killed a man in *self-defense*.

The hotshot Assistant U.S. Attorney hadn't even stopped to consider the possibility. Instead, she'd used some legal hogwash called the "felony murder rule" to charge my brother with life in prison with no possibility for parole.

I'd educated myself on the so-called felony murder rule and had learned any killing committed while a person was in the act of a felony could be charged as first-degree murder. It sounded like a law created by the sissy academic elites my father had hated so much. Back when I was a kid, I hadn't understood his dislike for higher education, but now I got it.

That prissy redhead didn't need to get it, though. All she'd needed to do was push for Evan to be sent to protective custody—to be kept separate from the general population. If she'd done her job, he wouldn't have had to turn to those bikers for protection, and he never would have...

Well, he wouldn't be dead. If one of those people—Carla Graham, Anna Denson, Cyrus Osborne, or Ms. Lead Prosecutor Cassandra Halcott—had made the recommendation for protective custody, my brother would be alive.

If Evan had been put in protective custody instead of thrown to the wolves, his lawyer could have fought for a new trial. Every inmate sentenced to life without parole was automatically granted one appeal.

Who knew what an appeal would have brought? It could have been a chance for Evan's defense to prove he deserved a new trial. We could have proven Evan had acted in self-defense. I was sure of it.

In the end, the opportunity had been stolen. Stolen first by Cassandra Halcott and Cyrus Osborne for pursuing the trial in the first place, then by Carla Graham for recommending life without parole, and Anna Denson for conceding to the suggestion.

Three of the four main offenders were dead now, and I'd made sure their passing wasn't easy or painless. The wives had all watched, bound and helpless, as I'd dominated their beloved husbands. I'd led them to believe I'd spare their children if only they remained quiet and heeded my instructions, but in the moments before their death, I'd let them know the kids had been dead the whole time.

Remembering my time with Cyrus was especially pleasing. He'd stripped me of all I had when he sent Evan to prison. With every fiber of my being, I'd needed to strip what mattered to Cyrus from him. First his daughter. Then his manhood. And his wife. Finally, only after he knew of his family's demise and had satiated my desires, only then could I end him.

Reliving each detail over again in the dark, quiet sanctuary of the RV imparted on me a sense of calm I hadn't expected.

My experiences with the Grahams, Densons, and Osbornes were the high points of my twenty-seven years of life. If I'd known what a sense of control such actions would bring me, I'd have started earlier.

Perhaps with my father.

I was used to my brain being a constant warzone. In my early twenties, the army had even discharged me for my peculiarity. I'd started therapy, taken medication, and had played the role of a respectable citizen. All the while, I'd been subconsciously aware of a dam in the back of my head that was approaching its limit.

While Evan was off getting high and selling drugs, I was left by myself. I made a couple friends, but none of them got it. They weren't schizophrenics trying to make their way in a world that didn't want them. They didn't know. How could they?

No one cared. Not even my so-called therapist. I wasn't the least bit surprised to learn of Dr. Ferguson's little side business. In every session with the man, I'd been able to tell he wasn't there to help people, especially *me*. It was clear from his tailored three-piece suit, his expensive Swiss watch, and his four-thousand-dollar gator-skin shoes what motivated the man.

"That's what dad always said, wasn't it?" Evan chuckled. "All those stuck-up elites are the same. They all want money, and that's it. But, hell, who can blame them? Money's what makes the world go round, isn't it, little bro?"

"Fuck off. You're not real." I rolled onto my stomach and pulled the dusty blankets over my head.

"Ain't I, though?" Evan's tone was mocking, laden with derision. No different from when he'd been flesh and blood. "I'm still alive in your head, Kenny. You're doing all this for me, aren't you? The lawyer...what're you going to do with her? Chicks aren't even your type, are they? How're you going to take control of her when you can't even get it up in the first place?"

"Shut up," I hissed, the words muffled by the pillow. "I'll figure it out. There are plenty of ways to dominate someone and make them suffer without using your cock."

Evan slapped his leg with a cackle. "I'm sure there'll be a guy at the safe house you can have your fun with. Some of those FBI agents are lookers, you know? That redheaded lawyer's boyfriend sure is a snack. Personally, I like 'em a little on the younger side, but you know that, don't you?"

Anger prickled the hairs along the back of my neck, but I grated my teeth to keep from spitting a rebuttal.

Evan wasn't here. I'd ditched my meds to allow the full use of my brain, as the pills had stifled me. The decision to avenge my brother had been made before I'd stopped taking clozapine. This wasn't a half-cocked plan cooked up by a guy who'd gone nuts after becoming unmedicated.

"You know, Kenny." Evan heaved a sigh. "You say you're doing all this for me, but I don't know how much of that I buy anymore. You're doing this because you like it, aren't you? You little fucking psychopath."

I squeezed my eyes closed and covered my ears. "You're dead, Evan. Shut up."

He wasn't completely wrong, but he also wasn't entirely correct. Evan *had* been the only family I'd had left. We'd lost touch for a time during my early twenties but reconnected when he'd moved to Chicago.

Evan got it. Evan knew what I'd lived through. He'd always been there for me, and I wouldn't let those who'd taken him go unpunished.

At the same time, I *did* enjoy what I was doing. And if I died doing what I loved, wasn't that most people's goal in life anyway?

There was nothing left for me here with Evan gone. Nothing aside from revenge and the sweet, sweet suffering of those who'd wronged us.

21

Stifling a yawn, Amelia stretched both arms above her head until her lower back popped. Aside from the muffled drone of the furnace, the living room of Cassandra Halcott's safe house was quiet. Amelia was seated in the corner of a small sectional, and Cassandra had stretched out in a recliner beside the couch. The lawyer's nose was still buried in a Stephen King novel that was approximately the same size as an unabridged dictionary.

Not long after they'd settled in, Cassandra had complained about the safe house's collection of books. Amelia had thought at first that the woman was being dramatic or high maintenance, but then she'd taken a peek at the shelves.

With nothing but stuffy old "classics" reminiscent of a freshman English class, Amelia had immediately understood Cassandra's complaint. Not a single novel on that shelf had been written after the sixties, leaving Amelia convinced the Bureau had truly stocked the safe house's bookshelf with secondhand paperbacks donated by a retiring English teacher.

Amelia had meant to get back into the habit of reading, so she'd taken the opportunity to swing by a half-priced bookstore to shore up their supply. She'd been pleasantly surprised to learn she and Cassandra shared similar preferences in books.

"Horror, horror, and more horror" had been Cassandra's exact words. The more gruesome and colorful, the better. She told Amelia she'd read her fair share of stuffy words during law school.

Maybe being concerned with how to spend their free time might sound inane to an outsider, but there was no telling when they'd find Kenny MacMillan. The search was on, but two days had passed with no sign of the guy. Amelia didn't intend to leave the books behind when they left—whenever the hell that would be—so the next person to inhabit the house would be on their own.

Glancing from her empty plate on the coffee table to the pizza boxes set out along the breakfast bar at the other end of the room, Amelia wondered if the time had come to help herself to seconds. No, not seconds. Thirds. She'd picked up dinner for the small crew at Cassandra Halcott's safe house, but she'd realized upon retrieving it that she'd gone a bit overboard.

It was New Year's Eve, and the only people *in* the house were Amelia, Cassandra, and Dean Steelman. Zane was stationed with Kate Denson, and Sherry had been fortunate enough to get the night off to be with her husband.

A disguised FBI surveillance van was set up across the street from their unassuming two-story residence to monitor traffic coming and going from the neighborhood.

Three large pizzas for three people? Yeah, it was a bit excessive, but Amelia would do her part to ensure there were minimal leftovers. Over the two days, she had to have gained a few pounds, at least. When there was nothing else for her to do at the safe house, she snacked.

Fortunately, the finished basement sported free weights and a couple pieces of gym equipment. Relocating people whose lives were in danger was only part of the battle to keep them out of harm's way. Once someone was in the safe house, they had to maintain security.

Boredom was the bane of the vigilant, and there were a finite number of tasks for the agents guarding the house to attend. Though Amelia had used much of her free time to go through the MacMillan case—both the current *and* former MacMillan cases—they'd reached a point where not much else could be done in the investigation.

Analysis on the DNA found at the scene of the Denson murders had come in the day before, confirming what all the agents working the case had suspected. The foreign hair taken from Stephen Denson's body belonged to Kenny MacMillan.

Even if the CSU hadn't managed to pull a DNA sample from the drain of Kenny MacMillan's sink, his deceased brother, Evan, was already in the national database. The mitochondrial DNA match alone would have bolstered their theory beyond a reasonable doubt.

Amelia uncrossed her legs and returned her focus to the empty plate. No, she didn't need any more pizza. And if she started up another game of Minesweeper on her laptop, she'd fall asleep. Though she was permitted to travel outside the safe house and even to return home to tend to her needy cat, Amelia preferred to minimize her departures. The more she drove back and forth between here and her apartment, the more likely she was to pique someone's curiosity. For the most part, the safe house had become her and Dean Steelman's second home.

When spring rolls around, maybe we can plant a garden.

Steelman likes pickles. Maybe we can grow cucumbers and make our own pickles. We can call them...Safe House Pickles. No, that's too boring and predictable. Maybe just Safe Pickles? No, still too bland. I'll have to come up with something better before I pitch the idea to him.

She rubbed her eyes and held back a sigh. There was work to be done that didn't involve the MacMillan case, but Amelia wasn't comfortable digging into Joseph Larson or Brian Kolthoff while she was at the safe house. The internet connection was protected by a number of FBI-sanctioned firewalls, but it still didn't *feel* secure enough. Joseph had been placed on the task force created by SAC Keaton to respond to any anonymous tips they received regarding Kenny MacMillan.

To Amelia, the decision to involve Joseph in an investigation centered so heavily around Cassandra, his *ex*-girlfriend, was bizarre. But then, SAC Keaton wasn't even aware of the relationship the two had shared. Following up on tips submitted online was often tedious and unrewarding, and the position gave Joseph a way in. Though Amelia had to admit she was amused that Joseph would be toiling away at the task.

He'd have been able to find us anyway. He's a piece of shit, but he's still an FBI agent.

An FBI agent who'd been friends with Brian Kolthoff for god knew how many years.

Which reminded her, she'd been meaning to ask Cassandra for her take on the charges the U.S. Attorney's office had tried and failed to press against The Shark. Cassandra and Amelia might not have started out on the best terms during the Ben Storey case, but the woman's sass and sarcasm had grown on Amelia since they'd been stuck in a house together. They weren't quite friends, but they had a sense of...comradery.

Amelia glanced to the hallway leading to the first floor's study and its closed door. The room had been converted into a sort of surveillance headquarters for the entire house. Each camera fed into its own monitor, and the internet VPN connection kept them up to date with the field office.

A half hour earlier, Dean Steelman had piled pizza slices onto a plate before disappearing into the office for his shift to watch the cameras. Amelia wasn't sure how wise it was to eat pizza in a room full of sophisticated electronic monitoring hardware, but Agent Steelman was a grown man and a tenured FBI agent. She'd have to trust that he could eat without smearing pizza grease all over the sensitive equipment.

Satisfied the door to the study remained closed, Amelia shifted in her seat to face Cassandra. "This is kinda out of nowhere, but I wanted to ask you about something."

The lawyer marked her place in the Stephen King novel with an index finger, taking off her black-rimmed glasses with the other hand. "All right. Shoot."

Amelia lowered her voice to a conspiratorial murmur. "You remember Brian Kolthoff?"

Cassandra's expression soured. "Of course. That rich creep didn't even wind up paying a fine, much less serving a prison sentence. That case wasn't mine, but I helped Cyrus with it. We both wanted to watch that guy go down in flames, but," she leaned back in her chair and shrugged, "you know how it goes with guys like him."

"You could say that. Do you think he's got any friends in the Bureau? Not in Chicago, necessarily, but…in general."

Though Amelia had worried she'd come across like a crackpot when she mentioned the possibility of Kolthoff being entwined with the FBI, Cassandra didn't bat an eye. "I wouldn't doubt it. He's a D.C. lobbyist. Those bastards always have their hands in every cookie jar they can find."

She was right. Kolthoff's network of friends in high places was part of what made him so dangerous. "Yeah, I was just wondering what your take on that whole thing was. I'm assuming the U.S. Attorney's office didn't have any plans to charge him with other offenses? Or to revisit anything in the future?"

Shaking her head, Cassandra set her book on the end table at her side. "No. Cyrus said he couldn't make anything stick. Without some kind of testimony against him, it was all just speculation."

Amelia had suspected as much. She wouldn't be surprised if Kolthoff also had a friend in the U.S. Attorney's office. "Right. That makes sense."

Cassandra lifted an eyebrow. "Why? Do you think you might have something on him?"

"I wish." Amelia lifted her hair off her neck and kneaded the tense muscles with her fingers. "No, nothing like that. It's just, that case still bugs me. That creep almost bought a sixteen-year-old sex slave, and he just walked off into the sunset like nothing even happened."

"I don't think it ever sat well with Cyrus, either. His daughter, Julie, is..." Cassandra's face paled, and she pushed a strand of stray hair behind her ear. "Julie *was* about the same age as Leila, and his wife was a child psychiatrist." She looked down at her hands and sighed. "If anything new ever cropped up about Brian Kolthoff, I'd be more than happy to put his balls in a vice."

Amelia chuckled. For a lawyer, Cassandra sure didn't mince words. "Legally, right?"

She shrugged. "Either way. I'd be happy to help."

As the two of them shared a laugh, the air of foreboding in the safe house seemed to thin. Once they'd dealt with Kenny MacMillan and assured Cassandra and Kate's safety, perhaps Amelia could enlist the lawyer's help when the time came to report Joseph. The more allies she had, the better off she'd be. Especially if she wanted any *criminal* charges against Joseph to stick. Obstruction of justice for his hidden relationship with Kolthoff during the Leila Jackson case would be a nice start.

Boom!

Boom! Boom! Boom!

Cassandra jumped out of her chair and Amelia was right behind her when explosions almost rattled the windows. Amelia had Cassandra pressed into a corner, gun pointed at the door before she realized what was making the sounds.

Fireworks.

Dammit.

With a soft chuckle, Amelia blew out a breath and stepped over to the window. Sure enough, a multitude of colors were lighting up the night sky.

"Must be midnight."

Cassandra's hand was pressed over her heart. "Happy New Year. Geesh. That nearly gave me a heart attack."

Amelia's heart had taken quite the licking too. "How much did that neighbor spend on fireworks, anyway?"

Cassandra moved to stand next to her. "Wow. A bunch."

A heart exploded into the sky, followed by a smiley face.

The click of a door captured Amelia's attention, and gun still in hand, she turned just as Dean Steelman appeared in the hallway across the living room.

Partway through opening her mouth to make a comment about Dean's pizza consumption, Amelia noticed the grave expression on the agent's face. The fleeting twinges of good humor turned to ice in her veins as she took a step his way.

Steelman's sapphire eyes flicked from Amelia to Cassandra as he beckoned them forward. "Something's going on. Come take a look. Both of you. I think we're under attack."

Amelia swore. They needed to act fast so their enemy didn't get the upper hand. Had the fireworks been a distraction? A cover for any noise?

Cassandra fell in behind Amelia as she hurried across the living room. Wordlessly, Steelman ducked back into the dim office, with Amelia and Cassandra right on his heels.

Ten monitors in total were mounted to the wall, with an additional two adorning an L-shaped computer desk. Each wall-mounted screen was linked to a different security camera around the property. One for the interior of the garage, another for the exterior. Another above the front door to capture the porch and the street in front of the house, then a fourth on the side of the house, and so on.

Though recordings inside were minimal in order to preserve the privacy of the occupants, just about every square inch of the exterior was covered.

As soon as Amelia stepped into the office, she knew what had piqued Dean's suspicion. Rather than provide a clear picture of the exterior of the safe house, every monitor flickered with grayscale static, like someone had turned a television to the wrong channel.

Adrenaline burned its way through Amelia's veins. "When did they get staticky like this?"

Steelman's gaze was locked on the monitors. "A minute or two after the fireworks started. I did some quick troubleshooting and checked to make sure the cables were secure to make sure I wasn't being an idiot. I even swapped one out for a new HDMI cable, but it didn't make a difference. The screens are just fuzz."

"Shit." The back of Amelia's neck tingled the same way it did when she was certain she was being followed. She glanced over her shoulder, half-expecting there to be a hulking, masked man standing in the middle of the living room.

When there was nothing, her unease deepened. Finding nothing there was almost worse than finding something.

She shook off the paranoia, pulled the door closed, and turned back to Dean and Cassandra.

Steelman's jaw tightened. "I've been listening to the scanner on and off for most of the night. It's been a weird one, and honestly." He raked a hand through his hair. "The scanner traffic is probably because it's New Year's Eve. But this..." His hand swept past the monitors. "I tried to contact the surveillance van, and they didn't answer. This is bad, ladies, and we need to take action quickly."

Amelia hadn't witnessed Steelman this tense since the night they'd raided Dan Gifford's cabin. The man's stiff posture and jerky eye movements weren't doing any favors for Amelia's rampant paranoia.

"There was no response from Phobos and Deimos? None at all?" They'd given the code names to the agents monitoring the neighborhood because, as the titles suggested, the duo orbited the safe house like the two dwarf moons that orbited Mars. Their names were Grady Navarro and Claudine Knapp, though Amelia wasn't sure who was Phobos and who was Deimos.

"No. Nothing." With each passing second, the anxiety in the room elevated another notch.

"Guys." Cassandra's voice was hushed, but the single word drew Amelia's attention as if the woman had shouted. The glow of the burner cell they'd given her glinted off the lenses of her glasses, lending her the eerie, enigmatic vibe of a crime show protagonist. "Check your phones. I don't have any service."

Steelman dug in his pocket. "You've got to be kidding me..."

Amelia held her breath as she waited for her phone to register her face. Just as Cassandra had said, an icon at the top of the screen advised Amelia that a service signal couldn't be found. "She's right. I had service the last time I checked my phone. Full bars, zero fluctuation."

"What the hell is going on?" Steelman pulled his gun from its holster. "There's no way these things aren't connected."

He was right. Amelia wasn't a tech expert, but she knew even the best technology was vulnerable to a hack, even in a safe house. Blood pounded in her ears as she racked her brain.

"Someone has to be jamming the radio and cell signals." To Amelia's surprise, the statement came from Cassandra, not Dean. The woman looked as if she'd just spotted a ghost, but her shoulders were squared, her head held high. "And whatever they're using could even be working on the cameras. Not the hardware necessarily, but their wireless connection to the monitors."

Steelman was on his feet in an instant. "We're wasting time debating the cause and let's not even start with wondering how we were found. Let's prepare for a breach of the safe house. We can figure out the culprit later. Right now, we need to—"

All at once, every screen in the room went dark, along with the dim floor lamp in the corner next to the doorway. The hum of the furnace, the even fainter sound of the refrigerator's motor, the whir of the fans spinning to cool the processor of the computer. Every source of white noise was abruptly replaced with silence.

If they weren't already sure there was trouble on the horizon, they damn well knew it now.

"He cut the power." Amelia was certain Dean and Cassandra had noticed, but she was compelled to state the obvious. "Why the hell hasn't the backup generator fired up? Shouldn't it kick in right away?"

"I thought so." Dean's voice was barely above a whisper. A

white glow lit up his face, followed by the bright LED light on the front of his phone.

Amelia took the cue and navigated to her smartphone's flashlight app, as did Cassandra. "We need to find real flashlights."

"I've got them." He picked his way over to the computer desk, knelt, and pulled open the bottom drawer. After killing the light on his phone, he passed a flashlight to both women.

The cell phone lights got the job done, but Amelia always felt more at ease when she had a real flashlight in her hands, something with some heft to it to act as a weapon if necessary.

"There's tactical gear in this closet, right?" Amelia shone the beam of her light on a closed door beside the desk.

"Right." Steelman straightened to his full height.

Pushing past the surge of adrenaline threatening to send jitters to her hands, Amelia pried open the closet. She'd have been grateful for a cache of high-powered rifles to go with the bullet suppression gear, but there was a good reason they didn't keep such firepower within reach.

Easily accessible weapons were a double-edged sword. If *they* could pull an M4 carbine from the coat closet, then so could an intruder. Aside from the service weapons carried by agents on duty at the safe house, other firearms were locked in a secure safe.

Amelia pulled out a Kevlar vest and passed it to Cassandra before pulling out two more for herself and Dean. "Put this on. We've got no idea what we're dealing with. It could just be some weird electromagnetic pulse, or a raccoon could've knocked over a trash can and started a chain reaction that left us without power or cell signals."

Cassandra shrugged back into her hooded sweatshirt, zipping up the front until the Kevlar was no longer visible. "A raccoon doing all this would make for one hell of a story. We could probably get a pretty successful YouTube series out of it, honestly."

Amelia wanted to laugh, but her sense of hyper-awareness wouldn't let her. Humor was important for morale and for avoiding blind panic. Keeping a level head was imperative. "We need to move. Just because we haven't heard anything break doesn't mean the intruder hasn't found a way into the house. This room only has one exit, and we're sitting ducks in here if they find us."

"Shit." Dean was standing in front of the closet that housed additional weapons. He stabbed a finger at the keypad attached to the wall.

Amelia groaned. "The keypad runs on electricity."

Face as hard as stone, Dean kicked the door. "Yep." He checked his only weapon. "We need that damn generator to turn on. I don't know when the thing was last serviced, but something's very wrong. Or...I don't know. I'm not a fucking electrician."

"My dad was an electrician." Cassandra's voice was still hushed, but the pallor on her cheeks was less noticeable. She adapted quickly. "We had a generator outside our house. I only ever remember us using it two or three times during thunderstorms, but my dad showed me a little bit about how it worked. I'm assuming the generator for this place has an automatic transfer."

The agents in charge of the safe house when it was unoccupied—Phobos and Deimos, who were presumably still in the surveillance van but not responding to calls—had shown off the generator during the rundown of the house's security features. Since they were in an FBI safe house, extra precautions needed to be taken to keep it from being tampered with.

To solve the issue, the Bureau had built a mini room outside around the unit. The walls and floor were concrete, and tiny openings were strategically placed in the wall to disperse harmful fumes.

Aside from explaining the precautions taken to protect the generator and offering assurances that it would automatically kick in if they lost power, Amelia couldn't remember many specifics. "I think it does. The other agents didn't say those exact words, but they said it'd start on its own if the power grid failed."

"Yeah, exactly." Cassandra shifted her flashlight from one hand to the other. "If the *grid* goes down, it'll turn on automatically. The automatic transfer is only as smart as its design. It's built to detect an outage from the utility, not a local power failure."

Understanding dawned on Amelia. "So, it *is* someone cutting the power to the house, and not a freak outage for the whole neighborhood." Her muscles tensed involuntarily. "We need to move…now."

Steelman snatched his coat off the back of an office chair. "We should split up. This reeks of an attack, and we're sitting ducks right now. Unfortunately, by cutting off the power from the generator—or whatever the hell has happened—the safe room can't be accessed. The damn door panel needs power to key in the code. It's worthless right now."

Amelia was stunned. "There isn't battery backup?"

"No. The generator was the battery backup." Dean rubbed his hand through his hair and looked each woman in the eye. "It doesn't make sense to leave Cassandra here when she's the target. I'll head outside with her and head to the surveillance van. We don't know the range on the signal jammer, so their comms could be intact. If Phobos and Deimos are…incapacitated, I'll have Cassandra head to the nearest police station and wait there for the all-clear."

"Okay. I'll provide cover until you're safely away. Once you're clear, I'll sweep the house and see if we've been breached." Unease swirled beneath Amelia's mental calm like a prehistoric beast swimming in the ocean depths. She knew the anxiety was there, but she'd become adept at ignoring its presence and pushing forward when the stakes were highest.

Dean shoved a finger into her face. "Negative. Wait for backup."

He was right, but...

Amelia racked the slide on her Glock nine-mil, offering Dean Steelman a stalwart nod. "All right. Let's get this done."

Though part of Amelia was reluctant to split away from Agent Steelman, they weren't in a horror film. They were in the real world, and they were dealing with a real human being, not a ghost. And Amelia reminded herself, they were both highly trained agents with the Federal Bureau of Investigations. The pain they'd endured at Quantico hadn't been for nothing.

If Cassandra wasn't with them and in need of protection, it would have been smarter for Amelia and Dean to stick together. But her safety came first. It was part of the duty Amelia had signed up for. She'd put herself between a bullet and the person she protected every time.

Steelman and Cassandra would make their way to Phobos and Deimos, and with Amelia searching the house, they'd cover their bases more quickly. And if one of them were caught...well, at least the other one would hopefully still be safe.

Unless Kenny MacMillan *did* have an accomplice.

Shaking off the thought, Amelia stepped out into the hall. The door to the basement was almost directly across from the entrance to the office. Although this was no horror movie, she planned to save her search of the basement for last. Walking down the open-backed stairs would make her a target from any angle.

Cursing the fact that no night-vision goggles had been

stocked with the Kevlar vests, Amelia began her journey through the safe house. In the pitch-dark, with every blackout curtain drawn and zero sources of illumination, she might as well have been in a cave. She knew better than to utilize the flashlight Dean had handed her. Turning that on would be like painting a target on her chest.

As quietly as she could, she opened the front door, and slipped onto the porch, watching for any sign of movement. Other than the fireworks still lighting up the sky, she spotted nothing else.

"Clear," she whispered.

Dean turned on his light but cupped the beam in his hand, allowing just enough illumination to guide their way. As he strode across the foyer with Cassandra closely behind, Amelia watched and waited. She wasn't sure what she expected to happen, but she knew she had to expect *something*.

Once Steelman and Cassandra had slipped from the porch and had disappeared into the dark, Amelia went back inside and turned her attention to the living room. Without the need to protect the prosecutor, Amelia's attention could be laser-focused on the task at hand.

Come out, come out, wherever you are. Yikes. She did not need to think like that.

She wasn't in a movie. Robert DeNiro wasn't stalking her seeking his revenge. No one had vocalized the sentiment, but Amelia knew the only person who'd risk his life breaking into this particular safe house was Kenny MacMillan.

He wasn't a ghost or a werewolf or a character in a Martin Scorsese thriller.

Kenny was real.

22

Amelia waited until her eyes had become accustomed to the dark before assessing the situation. She recalled that the sliding glass door was sealed shut, rendering it unusable and that its glass could withstand a bullet. That left the garage door, which was the most likely point of entry. Those locks weren't easy to pick, and he'd have to go through two of them. One to get into the garage, and another to get into the house. Of course, this was the same man who'd picked the locks to several secure homes with high-end alarm systems and went virtually undetected.

Great.

After searching the garage and its doors and locks, the rest of the home had turned up nothing. There had been no sounds of breaking glass, although she doubted anyone could bust through the reinforced glass block windows in the basement...certainly not without creating a lot of noise.

Wait for backup.

She couldn't, though. If Kenny MacMillan was indeed down there, she needed to take him down before he realized Cassandra had escaped.

Amelia inhaled as she finally reached the basement door. Each movement measured and diligent, as if the creak of a hinge would immediately summon the intruder, she pushed open the door.

A rush of cool air wafted past her as she took the first step. Mirrors were strategically placed on the bottom landing so that the entire downstairs could be visualized from the safety of the stairwell. It was too dark for Amelia to use them, though. Dammit.

With a quick glance around as much of the basement that fell into her view, she tightened her grip on her service weapon. She'd have preferred searching with the aid of the nonexistent night vision goggles. Knowing the use of a flash-light would telegraph her location to an intruder, Amelia had no choice but to venture blindly into the dank darkness of the basement.

All of Amelia's senses were on full alert for the slightest hint she was not alone. But the only sounds were those of her own breathing and her heartbeat thundering in her ears. There were no unusual smells. Only the slight mustiness from the concrete walls mingled with a hint of perspiration. She wasn't sure if that was her own sweat or from Steelman's earlier workout on the exercise equipment tucked in one corner.

With her eyes adjusted to the darkness, Amelia stepped onto the carpeted floor. She swung her service revolver toward the workout equipment on her right, noting the shelved free weights, the bench press, and the unadorned bench were all as Dean had left them.

After a quick examination of the visible part of the base-ment, Amelia moved to inspect the bathroom and closed storage area.

With her service weapon leading the way, Amelia stepped into the doorway of the storage room and quickly checked each corner. Corners were always the first area she checked —a small detail that, if overlooked, could spell disaster to even the most experienced soldiers.

There was only crisp, clean concrete. Not even a spiderweb was revealed, though the low light may have concealed those. That was probably a good thing. She already had imaginary spiders crawling down her neck. She didn't need to add the real kind.

Before Amelia could further explore the storage room, a tiny creak caused her to whirl. A door opened from the wall, and she registered a shadowy figure stepping out.

No…two shadowy figures. He had an accomplice after all?

But the second person was much smaller and seemed to be struggling in his arms.

Cassandra?

Fire burned through Amelia's eyes when a light clicked on and was shone directly into her face. She almost dropped her weapon in her haste to shield her dilated eyes from the burning beam.

"Drop your weapon or I'll kill him!"

Him?

Kenny MacMillan lowered the flashlight just enough for Amelia to see that he was holding a young boy in front of him. Kenny laughed and pressed his gun to the boy's head.

The child whimpered, tears streaming down his face.

"That was quite the show, wasn't it, Tyler?" When the child didn't answer, Kenny shook him hard. "Wasn't it?!"

Big brown eyes bore into Amelia's as Tyler nodded vigorously. "Y-y-yes."

In contrast, Kenny's blue eyes were filled with rage. His nose was slightly crooked after a couple bar fights during his time in the military. Or so his records claimed. The MacMillan family had a sordid past, with a long history of violence preceding Evan and Kenny. Both boys had upheld their family's bad reputation.

This was the face Cyrus and Mabel Osborne had stared down before Kenny had put a bullet in the back of their heads. The same face Anna and Stephen were forced to view during their final moments.

Would he be the last thing Amelia and little Tyler saw? She was wearing Kevlar, sure, but Kenny was a head man. She doubted he'd change his preferences now.

In the blink of an eye, the world sped up from the adrenaline-fueled slow-motion to full speed. She had so many questions.

When the hell had he gotten so close? Where had he hidden? How had he even found them to begin with? Who was the boy?

Amelia shoved aside the questions before she could devote any brain power to solving them. She needed her entire focus here, not fixated on what-ifs.

The sights of her gun trained on Kenny's face, she took a small step closer. "Let the boy go."

"Don't move." The calm in Kenny's voice surprised Amelia. Based on the unbridled hatred in his eyes, she'd expected more vitriol in the two words. "Drop your weapon. Nice and slow. No sudden movements or this little guy pays the price."

Muscles tensing, Amelia met his intense stare. "If I drop my weapon, will you let the child go?"

He bent and ran his nose through the boy's hair, making Amelia shudder. "It would be a shame to do so, but you have my word."

What are my choices here? If I hold on to the gun, the child dies. If I put down the gun, we're probably both dead. Unless...unless I can get him talking. Stall until Dean returns.

Swallowing past the desert in her mouth, Amelia lowered

her service weapon, each movement painstaking. Every fiber of her being was screaming for her to take a shot, but instinct wasn't always logical, and logic wasn't always instinctual.

She forced her fingers to relax their grip on the nine-mil. With a muffled *thump*, the weapon landed on the carpeted floor.

Dialogue. Amelia needed to get Kenny to talk.

"I did what you said. Are you going to do the same?"

Kenny pulled the boy closer to his body. "Kick the gun my way."

Amelia gave it a half-hearted kick, sending it about three feet away. "Now?"

The deranged man inhaled the boy's scent, turning the weapon on Amelia. "This is such a shame, but a promise is a promise." He walked the boy back to the door they'd come through. "Climb out the way we came in."

For a moment, Amelia thought the boy was frozen in fear, but with only a little shove from Kenny, he took off, climbed the generator, and disappeared.

The bastard had used the fireworks to cover the sound of him cutting into the generator room's ceiling. If the knowledge hadn't pissed her off so much, she would've been impressed.

Too bad this guy hadn't used his genius for good.

Now, she just needed to outsmart him.

"Cassandra's the final name on your list, isn't she?" Amelia's voice was hoarse, like she was a middle-aged woman who'd smoked a pack a day for the last thirty years.

Though slight, Kenny tilted his head to the side. "Are you trying to get a confession out of me, Agent?"

Amelia almost rolled her eyes. "I don't need a confession. We have a mountain of evidence against you, Kenny."

He took a step closer, his handgun pointed unerringly at

her. "I know you Feds love to trick people into admitting they've done something wrong."

As much as Amelia wanted to snap at him for his nonsensical logic, she refrained. Dialogue. She needed a damn dialogue.

Evan. He's doing all this to avenge his brother, isn't he? Pretend to be interested in his brother's story.

She licked her lips. "Is that what happened to your brother, Evan? Are you doing all this out of vengeance?"

"Not vengeance." His nostrils flared. "Justice."

She desperately wanted to give this madman a dose of Amelia Storm's justice.

Focus.

"Tell me about Evan."

A muscle in Kenny's jaw tightened, the first visible reaction Amelia had spotted. "You don't give a shit about Evan. He was the only family I had left, no, the only *person* I had left. But that didn't mean anything to your fucking agents or the worthless lawyers!"

Amelia turned her palms out toward Kenny. "Hey, the Drug Enforcement Agency worked your brother's case. I'm with the FBI, not the DEA. The Bureau didn't have anything to do with Evan's conviction. He got in a firefight with a street gang, didn't he? The Asphalt Knights?"

Kenny shifted his weight from one foot to the other, but his attention was rapt on Amelia. "Yeah. It was self-defense. He didn't know the guy he shot was a cop! He wouldn't have fired at him if he did! He just thought it was another gangster trying to kill him!"

Amelia doubted Kenny's assertion, but she could play along. "Look, like I said, that wasn't the FBI's jurisdiction. But here's the thing about that gang." She hesitated, playing the part of someone who was about to pass on privileged information. "I'm a Special Agent in the Organized Crime

Division at the FBI, okay? I know about the Asphalt Knights, but..."

She made a show of biting her lower lip. Aside from reciting her title, none of the words coming out of her mouth were true. She was pulling the entire spiel out of the usual place.

Kenny's eyes narrowed, and he advanced another step. "What? What do you know?"

Amelia heaved a fake sigh. "I haven't been on any cases that involved the Knights, but I *have* dealt with the Leóne family. You've heard of the Leónes, right?"

"The Italians? Yeah, who in Chicago *hasn't* heard of them? They run this damn city."

You don't know the half of it, buddy.

She'd thrown out the bait. Now, she needed to reel him in. "But the Knights, they work for the Leónes. They push heroin for them, even guns sometimes. I don't know if this is true or not, but rumor has it one of their leaders is Emilio Leóne's half-brother."

"What? How do you know this?" The dangerous edge returned to Kenny's tone. "And why are you telling me? Isn't this some shit the FBI ought to keep to itself?"

"I'm telling you this because I don't want to die!" Amelia didn't have to put forth much effort to feign an exasperated frown. "I know you want to avenge your brother, and I'm telling you I've been investigating the same people who might've played a part in landing him in prison. You want revenge, don't you? If you want to make the people responsible for your brother's death pay, you can't just cherry-pick the ones that're easy to get to. Only cowards target the weak."

Her aggressive phrasing was a gamble, but it was calculated. Kenny had damn near worshipped his older brother, and Amelia had learned a thing or two about Evan

MacMillan over the past couple days. *Aggressive* didn't quite encapsulate Evan's demeanor.

Vehemence and violence were Kenny's normal. If Amelia wanted to get through to him—or at least pretend to get through to him—she needed to match the energy he'd experienced throughout his life.

Besides, she didn't need to actually convince him. She was making this shit up because she needed an opening, a way to get the weapon out of Kenny's hands before he decided to pull the trigger.

Nostrils flaring, Kenny shook his head. "I'm not a coward. I'm not targeting the weak. I'm just getting started. What the hell would you even do for me, anyway? If I let you live, I'll go to prison!"

Amelia scooted forward a couple inches. Her movement was barely noticeable, but she'd shrunk the distance between them to six or seven feet. Almost enough. Amelia's opening was getting closer. She just had to keep him talking. Keep his focus split.

"You're going to prison no matter what you do to me. Even if you walk out of this house, how long do you think you'll last before the Marshals catch you? They're *very* good at catching people."

"No, nuh-uh." His jaw tightened. "I'm not going to prison. That's a death sentence, and you know it. It was for Evan, and it would be for me. I'd rather—"

The words died on Kenny's lips. His gaze, as well as the aim of his silenced handgun, jerked toward the stairs.

There were no flashing lights, no booming announcer voice, but this was it. This was the opening for which Amelia had been searching.

Kenny's attention was still on the stairs as Amelia launched herself forward. Like a tiger going for the neck of its prey, Amelia honed in on Kenny's gun-wielding arm.

Clamping both hands around his forearm, she used her forward momentum to yank his arm up and out to the side.

The handgun discharged with a quiet *pop-pop*, each bullet slamming into the modular foam panel wall with a much louder crack. Light swirled around the basement as the flashlight fell out of his other hand, spinning in circles on the floor.

Amelia tightened her grip and jerked his arm around to his back. She jammed the limb up, twisting his wrist until she felt the sickening pop of cartilage. With a howl of pain, Kenny's fingers went slack, and the weapon fell to the floor.

Rather than risk the lunatic finding an opening to scoop the gun off the carpet, Amelia kicked the weapon toward the base of the stairs. Well out of both their reaches.

Kenny's body went rigid, and Amelia released her hold on his arm, stepping back just in time to avoid a backward headbutt. As he spun around to face her, he led the charge with a left hook.

The damage to his dominant wrist had left him off-kilter, however, and his stance was weak. Based on the way he leaned into the blow, Amelia immediately knew he'd put far too much of his weight behind the punch.

Hopping aside at the last second, Amelia prepared to take hold of his arm. Using his own momentum, she'd throw him to the floor, giving herself an opportunity to either subdue him or rush over to grab her service weapon. She'd been flying by the seat of her pants during their dialogue, but hand-to-hand combat was her specialty.

She had the situation handled. Of that she was certain.

When a raucous *crack* split through her eardrums like an ice pick driving into her skull, a split second of blind panic erupted in her brain as she struggled to put the pieces together.

Warmth spattered her face, and she reflexively turned her

head to the side to keep the substance out of her eyes and mouth.

A gunshot. That had been the sound.

But there had been no suppressor, clearly. The report still echoed through her head. Did Kenny have a second weapon she hadn't noticed?

Mentally, she took stock of herself. Her heart knocked against her ribs like a championship boxer wailing away at a heavy bag, and her breath came in ragged gasps.

Nothing hurt. She was fine.

Amelia snapped open her eyes. A pool of dark blood expanded beneath Kenny's ruined head.

As Amelia turned her attention back toward the stairs, she noticed the unmistakable pale blue irises of Joseph Larson in the dim light. The man stood on the third and fourth steps up from the floor, and half of his features were in shadow. Since he'd just shot Kenny, Joseph's Glock was trained in Amelia's direction.

Without lowering the weapon, he looked down to the silenced handgun Amelia had kicked toward the stairs.

Amelia's blood turned to ice.

He wouldn't...would he?

Jesus, Amelia, you know he would. He's thinking about it right now! If he picks up Kenny's weapon, he can shoot me where I stand. He'll walk away from it scot-free. In fact, people will laud him as a fucking hero.

What did she do now?

What *could* she do? Her damn service weapon might as well have been on the moon for all the good it was doing her at this distance.

Kenny MacMillan had just unknowingly solved a serious problem for Joseph Larson.

"Agent Storm? You down there?" Dean Steelman's voice was the most beautiful sound Amelia had ever heard. The ringing hadn't subsided from her ears, and she couldn't tell how far away he was. But he was close enough.

"Yes!" Amelia was surprised she could even force the words past the tightness in her throat. "I am, and so is Joseph Larson. Kenny MacMillan is dead."

Steelman's footsteps creaked the floorboards above their heads as he neared.

Joseph's nostrils flared. It wasn't until the first footstep landed on the stair that Joseph finally lowered his weapon.

23

Dean had waited to announce his presence at the top of the stairs until he was sure the interference was absolutely necessary. A gunshot had ripped Dean away from his diligent search of the house's exterior.

He'd managed to get Cassandra to safety at the surveillance van and had returned to search the perimeter for any sign of forced entry or foul play.

Rushing back into the pitch black, Dean was careful to keep his footsteps light and quiet. If Amelia was in trouble, he wanted the advantage of surprise.

After clicking off his flashlight, he'd crept to the open basement door where voices could be heard, his service weapon leading the way.

To his surprise, he spotted Joseph Larson at the bottom of the stairs. The man's gaze, and the aim of his handgun, were glued to a scene out of Dean's field of view.

A careful examination of the mirrors strategically placed at the bottom landing of the stairs showed a man bleeding out on the floor and a weaponless Amelia Storm facing Larson. Though the lighting wasn't good, Dean could see well enough to make out the mix of surprise and worry on her face.

He'd expected Larson to lower his weapon. Even if the guy didn't care for Agent Storm, he was supposed to be a professional. A highly trained federal agent.

With each second Joseph held his aim steady, the alarm bells in Dean's head grew louder. Time crawled through molasses, leaving Dean with no true idea how long he'd been hidden at the top of the stairs, waiting for Larson to lower his weapon.

The man's threatening posture wasn't a figment of Dean's imagination. It was reminiscent of the scene he'd intruded on at Cassandra's apartment.

He had a really bad feeling about the man.

Stepping out of the doorway, Dean ran through his options. He needed to act. His instincts were screaming at him to intervene.

If he announced his arrival from the top of the stairs, a part of him suspected that Joseph Larson would be just as likely to turn and shoot him as he would be to offer a normal greeting, especially if the agent knew that Dean had witnessed the fear on Amelia's face or how Joseph had been pointing his gun directly at her.

It would be best if Larson didn't know what he'd witnessed. Dean didn't want the man to know he suspected anything.

That's how you play it, then. Act like you just got here.

Dean didn't have time to second-guess himself. Balancing on the balls of his feet, he crept back to the foyer. The adrenaline flooding his body wanted him to run, but he ignored the jittery sensation. As far as anyone in the basement knew, Dean had just gotten here. He'd been drawn in by the sound of the gunshot, and he just wanted to make sure everyone was alive.

"Agent Storm? You down there?" His voice was clear and confident, though the turmoil in his head was far from.

"I am, and so is Joseph Larson." Amelia's voice was faint, like he was hearing her through speakers at a supermarket. "Kenny MacMillan is dead."

Turning on his flashlight, Dean hurried into the basement doorway, unsure what to expect from Joseph Larson.

To his relief, Larson had lowered his weapon. As the man stepped off the bottom stair, the aggressive posture from moments before was nowhere to be found. His expression was damn-near unreadable.

Dean had already been under the impression Larson was a bit of a prick, maybe even a misogynist to boot, but was the chip on his shoulder really big enough that he'd murder another agent in cold blood?

In the heat of the moment, the answer had seemed like a resounding "yes."

But now, with Larson so calm and collected, he wondered if the wild glimmer was all part of his imagination. They'd been in a life-or-death situation, and adrenaline was undoubtedly coursing through all their veins. And the basement had been bathed in semi-darkness from where a flashlight lay on the floor next to a dead man. Dean's flashlight illuminated the scene further once he descended the stairs.

It wasn't out of the realm of possibility that Dean's imagination was getting the better of him. He dealt with psychopaths for a living and had for more than a decade.

What was the saying?

When you stare into the abyss, the abyss stares back.

Was that it? Or was he making excuses because he didn't *want* Larson to be a closet lunatic?

He pushed aside the contemplation. He'd puzzle over Joseph Larson's motivation later. For now, he needed to ensure the area was secure.

As he continued down the stairs, he nodded a curt greeting to Agent Larson. "Surprised to see you here. I thought you were handling the anonymous tips?"

A faint smile crept to Larson's face, and to Dean's continued relief, he tucked his weapon beneath his black peacoat. "Sure was. Still am, technically."

Dean snapped his gaze to the side as he descended the last few steps. The beam of his flashlight cast a bizarre, exaggerated glow along Kenny MacMillan's body. Though Kenny's face was shrouded almost entirely in shadow, the light caught the edge of the pool of blood beneath his head.

So, *that* was who Joseph Larson had shot.

Offering a quick thank you to any deity who might be listening, Dean let out a loud sigh. He wasn't as eager to tuck away his weapon just yet. "Mind if I ask what brought you to our neck of the woods? Not that I'm complaining."

"A lead." Joseph Larson lifted a shoulder. "One of the anonymous tips we got said they'd seen someone matching Kenny MacMillan's appearance driving up and down their street. They thought it was suspicious, like he was doing recon or something."

Dean glanced to Amelia Storm as she started to carefully pick her way around Kenny's corpse. "We didn't hear anything about that. Shouldn't you guys have sent that lead over to us?" He held up a hand to stave off a potentially hostile rebuttal. "I'm not complaining. It's just," he gestured to Amelia, "seems like we came awfully close to getting killed when it could've been prevented."

Larson's eyebrows scrunched together in what appeared to be confusion, but Dean spotted no signs of hostility. "I thought it did get sent to you. It's a brand-new lead, which is why I was here in person. The car was reported driving around a few blocks south of here. I was sent out to look for it. And you know we can't forward every single anonymous tip we get, right? Ninety-nine-point-nine percent of them wind up being total bullshit."

The guy wasn't wrong. Well-meaning civilians tended to go overboard with nonsensical details when the FBI asked for their help.

"What about Phobos and Deimos? What's their status?" Amelia Storm had moved closer, and Dean got the impression she was closely observing Joseph Larson's demeanor.

Dean stifled another sigh. "They're fine. They were doing their job. Had no idea what was going on inside the house."

The first hint of relief crept to Amelia's face. "Well, that's good. And Cassandra? She's safe?"

"Yeah, she is." Dean let out a self-deprecating chuckle. "I had them escort Cassandra back to the office and directed them not to leave her side at any point. They probably think I'm a bit of a jerk for how many times I repeated that point." He had been surprised by his own overprotective nature regarding the prosecutor. "The signal jammer didn't extend too far beyond the house, so I had them call for backup. I imagine the cavalry ought to be here any minute now."

Amelia turned to Dean and told him about the boy named Tyler and what had happened once she'd gotten to the bottom of the stairs.

Dean gave her a hard look. "I told you to wait for backup."

The agent's eyes nearly rolled to the top of her head, making him laugh. He might have actually joked a little more with her to cut the ongoing tension, but he didn't want to let down his guard with Larson still around.

Instead, Dean assessed the situation. "We're going to need to give statements when the rest of the team gets here. MacMillan is dead, but we still need to keep this all by the book. Chain of custody, and so on."

Amelia nodded. "We should leave the generator off until the CSU arrives. They might need it to be turned off to examine how MacMillan cut the power. Larson, you'll need to give your service weapon to ballistics when they get here, and we'll need to find the little boy, Tyler, and check on him."

Annoyance flickered in Joseph Larson's eyes, but he tempered the expression quickly. "Yeah, I know."

"What about an accomplice?" Dean flexed his fingers against the grip of his handgun to remind himself of the weapon's presence. "Larson? Any word on that?"

"The civilian who reported the car said they only saw one person driving it. I didn't see any sign of another person as I was pulling up."

Puzzle pieces slid together in Dean's head. *That* was how Larson had crept into the house without anyone knowing. Dean had been preoccupied with getting Cassandra to Knapp and Navarro.

One hell of a way to spend a New Year's Eve. I will definitely not *be doing this again next year.*

The faint wail of a siren drifted down to them. Plenty of people regarded the noise of sirens as a nuisance, but more often than not, someone out there was glad to hear the sound.

Tonight, that someone was Dean.

Straightening his spine, he finally managed to tuck his service weapon back into the holster beneath his arm. "Well, someone's gotta greet the cavalry. Agents," he swept an arm at the stairs, "shall we?"

Dean was eager to get the night over as quickly as possible but less eager about what lay in store for him when it came to Joseph Larson.

Whatever Larson's beef was with Amelia Storm or even Cassandra Halcott for that matter, Dean wanted no part of the feud.

However, what he *wanted* didn't matter much anymore.

Already entangled in the hostility, Dean vowed to do the right thing and stand by Halcott and Storm.

By the time Joseph Larson returned home to his apartment, Kenny MacMillan had been dead for six hours. Joseph should have been tired to the bone, but a lingering combination of rage and paranoia wouldn't let him rest.

Turning a mostly empty glass of water around in a circle on the coffee table, Joseph fixed his vacant stare on the foyer. He'd only removed his shoes and coat when he'd gotten home, though he had no plans to leave again until the following day.

He'd had her. All he'd had to do was pick up MacMillan's weapon—the silenced handgun that was right at his damn feet.

The universe couldn't have laid out the situation any better unless, of course, it would have put Cassandra in the basement with Storm.

But for the second time in the span of a few days, Dean Steelman had shown up at just the right time.

Before he could reach for that silenced handgun. Before he could permanently deal with one of his most pressing problems.

Growling low in his throat, he rubbed his eyes. He should be drinking booze instead of water, but he didn't want to risk letting down his guard. There was a time for letting loose, but he'd be damned if he could find it lately.

Amelia and Dean might not have believed him, but the lead about Kenny MacMillan scouting a neighborhood near the safe house was legitimate. A middle-aged woman had been out for a smoke when she'd first spotted the vehicle, and then she'd noticed him cruise by one more time before she'd finished her cigarette. When she went to walk her dog a half hour later, the car was there again.

Out on the sidewalk, she'd gotten a better vantage point when the driver passed her. She'd immediately made the connection to the man whose photo had been in the news earlier that night.

Joseph couldn't make that shit up. He couldn't have fabricated a better reason to be in the area when Kenny MacMillan had broken into the safe house.

The Bureau would have considered him a damn hero. He'd have ostensibly avenged the death of a federal agent, but also Cyrus Osborne, Carla Graham, Anna Denson, and so many others. Ballistics would've backed up his version of events and cleared him of any wrongdoing.

Then, with Amelia out of the picture, he could deal with Cassandra and finally get back to living life the way he'd come to enjoy. He could take trips to Florida and cruise around on Brian Kolthoff's yacht without worrying his nosy bitch of an ex-girlfriend had hired a private investigator to follow him. Or that Amelia was spying on him from a distance.

Dean Steelman just *had* to come and fuck up his perfect opportunity.

No. If I'd picked up MacMillan's weapon and shot Amelia, Steelman would've gotten there too soon. It's a good thing I hesitated and thought the whole thing through. Otherwise, I'd have had to kill Steelman too.

Not that offing the agent from Violent Crimes would bother Joseph. He didn't know much about the guy, aside from the fact he had a knack for arriving just when Joseph didn't want him to be around.

This is fine. You'll figure it out. You always do.

He couldn't argue that logic. He'd stay close to Cassandra, and he'd keep pressing her, just like he'd done with Michelle

Timmer. The lovestruck apologies had worked on Michelle, and he'd taken advantage of the first opening he'd sensed.

He'd convinced her to attend a make-believe shindig on Kolthoff's yacht, and the rest was history. She was still on the *Equilibrium*, as far as he knew. It was only a matter of time until he could add Cassandra to the collection of sweet things belowdecks. Then, maybe, just *maybe*, he'd even bring Amelia onboard.

Just the thought of the three of them naked and bound, forced to submit to whatever fantasy he dreamt up…

His cock stiffened, pressing against his slacks. Glancing at the clock, he knew that his newest plaything would still be fast asleep at this early hour. Her job as an elementary school teacher meant she had the rest of the week off work.

Joseph smiled. Perhaps it was time he started to establish exactly how their relationship worked.

With a grunt of approval, Joseph reached for his phone. He'd be able to craft a better plan to deal with Amelia and Cassandra after he'd gotten off.

He'd missed his opportunity tonight, but he'd be damned if he'd let the next opening slide.

One way or another, he'd get to them. The only question was when.

24

Cassandra drummed the end of her pen against a pad of yellow legal paper, her vacant gaze fixed on the microwave clock. Since Kenny MacMillan was dead, she didn't have nearly as much paperwork on her plate as she would if she'd been prepping for trial. The FBI had conducted an official hearing among the parties involved with MacMillan's death, and the case was considered closed.

The little boy, Tyler, had been found safe and sound. Apparently, the eleven-year-old lived in the safe house's neighborhood and had been lured away from his home with the promise of an "epic" fireworks show.

Kenny MacMillan had certainly delivered on that promise.

Joseph Larson, as a peripheral member of the MacMillan investigation, had acted on a piece of intelligence he'd received regarding MacMillan's whereabouts.

Cassandra still wasn't sure if the lead was real or if Joseph had manifested it so he could stalk her. Faking an anonymous tip wasn't difficult, especially for someone in Joseph's position.

The thought that he'd go so far as to fake evidence to keep himself close to her made her gut twist.

With Kenny—who'd been dead set on killing Cassandra in some horrific way—out of the picture, Cassandra *should* have been able to take a breath.

She *should* have been able to let down her guard a little, to sleep through an entire night without waking in a cold sweat. To drive to work without constantly staring at her rearview mirror to ensure she wasn't being followed.

She *should* have been able to relax, but she couldn't. Although Agent Steelman had gotten her to the relative safety of the surveillance van and those agents had never left her side back at the field office, she simply couldn't feel safe.

Anytime she thought she was safe, all she had to do was picture the crazed look on Joseph's face when he'd pointed his finger at her in her apartment. Her own damn apartment. Could she ever feel safe here again?

After hearing Agent Storm's personal, off-the-record account of what happened with Larson in the basement of the safe house, that only raised more questions. What was his beef with Amelia? He'd always painted them as good friends who'd drifted apart, and he'd left room for Cassandra to imagine more between the two of them.

Not that she'd believed him. She'd suspected Amelia was a one-time work fantasy of Joseph's, and he'd made the adult decision not to pursue a romance with his coworker.

Was the scuffed relationship the reason for Joseph's apparent dislike of Agent Storm? Had she turned him down?

Goose bumps crawled up her arms. From what Cassandra had learned of Joseph Larson in the past few days, she doubted he'd take such a rejection well.

But what about Amelia's warning to Cassandra, about Joseph's friends in low places?

During the time when she should have been giving

herself permission to relax, she'd taken up Michelle Timmer's missing persons case instead. Her friend in the Chicago PD had provided her with Joseph's statement, as well as all the information they'd collected before the investigation went cold.

After reading over Joseph's statement to the CPD, she was certain ninety-five percent of his account was fabricated. Joseph was an authority figure among bullshitters, but Cassandra was the fucking queen. She knew how Larson operated. She'd learned his tells, his go-to line of logic when he wanted to make a lie sound convincing.

Unfortunately, her intuition wasn't enough to brand Joseph a suspect. Aside from him being the last person to speak to her, there was no hard evidence to indicate he'd personally been involved in Michelle's disappearance. Right now, the CPD hadn't even established for certain that foul play had been involved.

In the case notes, suicide had been mentioned a couple times. Michelle hadn't had an easy life, especially during her childhood. The fact that she'd attained a scholarship to Yale was more than impressive. It was downright remarkable.

The more Cassandra mulled over Michelle, the more she noticed similarities between the two of them. Michelle was a natural brunette, but she dyed her hair a fiery shade of auburn. Just like Cassandra. Also like Cassandra, she'd lost her family and had wound up as a ward of the state.

Michelle's stay in the foster care system had only lasted six months before she'd been adopted by a kind, older couple. Both the adopted mother and father had since passed from natural causes, leaving Michelle all alone. Michelle had also attended a prestigious university and had obtained a respectable position in a male-dominated field.

As Cassandra willed herself to let go of the thoughts, unease increased the rate of her heart. Here she was, supposed to be making a grocery list, and she'd let her mind wander back to Joseph.

Maybe if she could find Michelle, she could figure out what in the hell was going on.

If she could find Michelle.

The more Cassandra researched, the more convinced she was that something terrible had happened to the forensics analyst.

At the end of the day, there was only so much Cassandra could do from behind a laptop. She needed someone who was experienced with fieldwork, with physically tracking down leads, and evaluating their legitimacy.

After the time she'd spent in Amelia Storm's company, Cassandra was more comfortable approaching the agent for non-work-related discussions. They shared more common ground than Cassandra had expected, and to her relief, Storm didn't harbor any ill will from the Ben Storey case.

Cassandra straightened, finally setting down her pen. For the first time since she'd begun to suspect Joseph's infidelity, she possessed a sense of purpose. The knowledge she wasn't helpless. That she had someone on her team.

Reaching for her phone, she put the grocery list on pause. She needed to schedule a time for her and Amelia to meet up *outside* of the field office or the U.S. Attorney's office.

And on this first day of the new year, there would never be a better time.

25

As Amelia pulled into the shadow of the abandoned warehouse, her gaze shot straight to a black Lexus parked along the curb. To her chagrin, the tint of the windows obscured any glimpse of the driver.

Yesterday, she'd walked out of Herman's Sandwich Shop to find another slip of paper beneath her windshield wiper. Aside from the address to a long-abandoned warehouse, the message had apologized for the delay and had requested her presence the following day.

With Zane's help, she'd scoped out the building and the area nearby. On the edge of the city, the place was bordered by two other vacant structures. One had been a store for boat supplies, and the other had sold CDs and DVDs. The location was bizarre for a retailer, and Amelia figured the choice to set up shop next to a textile factory warehouse was part of the reason they'd gone out of business.

Fortunately, the old CD store made a great hiding spot for Zane. If Amelia's meeting with...whoever in the hell this was went south, Zane was only a stone's throw away.

Twisting the GPS bracelet—the same style she'd worn

when Glenn Kantowski was trying to kill her—around her wrist, Amelia sighed. She hadn't wanted to wear a mic for the meeting with her secret ally, but as her time to exit the car drew nearer, she almost wished she had.

No. Whoever this is, if they actually were Trevor's confidential informant, I don't want to scare them away. If this is legitimate, it could be the only opportunity I'll ever get to figure out what happened to him.

Microphones were easy to hide, but a trained observer could still spot them. Not to mention, it was easy to scan for the devices.

She'd made the right call. Zane was close, and all she had to do was shout for his help. Not that she'd need it since the notes hadn't specified whether or not she could carry her service weapon. There was no way in hell she'd show up unarmed to a mysterious meeting with an even more mysterious messenger.

A flicker of movement drew her attention back to the Lexus.

Slowly, maybe even hesitantly, the driver's side door inched open. The person behind the wheel set one foot on the ground, permitting Amelia a glimpse of his black slacks and leather dress shoes.

Okay. The guy's a snazzy dresser. And he drives a Lexus. What kind of informant does either of those things? Who the hell is—

As the man rose to his full height, Amelia swore her heart stopped.

She recognized him. She'd learned all about him during the research she and Zane had done on Stan Young's agricultural empire, Happy Harvest Farms.

Amelia couldn't believe it.

Her brother's confidential informant was the dirty senator's son, Josh Young.

The End

To be continued...

Thank you for reading.

All of the Amelia Storm Series books can be found on Amazon.

ACKNOWLEDGMENTS

How does one properly thank everyone involved in taking a dream and making it a reality? Here goes.

In addition to our families, whose unending support provided the foundation for us to find the time and energy to put these thoughts on paper, we want to thank the editors who polished our words and made them shine.

Many thanks to our publisher for risking taking on two newbies and giving us the confidence to become bona fide authors.

More than anyone, we want to thank you, our readers, for clicking on a couple of nobodies and sharing your most important asset, your time, with this book. We hope with all our hearts we made it worthwhile.

Much love,

Mary & Amy

ABOUT THE AUTHOR

Mary Stone lives among the majestic Blue Ridge Mountains of East Tennessee with her two dogs, four cats, a couple of energetic boys, and a very patient husband.

As a young girl, she would go to bed every night, wondering what type of creature might be lurking underneath. It wasn't until she was older that she learned that the creatures she needed to most fear were human.

Today, she creates vivid stories with courageous, strong heroines and dastardly villains. She invites you to enter her world of serial killers, FBI agents but never damsels in distress. Her female characters can handle themselves, going toe-to-toe with any male character, protagonist or antagonist.

Discover more about Mary Stone on her website.
www.authormarystone.com

Amy Wilson

Having spent her adult life in the heart of Atlanta, her upbringing near the Great Lakes always seems to slip into her writing. After several years as a vet tech, she has dreams of going back to school to be a veterinarian but it seems another dream of hers has come true first. Writing a novel.

Animals and books have always been her favorite things, in addition to her husband, who wanted her to have it all. He's the reason she has time to write. Their two teenage boys fill the rest of her time and help her take care of the mini zoo that now fills their home with laughter…and yes, the occasional poop.

Connect with Mary Online

- facebook.com/authormarystone
- goodreads.com/AuthorMaryStone
- bookbub.com/profile/3378576590
- pinterest.com/MaryStoneAuthor